RULE

(A Mafia Romance)

by

CD Reiss

The Corruption Series – Book Three

ISBN-13: 9781942833093
ISBN-10: 1942833091
Flip City Media Inc

RULE

www.cdreiss.com

Cover Art designed by the author.

There is no fear in love; but perfect love casteth out fear: because fear hath torment. He that feareth is not made perfect in love.
—1 John 4:18

Would that life had the symmetry and passion of Italian opera, without the absurdity.
—Anonymous

Prologue

DANIEL

There was soot all over everything. Black ash and dust. Big stones made newly small. The size and shape of the Carriage House of the Gate Club had changed from the foundation upward with an explosion, much like my career. The building remained but had withstood the equivalent of a San Andres earthquake.

"She's not here," Kylie said, out of breath. She'd barely broken her run from the ballroom, in heels and a tight skirt, to deliver the news. "But she's on the tape and—" She stopped short and turned green.

The spot where a barely breathing gunshot victim had been found—male, early thirties, possibly Paulie Patalano, possibly not—was splattered with blood, bone, and flesh. A dozen crime scene technicians took pictures and laid markers.

"Don't look," I said, using my fingers to direct her eyes from the corporeal mess to my face. "Did you check the exit tapes?"

She swallowed hard and looked at me. "So many people are crowding out at once, it could take days to sort through."

My stomach had started churning as if poked with a sharp stick. And I had to stand up straight, because she'd taught me to do that. She'd made me a man, and in the wreckage of what I'd done, and with every bit of information that came to me, it became more clear she was gone. The tunnel had been sealed shut on the outside.

She'd been lured down there, or that piece of shit had, and she'd followed him. Then...

I couldn't dismiss Kylie to do her actual job of assisting Gerry in spin management, because if I sent her away, it meant I had no more leads and Theresa had been in that tunnel when the explosion hit. A ruckus broke behind me. Four men in smoking, wet rubber jackets came out of the closet. Aaron, the chief of police, approached them with questions, and I heard *collapsed. Nothing left.*

"Not much but junk down there," one of the firemen said as he handed a digital camera to a forensics specialist, and I saw a picture of the scene. "We're yellow taping it. It's not safe."

The forensics guy flipped through the pictures. A button. A diamond ring half-buried in the detritus underground.

I knew that ring. I'd chosen it. I'd gotten a bigger stone than I could afford. A stone that matched not my budget but my aspirations.

All the noise in the room fell away. Because that ring meant Theresa had been there, but it meant more than that. It meant nothing was cut and dried.

Why had she been wearing that ring? If Spinelli had wanted her to marry him, he would have gotten his own damn ring. I put the puzzle together. Was it that easy? It had been only hours since the Bortolusi wedding ended in fire, and the solution was already in my hands.

The question was, did I share my guess or keep it to myself? I wouldn't tolerate anyone shooting it down, because if I was wrong, she was dead, and that wasn't bearable.

"Kylie," I said, bringing the young intern away from the noise and clutter of the investigation. "For the past and next twelve hours, get me flight manifests into and out of Rome and Milan."

She cocked her head. "What are we look—?"

"Just get them. And Palermo and Naples."

***

I'd cheated on her, ruined her ability to trust in men. I hadn't spent one minute being faithful to her or doing what I'd promised, then I'd manipulated her, used her, done everything to push her into the arms of a man who destroyed her.

I didn't even know how to be pissed at Spinelli. I kept redirecting the energy back at myself.

It was my fault she was in the position she was in, whatever that was, living or dead. I'd pushed her, with my distaste, toward a criminal. I'd used her to plant bad earpieces and tried to manipulate her back into my bed. But even before that, I'd set her up. I'd left her crying and broken and wondering what was wrong with her. I'd betrayed her for years behind her back. Whatever happened was my responsibility, and if she was dead or a mob wife, I had to save her to save myself.

If that meant the mayor's office and the governor's mansion would go to someone else, then fine. Suddenly, gaining political office and losing my soul seemed like a fool's choice.

The seed of an idea grew in my head, watered and nourished by the reams of minutiae that came into my view over the following hours. Small things were my job. Details that fit together like a puzzle, telling a story of guilt or innocence, were how I put men in prison. And later, retelling that story to thousands of people became another part of a job I wanted and would do anything to gain.

The idea that grew, though, wasn't the story of how the Bortolusi wedding was handled, or who shot Patalano. It wasn't a story around how we would nail Spinelli. The story that grew was the tale of my own life being lived differently. It was a story of opportunities I had missed in choosing my life's ambition. It was a story of freedom and, wrapped up in it, was the story of a life lived parallel to Theresa.

The story was a deal with God. If I made up for the pain I'd caused her, I would lose the election and be free of my ambition. Then what?

Who knew? Maybe a life with her. Maybe without. But a life where she was somewhere safe in the world and my responsibility for her hurt would be gone.

If she was alive. And that looked less and less likely. Her phone was dead. Her apartment hadn't changed. Her family was dealing with their own crisis and hadn't been able to get her on the phone.

I let everyone prove she and Spinelli were dead, and I wove the story of her life in the midst of it.

The details came in. I let my staff run in circles, because the story I built wasn't for them. It was for me. I was a full-on fuckup no more. That was my new story.

Theresa hadn't taken a bag with her.

The stash of cash was missing from her closet.

Years ago, the tunnel had led to a house across the street, but it was blocked by rubble and brick.

That ring. That ring that ring.

They'd split. It was so obvious to me, yet my staff was easily misguided. I told stories. It was what I did.

Did I have to save Spinelli to save Theresa? That was my only concern. I didn't want to. I hated him. I hated him for breaking her down. But if I was going to stop bullshitting myself and do the job, I had to consider it.

I was exhausted when the manifests came across my desk.

"You have a press conference on the wedding in three minutes?" Kylie almost asked.

"Why do you look like I'm going to snap at you?"

"I was supposed to get you into makeup seven minutes ago, but these came and I forgot."

I stood and got my jacket on in the same move. "Don't worry about it. Looking tired's going to help more than hurt." I picked up the manifests and walked into the hall before I'd even gotten my arms through both sleeves.

"What the fuck, Kylie?" Gerry said, walking with a purpose, flanked by the usual team. I was sick of seeing them already.

"Leave her alone. It's better." I flipped through the manifests. The third set I'd seen with nothing nothing nothing…"These are incoming to LAX." I handed them back.

But they caught my eye when I handed them over, and I saw two names right next to each other.

SPINELLI ANTONIN M 35A
SPINELLI TINA F 35B

I snapped the papers back. The flight was arriving in two hours. Impossible for them to get to Italy then back. Physically impossible. Was this some sort of trick he'd set up to misguide me? Or was every assumption I had made incorrect?

I was about to have Kylie set up a car to go to LAX after the press conference, but I decided against it. I was telling this story hour by hour, and I didn't need anyone sending it off the rails. I'd get there myself.

Chapter 1

Antonio

FIRST NIGHT IN TIJUANA[1]

She slept on her side with her hand resting on my arm and her toes pivoting against my calf. The bed flattened the side of her against it, so the curves above were accentuated in the moonlight. Her left hand was turned palm up, the burn ointment doing its work.

I didn't want to wake her, so I ran my hand along her neck, shoulder-to-ear-to-lips parted in innocent peace.

Paulie was dead because of me. He had been a confused, violent man I used and loved like a brother. And where was my grief? I rooted around my deep corners for it, but I was empty. I only had love for the woman who had killed him. That hand on my arm was murderous and capable. I should have been repelled by its touch, but I wasn't. I was connected to the soul who wielded it.

When she'd pulled the trigger[2], I saw the intent in her eyes. It terrified me in a way that was coiled tightly with exhilaration. This woman was no more than a stranger and no less than a kindred animal.

---

1 This is their first night after the wedding. Now, if you're going to count days and nights, let me just say here that there's an extra day in Corruption that doesn't happen in Submission. I hope you can just read and enjoy the books. But if that extra day bothers you, I really do apologize. I know it can be disorienting.

2 To reorient you, Theresa shot Paulie at the Bortolusi-Lei wedding.

Everything happened too quickly after that. The practical matter that I couldn't leave her took a backseat to something bigger. I couldn't put a name on it. Not yet. I couldn't call it something I didn't understand. But she belonged to me. Her eyes, fluttering in sleep, were mine because they saw what I saw.

And still, that didn't begin to define it. It wasn't something I felt. It wasn't lodged in my heart. This possession wasn't the stuff of operas and art. It was made of bone marrow and earth. Roots and reality. I could almost touch it, but still, I couldn't find the words in any language to describe it.

I touched her bottom lip, as if words would be released. She sighed and rolled onto her stomach, her elbows making a V on either side to keep her burned hands to the cracked ceiling.

The whole way to Tijuana, I'd wanted to fuck her, to see what was different, to touch this definition at the center and unearth its meaning. To dig through our separateness and feel what it meant to own someone. Until then, I would be at this same loss for understanding. I'd had half a hard-on the whole way south, and it wasn't the curve of her breast under her shirt, though that was as arousing as always. She was beautiful, and I knew she always would be to me. The source of my arousal was deeper. I wanted to fuck her to find this shared core.

But there had been matters. Things. First thing, get past the line in the sand. Then get a place to hole up for the night. As we'd waited in the bar for the hotel to clean the room, we found out about her brother.

Jonathan, who I'd met once, was as sick as a man could be. I couldn't take her from her family just yet. I couldn't do that to her. As if he were my own family, I had to go back, for her, for our shared fate, for that connection in the marrow. I didn't even want to return to LA for myself, but knew I was going as surely as my balls ached.

So on the beach, I'd spoken to her about plans. None of it meant anything, because plans changed in the doing, but we agreed on a goal and a first step, which had to be undertaken immediately.

I called my father, who cursed me for breaking his heart with my death on the one hand and being alive with the other. He'd arranged the marriage I'd run from.

"Do you understand what this means? Do you understand the level of betrayal?"

He was almost too enraged to speak, but he gave me the number for a man who knew a guy who could forge two passports.

I thanked him, but he'd hung up before I finished. My father's reaction hurt me, but it hadn't surprised me. I didn't know if I could ever repair things with him. Which was too bad. I loved him.

I ran my hand over the slope of her back. She didn't wake up.

We'd found a little hostel with the entire desert in the backyard. I spoke a little broken Spanish to the man behind the desk. When I signed us in as Mr. and Mrs. Spinelli, she blushed and got the smile people get when they can't help themselves.

The passports wouldn't be delivered until the next afternoon, and I had business to attend to. Important business.

I'd closed the hotel room door behind us. The room was done in cheap Mexican artifacts imported from China. The air conditioner hummed, and the windows were shut tight. The white curtains hung dead in the heavy afternoon air, and the flies were too lazy to buzz.

Theresa had slipped her bag off her shoulder onto the straight wooden chair as if she had all the time in the world, then peeked at herself in the peeling dresser mirror at the foot of the bed. She'd touched the bump on her head.

Against the sound of crickets and her breathing, I ran my finger along the angle of her shoulder blade, remembering the afternoon.

"I know what you're thinking." She'd passed the bed. The mattress was as high as a slice of bread over a metal frame.

"The bed will creak? I think it will, and I don't care."

"There's too much, Antonio. Too much to think about. I'm anxious."

If she hadn't said it, I wouldn't have known. Not a line of worry crossed her brow.

"Get on that bed, Contessa, before I give you something to be anxious about." I bolted the door.

"I don't feel like it."

I pushed her onto the bed, and she fell in a sitting position with her hands behind her. Her denim-covered knees parted slightly, and when she tried to cross her legs, I yanked them open.

"I mean it," she'd gasped.

I got hard remembering that little bit of resistance I'd had to get through.

"Give yourself to me," I'd said.

"Not now."

I wedged myself between her legs, and she fell supine. "Give yourself to me." I pushed my cock against her.

She put her hands on my chest and pushed me away. I took her wrists and held her hands over her head. She cringed. I let her hands go, and she held them up to me.

They were red. Streaks of white crossed the palms where they'd blistered.[3] When I looked in her eyes, the bump on her head laughed at me. I'd gone to the tavern and walked on the beach with her and not tended to her injuries. I was already a failure as a husband, and we weren't even married yet.

"Stay here," I said, getting up. I was out the door and on the street in seconds.

I had crossed the border a different man. Had it been the border? It was only a line in the sand. Or had it been before, on the drive south? Or the moments when I let her think I was dead, and I couldn't do it, couldn't leave her with the corpse of my best friend and a warm gun. The thought of leaving her there seemed wrong. Against the laws of physics and logic. I had been trying to be *forte* and turn my back, find some other life to ruin. I couldn't. I was a selfish brute. I was worse than my first wife's accusations. An animal. A destructive force wherever I went.

I got a tube of antibiotic cream, burn ointment, and white tape and gauze from the drug store, then I ran back. I was paranoid, convinced I saw enemies ducking around corners and behind doors. Would I always look for them? See them? When we got out of Los Angeles the second time, would I be able to live like a normal man? Ever?

---

3 This is from when she was in the old well underground and she pushed the wood trapdoor off her. She also bumped her head on a marble tabletop in the Carriage house, and Paulie whacked the side of her face. So she's got a pretty good bang on the side of the head.

When I got back upstairs, she hadn't moved. It might be the first time she'd actually obeyed me.[4]

The bed creaked and bent when I sat on the edge. "Let me see your hands."

She held them out, and I bit the end off the burn ointment.

"I'm sorry about this. This is not how we start." I gently coated her palms with the clear gel.

"We're not exactly normal. Ow." Her wrist twitched, but she didn't pull away.

"Are you sure you want to marry me? You're committing yourself to a man who gives you burned hands."

"Oh," was all she said.

I looked from her hand to her face. Her eyes were cast down, only slivers of blue visible from my angle, but her answer was in the shape and twitch of her mouth. Her lips were held tightly together, narrowed, straight across, and her cheeks dimpled. She was trying not to smile.

"I mean it," I said, capping the tube. There wasn't much I could do about the bump on her head besides clean it off. I pulled her hair away so I could see it. "You'll have to learn to speak Italian so you can curse me like a good Neapolitan wife."

The smile broke into a full crescent of teeth. "I'll invent new words to curse you with. Promise." She put her fingers on my shirt buttons and slipped them through the holes. "Now get this off. Your arm and your head need attention."

I got out of my shirt. I thought she wanted to get us naked so I could take her, but the sleeve stuck to my bicep and hurt when I ripped it away. I looked at the raw wound, bordered in gunpowder[5] and angry pink between the split skin.

"This is going to scar," she said.

"More proof I lived."

She spun on her bottom, hopped off the other side of the bed, and padded to the sink. She snapped a worn white towel from the rack and wet it, twisted it into a rope to get the last of the excess water out, then sat next to me.

---

4 This is actually untrue and more a matter of perception than reality.

5 Paulie took a shot at Antonio, and when Theresa saw his blood, she freaked out.

"No crying now," she said. "Be a big boy."

She pressed the towel to the wound. It hurt enough to make me bite back a grunt, but I didn't make a sound as she cleaned it off. She patted my head with the same cloth. The blood there had been wiped away on the drive down. We'd covered it with my hair so we could pass through customs.

"This already looks better," she said about my head. "You have amazing healing powers. The arm though..." She dabbed my arm again.

"I guess you'll clean the children's knees with a wet cloth too? I can see it."

"If the children have gunshot wounds, you're the one who's going to need first aid, Mister Spinelli." She squirted my arm with antibiotic gel and ripped open the packet of gauze with her teeth. She didn't remove the gauze from the envelope. Didn't move.

"What?"

"I was so busy thinking about myself. I didn't even think about children."

I took her chin and pointed her face at me. Close up, I could see tiny pieces of grit inside her scrape. "We're out."

"I don't feel out."

With the other end of the white towel, I patted the bump on her head, cleaning it. "You're out. I'm out. We go back to being civilians. We just have to get into LA without being seen and back out again. Should be easy."

She plucked the gauze from the paper package and looked around for the tape. "I don't want to be a burden to you." She taped the square of gauze to my wound, swallowing her nerves. "I'm scared, Capo."

I took the tape and put it to the side. "You're not to be scared."

I'd said it as if it were an instruction. I should have soothed her, but I didn't know how. So I kissed her. I kissed her long and hard. To suck her fear out of her. To eat it alive and spit out the bones. I pushed her back onto the mattress and kissed her harder. Her hands stayed burn-side up, but the rest of her body arched up to meet mine.

I moved my hips against her, the clothing between us getting hot with friction. "Give yourself to me, and I'll fuck the fear from you."

Her eyes fluttered closed as I pushed myself against her, increasing the pressure until I thought I'd burst.

"Your answer, Contessa," I whispered in her ear. "Your answer. Answer. Answer." I was ready to get off her if she said no, but I knew she wouldn't.

"Take me," she breathed. "You crazy, beautiful bastard. Take me."

I got up and peeled off her pants, yanking her legs open so I could see her pussy. She tried to close them, and I pulled her legs open again, bending the knees.

"Don't move." Standing over her, I got my pants off. I was going to fuck her so hard that we were one person, to touch that sameness between us so I could understand it.

Two fingers in her, and she was soaked. She bucked against the thin mattress, and when I ran my wet fingers over her clit, she cried out. I wanted to taste her, to tease her, to spend hours swimming in our heat. I wanted to fuck her hard and fast. Plant myself inside her and drive to the finish. I wanted to fuck her mouth, her ass, her cunt, her very being. I didn't know how to do all the things I wanted to do to her.

I got on my knees quickly, pulled her seam apart until everything was exposed, and I ran my tongue over her. She dug her fingers into my hair as I fucked her with my tongue and hands. Two fingers in her ass. A thumb in her pussy. My mouth sucking her clit. Other hand squeezing her nipple tight to hold her still. When she came, all of Mexico heard.

I didn't wait until she breathed. I had to have her. My spit had to be on her cunt when I fucked it, the last of my fingers in her ass still. She was so wet, so soft when I fucked her, and her mouth was open, unfucked. Unacceptable. I rolled her over so she was on top. I pressed her tongue down with three fingers and took her face too. I was everywhere inside her. Ass and mouth and pussy. All mine. All of it.

And still, a few hours later, in the dark of night, with her breathing next to me, touching every part of her as if committing to a sacrament, I didn't know what we were. But I knew I'd have to leave her alone on the earth. One way or the other, they would get me. Going in or going out. I was a dead man and something else. I was the man who would prepare her for his death.

Chapter 2

The Next Morning

THERESA

Jonathan had tried to kill himself when he was sixteen. It had been over a girl, my friend Rachel. At the time, I'd thought it was because they split up, but it had been much, much more complicated. He'd suffered, and I hadn't been there for him, not in the way I should have been. I was beating myself to a pulp over it in the hostel, brushing my thumb over Antonio's arm. I would be there this time, and as stressful as it was to go back to Los Angeles, reestablishing that balance released a different source of tension.

"This has a texture," I said, running my fingers over the volcano tattoo inside his left wrist.

He'd just brought me to orgasm twice, and I was on my stomach, getting my brain reorganized. Once I'd stopped screaming in ecstasy, he'd opened the windows. Children played in the street two stories down, and we spoke softly as if they could hear us.

"It's not a tattoo. Not really." He got up on his elbows and held out his wrists. "The shape is cut with a knife, and they rub ink from a pen on it."

I looked closely. Every line was a bump. "Blue pen?"

"I asked for the blue. I liked it."

"Did it hurt?" I stroked the lines of Vesuvius.

"Yes."

"It's dangerous to cut the inside of the wrist. Did it bleed a lot?"

"Are you going to ask me if I cried?"

"I know you did."

He took me in his arms and kissed my face. "Like a baby."

I looked at the ceiling for a second as his hand trailed up and down my body like a boat on still water, leaving widening wakes of sensation.

I rolled over. The window faced north, so the morning sun was cool and soft. "We have a few hours before the passports come."

"I have plans for you."

"More of the same?"

"No, I'm sorry to say," he said, sitting straight up. "I've left you vulnerable. We are going back as civilians, but that doesn't mean we go back stupid."

He took the gun off the table and checked the ammunition. He pivoted on his ass then stood above me with it, naked, shoulders at an angle that balanced the pedestal of his neck. His waist, his hips, his tight stomach with a line of hair leading to the perfection of his half-erect cock, all were meant for me.

He snapped the gun closed, reminding me of everything hard and hot and dangerous. All the reasons we were going to hell. I felt two jolts. One between my legs. The other in my heart.

"I did it," I said. "With Paulie. I shot him. I held the gun, and I pulled the trigger. That's on me."

"Because he was coming at me."

I sat up. Paulie had been coming at Antonio, and if I was ever unsure whether or not I'd kill for him, I wasn't anymore. But in the haze of thinking Antonio was dead, to needing to stay completely and utterly calm for the trip to TJ, to finding out about my brother and planning for our return, I hadn't had a moment's peace to think about what killing for him meant.

I looked away from Antonio at the foot of the bed. Past the wrought-iron footboard, the mirror stared back at me. I was naked, hair hanging over my shoulders in a post-coital nest. I looked as I always had, and him above me, dark hair contrasting with the whiteish walls, body lithe and tight and perfect, dark eyes with lashes longer than should be legal. The mirror couldn't see Antonio's taste in my mouth, his cum dripping from me, my aching pussy.

It couldn't see the change in my brain caused by the sex and the safety, the dam of avoidance dropping and the torrent of truth.

I held up my right hand to block my face in the mirror, and I saw something I shouldn't. The little black stain was probably caused by the dirty mirror, because when I turned my palm around to look at it directly, it was red from a burn, not black with sin. Downstairs, a child's scream turned to laughter. I pressed my lips between my teeth.

Antonio looked down at me. "Theresa?"

"I didn't..." I pressed my finger to his lips. "I can't accept that you forgive me."

He sat down, twisting to face me. "You didn't mean it."

Mean it? What did that even mean? No one *means* to shoot anyone, except psychopaths and nihilists.

"I did mean it."

He pulled my fingers away from his lips, but I shook my head violently and put both hands over my face. I couldn't look at him, or anyone. Especially not myself. That mirror, it bothered me. It flattened everything into truth.

Antonio straightened like a shot, straddling me. He took my hands from my face and filled my vision. The eye of the storm: a place of peace and calm, and the most dangerous space to be in. The eye made you complacent and comfortable, and the next minute, while you were enjoying the cloudless sky, you'd be swept into a violent wind.

"Theresa," he said, his accent like music, the concern on his face as real as his taste on my tongue. "Contessa. *Amore mio. Ascolta.* We are animals. You. Me. The kids playing outside. We wash ourselves. We cook our food. We speak in big words and have ideas. But we are animals. We fuck and we shit, and when we have to survive, we kill."

We kill. Did that mean everyone, or just me? Just us? Just the family I'd forced my way into for reasons that even I couldn't articulate?

"No. I don't believe that," I said, knowing he was right no matter how I let the light hit it.

He cupped my chin and held my head fast, as if keeping me still would ensure I heard him. "Your life will be easier if you accept it."

What about me deserved an easy time of it? I'd never earned the ease I'd been given, and now that I'd done what I'd done, my worthiness was even more questionable. His eyes met mine, and I saw nothing but the depth of his troubles. Decades' worth of weight. Would I add mine to his? Would I harp on my sin until he took responsibility for my corruption? I could break him. I knew that. If he thought I was destroyed beyond recognition, he'd take it all on himself.

"I'm fine," I said. "Just adjusting."

"Don't adjust too much. If something has to be done again, it's for me to do."

"I know." I turned away, and he let my chin go. "Trust me."

"First thing, we don't separate. I am with you always. If you need defending, I'm going to do it."

I admired the way he assessed and took control of a situation. I admired his passion and heat, his old world attitudes and how he was willing to bend them to accommodate his respect for me, and how unwilling he was to let go of his responsibility to protect me from all the evil I'd brought on myself. I couldn't have asked for better, and that made me want to shield him from the worst of me.

"I love you, Capo."

"Say you understand."

"I understand. We stay together. All the way back to Los Angeles."

"And you do not pick up a weapon to defend me. As long as I'm alive, I am your weapon," he said.

"You're not dying."

"Say it. Say I am your weapon."

"You are my weapon."

"I see you, beautiful Contessa. Don't think I'm blind."

"What do you mean?" My voice was sharper than I wanted it to be. I was afraid he saw my emotional discomfort and mistook it for guilt. But it wasn't guilt he saw. I'd turned my back on heaven when I pulled that trigger, and I felt no regret. I didn't want him to see the empty hole where guilt and sorrow should have been.

"You don't have as much practice at this, and today, before the passports come, I'm going to teach you to defend yourself for the day I may be gone."

"Please don't say that."

"Call it a sleep then. I need you to know what to do if I sleep."

I nodded, because I knew what I'd do if anything happened to him. I'd find the bastards who did it, and I'd put them to sleep with Paulie. I was a talented psychopath. I had a real God-given gift.

I kissed Antonio so he wouldn't be able to look in my eyes and see what was broken and what was whole. He owned me with his lips, protected me and told me I was worth saving when I felt less than worthy. I loved him for trying, for telling me how precious I was without saying a word. I wanted another hour with him, so he could fuck me so hard I became the human he thought I was.

Chapter 3

THERESA

t felt hard and warm, the surface supple to the touch, with curves designed to comfort the force of a closed fist.

"You know how to use it?" Antonio asked, even though he knew the answer.

The long brushy desert behind the hostel was perfect for target practice, and the owner didn't seem to mind bullets flying as long as we didn't disturb or shoot the guests. It was as good a pastime as any while we waited for passports to be fashioned out of lies.

I took aim at the empty Coke bottle, putting the pin of the front sight into the notch of the rear sight. Squeezed. Missed.

He smiled on one side of his mouth, lips full in the blasting Mexican sun, face cast in hard shadows that accentuated the flawless angles of his face. "I can see that it bothers you."

"What? That I missed? Everyone misses. It's a small object, and you put it far away." Was I whining? Maybe.

"But it bothers you."

He put his fingertip on the back of my neck and started to say something, as if he would teach me how to shoot. That was why he'd brought me out here. Before he could start, I leveled the gun on the bottle and squeezed, expecting to waste a bullet.

The bottle shattered.

He pressed his hand to the back of my neck.

"I'm getting anxious." I pulled the trigger again. A *ping* echoed over the rocks when I hit the bottle just at the edge. It spun then fell. "Every hour that passes...I might miss him."

"I think we can make it," he said.

"Then what?"

He ran his hand down my neck. "The Carlonis can't find out we're alive. I shamed Donna Maria by running from her grand-daughter. She'll want me dead and pay good money for someone to do the job. But these are the American mafia. They watch too many movies. The Italians I think I can make peace with. Once that's done, I'm going to marry you."

"Can't be a big church wedding." I bent my elbow until the gun pointed at nothing but the sky. "Not without family."

"No. Maybe." He ran his hand up my arm and over my body until he found my chin. I felt safe and loved when he looked at me like that, eyes shadowed by the sun but still intense enough to compete with its blaze. "I want something so badly, and I'm afraid to even say it."

"Why?"

"I don't want to tempt God."

"Say it." I felt more than heard the breath he took. "God can't hear you out here."

His glance toward the heavens was almost imperceptible. "I want to go home. I want to take you into my family. To make you a part of...we've always looked for a new life. Maybe that was the mistake. Maybe we need to make the best of the old life."

"How? I don't even know how."

He leaned forward, and I leaned into him until I felt his stubble on my lips. "Me neither," he said. "But come home with me and try. Come home with me."

I wondered, not for the first time, when it had happened. When I'd fallen in love. When I'd committed myself so irrevocably. When the thought of a world without him hadn't seemed grey and flat.

It wasn't the sex. It wasn't the way he fucked me as if he wanted to peel my skin off and enter my soul. It wasn't the way his unreasonable demands made me wet rather than angry. It wasn't the violence, or the knowledge that he would do anything he had to in order to get what he wanted. He'd murder, steal, hurt himself. Hurt me.

Nor was it the way he took on responsibility for my brother as if Jonathan was his own. Daniel would have asked me what I wanted to do then explained why he was too busy to be with me for it. Or we'd talk about what to tell the media. But my problems would be inconveniences, puzzles to be solved. He wouldn't own them. Antonio owned me, meaning my body, my soul, and my family. I didn't know how to own him with the same surety. I didn't know how to want things for *us*.

But he was teaching me how to be his. When we'd arrived in Tijuana, I'd been under the influence of such momentum, I couldn't imagine going in reverse, not even for my family, not even to see Jonathan one last time. Antonio had slowed me down, pushing against the inertia of movement from here, to there, to the goal that blinded me. Thank God for him, in that moment and every moment since. Thank God for his level head and his perspective.

Except now, behind a filthy hostel as we waited for our fake passports.

Now he seemed desperate as he whispered, "Come home with me. Be a part of me."

I could have just said yes, but there was no lying between us, not even to make the other happy for a second's breath. "They'll never accept me."

He nodded and stepped back, his hand dropping off me. His white shirt and linen pants clung to one side of his body when the desert breeze picked up, and they fell in a graceful drape when it died.

"You have one more bottle, and two bullets," he said. "You're a little to the left, so when you aim, you have to compensate."

I aimed carefully, holding the gun at the sharpest point of the triangle of my arms. Squeezed. I had no idea how far off I was, but the bottle was unimpressed.

"Little right," he said, putting his fingers together.

I tried again. Another fail. I shrugged.

"Missing bothers you," Antonio said, taking the gun. "I see it in your face."

"It's not a big deal. I have you."

"You do. And if you never destroy another bottle, you're still perfect." His eyes grazed my body, running over it in a zigzag, as if imprinting the details into his mind. I felt brazen and desired, the center of a vital universe.

"Do we have time to go back to the hotel room?" I asked, imagining his body twisted around mine, his rough hands on my ass, his mouth on my...

"No," he said, popping the empty mag and sliding in a new one. "Because...don't look. Don't change anything, but...take this." He handed the gun to me, sliding his fingers over my wrist. "There's a man behind the water heater at the back of the hostel, and one behind the big rock to my right, back there. If they kill me in front of the right witnesses, they get my title. My territory. My crew. So I can't reclaim it when I return."

"What?" I didn't move, but the conversation had turned so casually, I felt like a purse someone had turned upside down and shaken.

"They're going to try to take me alive."

I had to take a second to absorb what he said. "How did they find us?"

"The forger, maybe. There might not be any passports." Nothing about him indicated panic. He looked as if he were about to stroll in the park.

"Don't leave me." I choked on the words.

"Are you ready?"

I barely took a breath when I nodded. I was ready.

The whole of my vision went as far as the light that surrounded him, and the hard metal of the pistol between us became a world. I didn't see either of the men he spoke of, only a light patch of dust behind the shed.

"One behind the water heater," he said, tipping his head to the hostel behind him. "One behind the big rock to your right."

"What do you want to do?" I asked as if considering where to go for dinner.

"As soon as I raise my arm, drop to the ground."

"Then why the gun? If you're putting me in a defensive position?"

"Only shoot to survive."

"I'll shoot anyone who tries to hurt you."

"Don't. Trust me."

I trusted him. I did. The salt of the entire visible world was at my command with him. I feared nothing. Not death, not pain, not my own sin. God was my ally, and evil was my slave inside the quiet torrent of his eyes.

I trusted him to protect me, but not to protect himself for my sake.

He squeezed my hand, then he walked away, his own gun sticking out of the back of his waistband.

What happened then happened so quickly, I didn't have a chance to think about the feeling that he was shrinking in my vision, or the way the landscape seemed to squeeze him into a smaller space. He was ten steps to shelter. I still didn't see anyone. My gun weighted seventy pounds or more, and the Sicilians, who wanted him alive more than they wanted me dead, were waiting until he was close enough to get a clear shot.

That, I knew.

And I knew he walked slowly to draw them out.

And I knew the pain in my chest that grew with every step. The twisting feeling, as if my lungs were being played like an accordion.

I was afraid. Desperately afraid.

And my patience ran out like a broken hourglass.

I raised my arm and pointed the gun at Antonio's back as if I could ever shoot him. "Capo!"

He didn't spin toward me but pulled the gun from his waist, and shots, everywhere, pinged, popped, cracked against the mountains. I dropped, but not like a child in an earthquake drill. I dropped with intention and pointed the gun in the direction of the shots behind the boulder, while Antonio dropped and rolled to aim behind the water heater.

A rough scrape to my right left a divot in the dirt, missing me by inches. I'd never felt so vulnerable. So distant from my sun, like Mercury cast into Pluto's orbit. Like a child in an earthquake drill that turned out to not be a drill at all.

I exhausted my bullets and froze. Antonio rolled. Alive? With no more forward movement to take and the center of my orbit down, I was out of ideas, out of thoughts, only knee-deep in a fog of fear that I hadn't kept pressure on the guy behind the boulder long enough to keep Antonio from getting shot in the back. Oh god, he was out there, alone, and I was light years away.

He rolled onto his stomach and took another shot at the water heater.

One thousand years passed in a split second.

Then the explosion.

I screamed as water poured from the water heater, bathing the sand in a miniature ocean that grew and flattened while the noise and light of the pilot light hitting the broken gas line sent flames everywhere. Cracked masonry. Smoke. Steam. If I had been confused and afraid before, I was wrecked when I tried to stand.

Until he came to me. Through the dense air, he came and yanked me up. As if slapped back into reality, I felt safe again. My guts stopped twisting, and the world slipped back onto its axis.

"What the hell were you doing?" he growled.

"If they thought I was going to kill you, they'd shoot at me, not you!"

He squeezed my arms so hard, I thought he was going to cut off my circulation. His jaw was tight against his skull and his lips were parted. I wanted to kiss the snarl right out of him, but he pulled me into the smoke and steam. I ran with him, step for step, in complete synch like the winners of a three-legged race. If gunshots still rang out, their sound was muffled by the roar of the flames we headed right into.

Heat. My skin didn't have time for sweat, just hair-curling heat. I didn't ask what he was doing by pulling me into it. I just did what he asked, and I feared nothing.

"Get to the street!" he shouted, pointing left while keening his body right.

"No!"

"Theresa!" He said my name like a command.

We had no time for words. Under the thunder of the flames came another gunshot. I felt nothing, but Antonio looked at my arm. Following his gaze, I saw where a bullet had torn my sleeve.

The edges smoked from the heat of the projectile, or the fire from the water heater. It didn't matter. The calm in his face was gone.

He dropped to a crouch, pulling me with him. "The street."

He had soot across one cheek, and his face glistened with sweat. I couldn't change his mind about sending me away from danger, I knew that. I also knew I couldn't stand being away from him for a second.

He curled his fist and held it up as if keeping his patience inside him. His voice held a tension between uncontrollable rage and forced peace. "I'll be right out. I swear it."

I nodded. Took one step backward. The hostel was five steps away. The water heater was set away from it by ten feet, so the building hadn't caught fire, but it was only a matter of time before that escape route was closed off.

"Go!" He pointed at the hostel then took off at a run in the other direction.

The flames and the space around him squeezed him tight as he got smaller, and I couldn't stand it. I followed him.

Antonio stood by the boulder, looking down. A man crawled from the other side in a dark zip-up jacket and jeans, leaving a trail of blood in the sand. I knew him but couldn't place him. Young. Goatee. With the way the desert sun lit his face, I almost lost the memory, but the goatee jogged it. I remembered a night on Mulholland[6] when I brandished an outdated car security device. I'd been ready to kill this man, and Antonio dragged me away, promising to do it himself. Antonio had obviously let him live so I wouldn't have his death on my conscience. And there he was, armed and ready to return the favor with murder.

"Bruno Uvoli," I whispered.

Antonio made a *tsk* sound and shook his head. "His brother. Domenico."

Domenico pointed his gun at Antonio, and my spine turned to ice, but I didn't hear any shots. Out of bullets? Maybe. Antonio took three steps toward him and pulled the gun away, standing over Domenico with his own gun pointed.

---

6 Spin, Chapter 20, if you're interested in going back.

"Antonio," I said.

He looked at me then at my ripped sleeve where the bullet had almost hit me. "Go back."

Domenico had his hand up to fend off death. His leg was bleeding where he'd been shot. Had I done that? I hadn't seen Antonio shoot at the man behind the boulder. It could have only been me.

"You fucking bitch," he said.

Antonio cocked the hammer.

"Don't," I said. I had followed him intending to do no more than close the space between us. I hadn't intended to stop him from killing the second man. "It doesn't do us any good. And we're on foreign soil."

He was going to shoot, or so I thought. Instead he lowered his gun and licked his lower lip. He took a single step back as he put the weapon away. "You're right."

My eyes met his with an emotional click. He'd heard me and acted accordingly, as if I'd had the thought for him. Everything in that moment was right.

He took my hand and guided me toward the hostel, which had already cleared out, and through to the street. We ran across. Traffic had stopped, and dozens of people watched the flames.

I slowed. I didn't see anyone hurt but wanted to check, just to be sure. Antonio yanked me down the block toward our white Toyota. A Cadillac with the size and paint wear of a cruise ship pulled out from behind our car. Antonio ran to it and leaned into the driver's side window, where a straw-hatted man in his fifties turned the wheel.

"I'll trade you this car for mine," Antonio said as sirens got louder in the distance. He pointed the Toyota's key fob at the nondescript car we'd come in. He pressed a button, and the car squeaked. "Title's in the glove compartment."

Smoke rose from the desert behind the hostel, lighting the evening sky orange. A woman cried out behind me, bolting across the street. Two teenagers brought out a man with a bloodied shoulder, and she kneeled in front of him.

Guilt. There it was. I felt it for the innocent people I'd hurt. No more explosions. That guy was in pain because of me, and I didn't like it one bit.

Caddy Man shifted his hat, looked at Antonio, then past him at me. I smiled coyly, as if this was no more than the act of a crazy-ass boyfriend.

"Transmission's no good," the man said in a thick accent. "Bad." He laid his hands flat and wiped the air with them.

"It's okay."

The exchange of titles and keys was made in fifteen seconds, and our bags were removed from the Toyota in another five. Antonio drove away in a beat-up boat of a Cadillac with me in the passenger seat. An ancient fire engine pulled up behind us, and four police cars passed us coming from the other direction, sirens blaring and lights flashing red and blue.

Antonio put real weight on the gas pedal when the police cars passed. He pulled onto a scraggly highway, going in a direction I couldn't figure out. The car went into fourth gear and stayed there no matter what speed we went, lurching and jerking.

He looked ahead with an intensity that couldn't be attributed to the dark of night, one hand tight on the top of the steering wheel and the other draped out the window. The highway was mostly empty.

"Antonio?" I said.

No answer. Nothing moved but the small adjustments of the steering wheel.

"Antonio. Are you all right?"

Nothing.

"Antonio!"

He jerked the wheel, swerving to the side of the road in a crunch of sand and rock. The car pitched, flopping gears as the sheer length of the thing kept inertia from throwing us overboard. He slammed it in park and, in the same motion, reached for me. I didn't like the look in his eye. It looked like murder.

When his hand went around my throat, I liked it less.

"You did *what?*" He was stuck on some old conversation, as if rewinding a tape and playing it randomly.

"What are you talking about?" I asked, grabbing his wrist with my hands. He was holding me still, not choking me, but it was uncomfortable.

He thrust himself across the seat. Nothing stopped him. No armrest. No brake. Just a leather surface he put his knee on to get leverage. He was livid. Spitting mad. Hair in front of his face, beautiful mouth curved into a snarl.

"You drew fire to yourself?"

"It was—"

"*Basta!*" He put his face an inch from mine until I smelled bullets on his breath. "You do this again, and I'll…" He gritted his teeth so hard he couldn't speak.

"What?" I croaked. "What will you do?"

He pulled me toward him, fingertips digging into the space behind my jaw. I leaned into him, taking my hands off his wrist so I could push closer. I wasn't afraid.

"You do not—"

"What are you going to do, Capo?"

He didn't soften. Not a millimeter. He did not waver. He pushed me back against the door, and with his other hand, he twisted me around until I lay sprawled across the front seat.

"This is a fact, and it's a threat. You get killed, and I am as good as dead. Kill me first. If you die, you should just kill me."

I put my hands on the sides of his face. "It was the right thing."

His thumb stroked under my chin, and he lowered his head to put his lips to my cheek. "No. Don't…ever…do that again."

"I'll do what I have to."

He let me go and got as far up on his knees as possible under the car ceiling. I gasped as he reached for his waistband.

"There is one thing you have to do." He popped his button and held up a finger. "Stay still while I fuck you. That's your job. Spread your legs. That's all."

"You're so fucking backward." I tried to get up, but it was cramped in the car, and Antonio pushed me down. "Get off me."

He didn't get off me. He yanked my pants down with one hand and pressed on my breast with the other. He ripped off my jeans, stripping me of my shoes. "I'm going to fuck sense into you."

I had arguments on top of wisdom. I had logic and strategy on my side, but he pinned me like an animal and pulled my leg up until my knee was at my ear.

He slapped my ass and paused.

I groaned. "I'll do it again if I want."

"And I'll spank you for it if I want."

He slapped my bottom three more times. God, I should have been humiliated, but it woke my skin, sending a fire of pleasure through me. I couldn't move. Bone to skin, I was made viscous from the intimacy of indignity.

He pulled my legs farther apart, and I let him. He was hard with me. Merciless. His roughness silenced me into short breaths.

"Who's backward?" he growled. "Who has her legs open? It took me nothing to get you naked with your pussy out." He jerked up my shirt. "Now your tits. I can do anything to you. You're going to take my cock, and when you do, I want you to know I'm never letting you alone again. I own you, and you'll do what I tell you."

Before I had a chance to erase the thought, he rammed into me. My head was bent into the door handle, and one leg leaned on the dashboard as he took me without regard to my pleasure or pain. Outside, cars blew by so fast, I felt the air pressure change. I reached for him.

He swatted my hands away and pressed them to the window. "Look at me."

And I did, because he was still the most beautiful man I'd ever met.

"Never again. Say it." He pressed into me, deeper than deep, rubbing my clit with his body. "Look at me."

"Always, always."

"Never look away again."

He thrust into me again and again, and the fullness between my legs grew like a balloon ready to burst. I could have looked at the intensity in his eyes forever. There, I could believe he'd always be by my side, that I'd never be afraid again, that the safety he promised was real not just for me, but for us.

I believed it. In my heart I did, for just a moment, and the orgasm that came in that moment became tangible, with its own weight and mass. He let my wrists go and leaned on me. For those few moments, his roughness was gone, and he made love to me while I came, clawing his back as if that would get me inside him.

He buried his face in my neck and stiffened, releasing into me. He groaned again and again, then he was done.

He whispered my name. "Drawing fire can get you killed. There is no world without you in it. Nothing. I'm not talking about despair. I've lost people. This isn't me being a child. There is one universe. Just one. And it's between us. If you destroy that universe, you destroy me. Do you understand what I'm saying? You cannot do that again. Ever. For me."

"I was scared," I whispered. I could barely hear myself over the cicadas.

"I know." He dragged his lips over my cheek and to my throat.

"I was scared you were gone. That you'd be hit while I couldn't reach you."

"I know." He picked his head up and looked me in the eye. "I don't want you to be scared ever again. I'm going to teach you how to survive without me."

I pushed his chest so I could look him in the eye. "Enough of that."

I took his hair in my fists, I was so angry at him. How could he even consider that nonsense? Some idea that he was mentoring me for a life of misery?

Cars had been blowing past us sporadically, so the presence of another car on the highway didn't surprise me until it slowed down, and a car door slammed.

"Oh, crap," I said, pulling myself away.

Antonio picked his head up while holding me down. "Stay."

"I'm naked."

"That's why I'm staying here."

I heard the crunch of footsteps outside, and my door opened. Upside down, the man in the dark brown shirt looked ten feet tall, with a cowboy hat and a silver star like a sheriff in the old west.

Just above me, the underside of Antonio's chin cut a triangle into my view of the night sky

"Spinelli," the Tijuana cop said with a tinge of annoyance.

"Oscar."

"Hotel rooms too expensive for you?"

"We couldn't find parking."

"Get dressed, fucking gringos."

He slammed the door, and Antonio and I wiggled back into our clothes.

"You know him?" I looked behind us. Looked like that cop and another, shorter guy.

"His daughter."

I stopped what I was doing and looked at him.

"She got into trouble with a guy." He buttoned his pants. "Some drugs. The guy ran to LA, and I brought him back to TJ."

I jerked my legs through my jeans. "So he owes you?"

He buttoned the last button of his shirt. "Why?" A smile stretched across his face as if he knew what I thought but let me meet him there.

"How fast does this thing go?"

"In fourth gear all the way? Even this shit American car can hit a hundred fifty."

I made the rest of the journey in my imagination. He'd start the car and take off. We'd be followed for a time so the cop could say he did his best, but they'd give up, report us, and move on. We'd have nowhere to go. No passports. No way back. Then for sure we'd never get back to Jonathan.

Antonio caught my train of thought. "I don't think he'll chase us far."

I put my hand on his knee. "I have a better idea. There're no passports coming, right? If the forger sold us out? There's only one way out of here."

***

When we got out of the car, Oscar held out his hand to shake Antonio's. Oscar looked older, early fifties, when I was right side up, and his deputy looked to be a couple of decades younger. We made introductions in the middle of the desert, the afternoon wind forcing us to shout.

"You're in the shit, my friend," Oscar said.

"Keeps life interesting."

"Okay, I get it, but letting you walk's gonna cost you. You get outta LA with any cash?"

"I did," I interjected. I had a few hundreds in my pocket and no more. "But not to let us walk. We need to get back over."

Oscar, looked at his deputy, then at Antonio. Tipping his head to me, he said, "Live one you got here. She know she's jumping into the lion's mouth?"

"You can do it." Antonio waved as if it was nothing. "You got a badge. You can do anything."

Oscar laughed. "How? Tell them not to look at you?"

"Yes."

Oscar looped his thumbs in his belt as if they were too heavy for his shoulders to carry without support.

"People see what they want to," I said. "If they trust you, we can get across."

He laughed so hard his elbows shook. "You want me to be your coyote?"

I didn't want to look at Antonio. I didn't want to see his disapproval or disdain. Didn't want to see the thousand reasons this wouldn't work. But I did look at him, and he was fixed on Oscar, steady and strong.

"Yes," I said. "We want you to be our coyote."

"You know what stinking coyotes get paid?"

"Money isn't an object, generally speaking," I said, now totally out on a limb, "but transferring it can get sticky. So I think you may owe Antonio more than an escort out."

Oscar huffed. "One ride still pays for two." He held up two fat red fingers.

"I will find a way to pay you if we get across alive," Antonio said.

"And not into the hands of the Sicilians," I blurted.

"If they have you," Oscar said, "you'll be paying me from the grave."

Chapter 4

Seven Weeks Earlier[7]

ANTONIO

I didn't know how I felt about her.

I wasn't used to thinking much about how I felt or what I wanted. If I wanted a woman, I made sure she was someone who knew *omertà*, the law of silence, and practiced it. I was a lawyer and former consigliere, and I had too much information in my head to leave unprotected. So I found women already in the circle. I never had to even tell them to keep quiet. I didn't worry. If I was attracted to a woman outside the circle, I didn't fuck her. That was all.

But this one? Theresa? I wasn't even in control of myself with her. It was easy to see her on the television and admire her. The way she stood brought out her curves, and her eyes let you into a mind that turned and churned with something spoken in a language only she knew. She was inaccessible through that screen. I didn't have to think about what I wanted to do with her body because I couldn't touch it.

Then when I did, my mind was poisoned and I thought of nothing else.

I fucked her to get it out of my system, then thought, maybe one more time. If I could crack her and hear that language spill, I'd be done.

---

7 Time orientation – This is a few hours before Paulie found Theresa at *l'uovo* and accused her of working with Daniel to nail him.

In the shop office, with Paulie giving me a hard time about the Catholic Charities donation from the day before, I thought about how I could bend her until she broke just one more time.

And that was when Daniel Brower drove into the lot.

I'd never seen a man so bold in my life. He walked onto my property as if he had a right to be there. As if he had an Aston Martin making a high rumble when low was required. I saw him across the lot, through my office windows.

Paulie took his foot off the table. "What the—?"

I turned my back to Brower, who still had half the property to cross, in his beige jacket and flapping black tie. Paulie stood and put his hand on his weapon, which he had no license for whatsoever.

I waved my finger in the direction of his gun. "He's alone, and I know what it's about. Put that away."

Paulie had never looked at me with distrust in all the years I'd known him, but then, I saw it. It was so obvious, it jarred me.

I caught myself. I was acting as if I had done something wrong. I wasn't doing something wrong. I was doing something stupid. There was a difference.

"This is personal," I said.

He must have read my face, because his body went slack at the same time he rolled his eyes to the ceiling. He was so American. "You banged his wife."

"They never married."

"Jesus fucking Christ, Spin. We agreed not to do this. We agreed no women get in the way of business."

I shrugged. She'd been more than worth it, but I couldn't tell him that any more than I could tell him that I intended to do it again.

A knock at the door before it cracked open, and Lorenzo poked his head in.

"Let him in," I said before Zo could announce him.

Paulie stood and buttoned his jacket, which did nothing to hide the bulge under his arm. "Do not fuck with me on this."

Before I could decide if I should feel threatened or not, Brower came in. He looked naked without his security detail and trail of press.

"Danny DA," Paulie said with a thick coat of disrespect.

"Mister Brower, come with me." I indicated the door.

Before Paulie could protest, Brower and I were on our way into the lot. I didn't want to argue with Paulie in front of the DA, and I didn't want to shame him by asking him to leave.

"I know what you're here about," I said as we walked behind the building. We barely had room to walk two abreast. Oil cans stacked against the chain-link fence blocked the view of the graffiti'd cinderblock wall on the other side.

"You have no idea," he replied.

"One man's trash," I said, smiling. "You threw her away."

"Don't tell me she's your treasure. Let's skip all that. Let's not pretend you have a bone in your body that can feel anything. No one has time for discovery."

I didn't care what he thought about me, or his opinion of my intentions with Theresa. I didn't even know how I felt about her. But oddly, I couldn't read him.

"You have something," I said. "So why not just tell me what it is?" I tried to act casual, as if he had nothing on me.

"I know about your sister. I know there were four men who gang-raped her."

He did it on purpose. He used words that opened my glands and filled my bloodstream with violence. I wanted to choke him, and he smiled as if he knew it. He was trying to weaken me with my own bile, and I was letting it work.

"That was in Napoli," I said. "It's not your business."

"Four Neapolitans from a rival family. Three are dead, and you took their territory."

"I already thanked God for striking them down."

"You lit a candle to yourself," he said.

"You going to arrest me? In the back of my property? No. You didn't come here unarmed, by yourself, to take me in."

"I came to make a trade."

"This should be good."

"Do you want to hear it?"

I wanted to check him for a wire was what I wanted to do. I wanted to walk away, because there was no good end to this. He wasn't offering me anything that would benefit me. It wasn't in his nature. But I wanted to hear it, because it would tell me more about him than about me, and he was not to be underestimated.

I reached inside my jacket, and Daniel didn't stiffen or flinch, as if he knew I wouldn't pull my gun on him. He was confident of it even in his bones. That in itself was cause for concern.

I took out my cigarettes and lighter.

I poked out a cigarette for him, and to my surprise, he took it. I lit his, then mine, watching him for signs that he didn't smoke. But he blew a ring.

"I know what I did," he said. "I know, in the end, it'll fuck me. People don't vote for men who can't be monogamous. They think it means I'm not focused. Well, fine. Just fine. I'll fix what I can and fuck the rest. But Theresa takes it on herself. She thinks there's something wrong with her. And this is a problem for me, because there's nothing wrong with her."

"I agree."

I'd gotten to him, because his lips tightened. I knew he was imagining us together, and that made me happy. I'd fuck her again just to see that look on his face one more time.

"I know men," he said. "I know how we are. She's not some whore. She's not a tool in your drawer. She's sensitive, and she's been hurt enough."

"By you."

"By me."

"What do you want me to do about it?" I asked.

"Here's what you're going to do about it. You're going to take whatever happened yesterday and file it under stuff in the past. You're going to politely refuse to see her again. You'll leave her the hell alone, and she'll find someone else."

"How noble of you."

"Fuck you."

"No," I said, stamping my cigarette under my shoe and speaking softly. "Fuck you."

I walked off, back to my office, to my life, to figure out what I wanted to do about this woman. I wouldn't be told who I could and couldn't fuck, but I wouldn't be pushed toward her in the name of spite either.

"Spinelli," Daniel called behind me.

He didn't seem flustered. He didn't shout, he just said my name, and that made me listen. I stopped at the corner and looked at him as he flicked his cigarette through the chain link.

"I know where the fourth man is. If you want him, you know what you have to do."

Chapter 5

The Return to Los Angeles

THERESA

Oscar had gotten us into the back of a truck without being seen. He kept making jokes about being a newly minted coyote, since it seemed Antonio had rescued his daughter from one. I sensed an edge to the jokes.

"You didn't sleep with her, did you?" I'd whispered in a free moment at the depot.

"No. Can't speak for Paulie though."

"Jesus. He's not going to try to get back at you for that?"

The truck had come before he had a chance to answer, and we were all smiles and handshakes.

Hours into the journey, I'd forgotten all about Paulie's indiscretion. I was getting antsy in the back of the truck. It was dark outside, so it was black inside. The hours blew by in the *hup-shh hup* of the tires hitting regular seams in the road. The heartbeat sound made me anxious about Jonathan. We'd made the deal to take us all the way to Los Angeles, and the drive seemed to take forever.

"Do you smell that?" Antonio said in the dark.

I felt him next to me, a stalwart presence that kept my pounding heart from exploding. "Smells like trees."

"Olive trees. There are olive orchards in southern California. We must be passing a stretch along the 5."

I nodded and took his hand, memorizing that scent. It was important to Antonio. It reminded him of his childhood, and it seemed as if knowing an olive orchard when we passed it brought him closer to me.

"What's your mother like?" I asked.

"Sick, always sick. Since Nella...since the thing with those men, she doesn't get out of bed much. But she talks on the phone and leans out the window. When you meet her, she'll make you listen to opera. She'll tell you Italian culture has nothing to do with crime. And she's right. We're aberrations, my father and I. She'll show you art and read you poetry. She'll play you opera until you can sing it in the shower."

"I love opera." I was charmed by the idea of meeting his mother. It seemed like a fantasy that could happen. "And your dad?"

"Never. You'll never meet him. By running away from this marriage, I put him in a terrible position. If I see him again, fifty-fifty chance he'll kill me. Let's stick with my mother for now." The dim light glinted off his teeth when he smiled, but what he said couldn't be more serious.

"Opera and art then." My mind wandered to my own mother, her cultured aloofness, and my brother's love of art.

"Jonathan's probably fine," I said into the dark after a long silence.

"Yes. Probably."

"Fine. I'm sure of it." I recited it more than said it. "Fine."

Because I couldn't see Antonio, when he squeezed my hand, I felt every bit of his skin, his warmth, the pressure of his touch. We'd be home soon. The border patrol hadn't checked the back of the police van. We just withstood the heat, the stink of gunpowder and old sweat heavy in the bare box.

Oscar had been so confident, he'd sat us in the back without a contingency plan, and he'd been right. He'd taken our guns though. Antonio had been reluctant, but Oscar wasn't moving armed passengers. End of story.

Antonio and I sat next to each other on the wood bench, barely moving, ready for everything to go wrong. We weren't resigned to failure, only sitting in a state of preparedness.

"I don't know how I can face my family after what I've done," I said. "I hurt them. I try not to think about it...but I'll have to deal with it."

"Don't explain to them. You're back, and that's all there is to it."

"I'm not worried about explaining. It's...of everything I've done...I wronged them. All of them. They love me, and I made them grieve for nothing."

"You should sleep," he said.

"I can't. I can't think about anything but losing you and facing them."

"Do you still have the medal I gave you? The St. Christopher?"

"Yes." It lay flat against my chest. I forgot it was there most of the time.

"Touch it."

I did. I couldn't discern anything but an overall bumpiness on the nickel-sized charm. He put his arm around me and pulled me toward him. I didn't feel as though I was resisting, but apparently I was.

"Down. Put your head on my lap."

I rested on him, letting his thumb stroke my cheek. "That medal came from my great-great-grandfather, one of the first *camorrista*. It protects you from harm. All harm. Even when you beat yourself, you're protected."

"What about you?"

I felt a shrug in the movements of his body. "I don't need as much protecting."

I sighed. Arguing was pointless. "You should sleep too."

"I'll sleep when I'm dead."

"Stop that."

He pulled my hair off my face, stroking it gently back. "It's inevitable. One day, Theresa Drazen will close her eyes." He drew his fingers gently across my eyelids and down my cheek. I felt the need for sleep cover me like a blanket, as if my limbs and senses were in the first stage of shutting down. "She'll close them while thinking a happy thought. About when she was younger, and she and her husband drove across the border in a police truck, before he got old and ugly."

"You will never be ugly." It took an enormous amount of energy to get those five words out, but they needed to be said.

He continued as if I hadn't said a thing. "This is the day she'll remember. The day her brother's heart was healed, and she and her husband made peace with the Sicilians. The day they went to live in the olive orchards. When you close your eyes for the last time, it will be this day you remember as the first day of the long happiness of your life. You will smile your whole journey to heaven."

I didn't know if he said anything else. My thoughts started to go pre-dream, and I was far away from the heat and smell of the truck, held down only by Antonio's touch on my cheek and the thrumming of the wheels on the road.

I woke with a mouth full of white school glue when the truck jerked to a stop and went backward, beeping. The light through the tiny windows in the door was daylight bright, then grey, as if we'd glided indoors.

Antonio's head rested on the side of the truck, but his eyes were open. *"Buongiorno."*

"Hi. You look good for a guy who slept sitting up." I rubbed my eyes. He couldn't possibly look that good on no sleep, but he did. Unshaven. A little rough around the edges, but still perfect.

He cupped my chin. "I want you to be ready for anything." He gently pulled me up so he could stand. "I don't know what we're going to see when those doors open."

"As long as you stay with me, I'm ready."

The windows in the rear bay doors were set so high, Antonio had to stretch himself to see through them.

I heard a conversation outside the truck. It sounded like English, but I couldn't string two words together. Contentious, sharp, businesslike. Antonio rubbed his eyes and sighed and motioned me to him.

"What is it?" I tried to get tall enough to see through the wire-meshed windows, but I couldn't.

He didn't answer, just looked at me for a few seconds, then took my hands. "Listen to me, this is not negotiable. This is the rule. Whatever I do, you stick to the story we agreed on."

His tone was so sure, so confident, as if I were an employee and he were the head of operations for Theresa and Antonio Inc., I got a little ruffled.

"I'm not agreeing to anything until you tell me what you've got on your mind."

He put his finger up. Tightening his voice like a rubber band wrapped twice around something just a little too big, he got his tone down to a low, tight-jawed growl. "We don't have time for this. Just do what I say."

I put my hands on my hips, more to give my body a message from my mind, because my physical self wanted to do whatever he said, almost as a reaction. But my mind was infuriated. "Tell me first."

The clack of the lock echoed in the empty space, and he let go of me.

"Do not defy me," he said.

I didn't have a second to tell him I didn't want to defy him, only know what he had planned.

The back door lifted, clattering open as it slid up.

There wasn't much like the squawk of a police bandwidth, both urgent and incomprehensible. Like the scrawl on a prescription pad, it was only clear to the initiated. I tingled from between my shoulders to my fingertips, as if my central nervous system demanded I do something violent.

We were supposed to be dropped by Sequoia in a building Antonio's company owned. Had the cops infiltrated it? This was bad. So bad. My skin got tight around me, cutting my ability to breathe, to think, to see a foot in front of me.

The muscles of my hand tightened and the skin...

No. That was Antonio. He was holding my hand. I took a short breath, all my lungs would hold, and looked at him. He oozed a type of awareness and alertness that made me feel safe next to him.

I exhaled, and my chest opened. It would be all right. Whatever it was, I could handle it.

Half a second later, with my every nerve ending on fire, the front cab doors slammed shut, and the man pulling up the truck door was revealed.

It was Daniel. The squawk was from two cops passing behind him.

"What the—?" I gasped, realizing we were in a loading dock in the First Street police precinct.

"I knew it!" Daniel cried, pumping his fist. "God! You!" He pointed at me. "You're just…sight for sore eyes doesn't even begin."

He took two steps into the truck and put his arms around me, invoking God and Jesus in a litany of gratitude I didn't feel I deserved. He rocked back and forth, squeezing me until I thought I'd suffocate. I turned my head just enough to see Antonio. His face was impassive, but the clenched fists at his side told me how he was reacting to the hug.

"Dan, I can't breathe."

Daniel pulled away but held my shoulders. "Are you hurt?"

"She's fine," Antonio said, putting his hand on my shoulder.

Daniel didn't seem the least bit threatened. He was so close to me, I could see the white rings around his blue eyes. "What happened?"

"It's a long story," I said.

"We thought you were dead."

"I know. I…we escaped. They were after him. They had Paulie lure him into the Carriage House and—"

"Slow down, Theresa," Antonio said. We'd gone over the story and who would tell it.

"No! I won't!" Was I being too petulant? Did the lady protest too much? To hell with that. I had to sell it and sell it fast. "It was the Bortolusis. They were afraid Antonio was going to make a marriage that would compete with them, so they planted a car bomb at the shop then tried to do the same at their own wedding. Those people are nuts, Dan. They won't leave him alone. He needs protection."

"And you ran," Daniel said, crossing his arms.

"Damn right we did," I said.

Daniel looked over my shoulder at Antonio, who held up his hands. He'd slept sitting up and had a day and a half of growth on his face, but the sparkle in his eyes made him look as if he'd just stepped out of the shower.

"I make no accusations," he said, "and for my own protection, I don't argue with her. But we're back."

"And the shooting of Mister Patalano?" Daniel asked.

I swallowed a bucket of ice.

"Shooting?" Antonio said casually, as if talking about the weather. "So he's not dead?"

"Not entirely."

"I was there when he shot himself," Antonio said, shaking his head in mock disappointment. "He always had this problem. He couldn't hit the side of a garage."

"We'll see what forensics comes back with on that. In the meantime, come with me. I have something to show you."

Chapter 6

Six Weeks Earlier[8]

ANTONIO

The day I killed the last man who'd raped Nella, I forgot my own name.

I did it four days after Daniel came to me with his name in exchange for turning my back on Theresa. Four days after I kicked her out of the shop because I suspected she was partnering with him, even while I didn't believe it. Four days of making sure Daniel's man was really the culprit. Knowing I might be getting set up, I killed him anyway.

At the time, I'd been confused. Confused about my purpose in life, which was vengeance for my sister. Confused about how to proceed now that I'd killed the last of them, and confused about this woman who wasn't supposed to mean anything to me.

I felt a curious emptiness when I stood over his body. Brower had given me his name, and despite the fact that the DA thought I was an animal who would kill anyone, I had to check his facts.

It all lined up.

Four days of forcing myself across the town, asking questions that would only be answered when accompanied by gunshots or a beating so deep inside Griffith Park, the threat of starvation on broken legs was real.

---

8 Spin, Chapter 20 (ibid footnote 6). The road rage incident.

Four days of petitioning old Italians to let me finish my business.

Half a day of chasing him, because he knew I was coming. When I finally stood over the rapist fuck after the light had gone out of his eyes, a piece of myself went with him.

That was it. I was done. I had no more vengeance to wreak. I had no more debts to pay.

I dialed my mother's number to tell her Nella was safe, that the men who'd raped her were gone forever. Down to the last one, they were wiped from the earth. But I couldn't tell her. I couldn't make it real. I had to figure out what it meant for me first. I drove to the mountains and took a dead dirt road up, up always up, and walked past a yellow-and-black gate until I could see California in front of me.

What would I do now?

That empty space filled itself with an ache I couldn't control. I even felt it happening and pushed it away. Denied it. But the anger-shaped space inside me changed into a vacuity designed for her sweet smell and her cinnamon hair, the sound of her laugh, her tone when she was haughty, and the silk of her skin in my hand. She took up residence, kicked off her shoes, and sprawled out inside my soul.

I couldn't have her. It was crazy. But the place where the want for vengeance had resided was filled with the want for her, as if I had a proscribed amount of space for desire in my heart and it had to be occupied.

I felt the warmth from my chest to my fingertips as she infected my blood. Every part of me vibrated. I had agreed to stay away from her. I'd made a trade. Vengeance in exchange for erasing her from my life.

But in exacting the vengeance, she became impossible to erase, and when I got a call that Bruno was going to grab her because he was ambitious and stupid, I had to nip it in the bud. Not to protect myself, but because I needed to send a message. Theresa Drazen was not to be touched.

I couldn't be with her. My world would break her, and hers would never accept me. I was fine with that. Just fine. Up to the point where she was hurt. Then the space in me where vengeance was, that was now filled with thoughts of her, widened a little, and the old rage seeped in.

At exactly the right time, I found out she was being chased up Mulholland Drive. We found her wielding a stick against a man who had made his bones at twelve.

"Make no mistake," I said after closing her car door. Her eyes were cast in shadow from the car roof, until she moved, and I saw her broken. "I will hurt you to protect you."

Her lips parted another millimeter. I had to bite my tongue to keep from kissing her. I was trying to scare her, but I hadn't. I'd excited her. It was in the curve of her lips and the growing tension between my legs.

"Now go." I turned my back to her. I heard her back up, and the glare from her headlights swung against the trees and disappeared.

Lorenzo got off Bruno when I approached. Bruno's hand was shot up, and he had one foot in nothing but a black sock like old men wore. Paulie kept a foot on Bruno's shot up hand and a shoe in his mouth to muffle his screams. I stood over Bruno, considered the flame at the tip of my cigarette, then looked at him again, stretched before me.

"Bruno," I said, flicking the ash on him. "How are you?"

Paulie removed the shoe. Bruno spit defiantly, but gravity sent it back in his face. Paulie put his foot on the man's throat. I'd had that done to me once. It was very uncomfortable, and the next day I'd looked as if I'd danced with a noose.

"What did you think you were doing?" I asked.

He grunted. I didn't know if he could even pay attention to me with the fear of death clouding his vision. I retrieved the shoe that had been pulled from his mouth and tapped it on his forehead.

"Don't you know nothing, *stupido*?" Paulie mangled even the simplest Italian words. "You can't get to us through a woman."

I crouched until I took up all of the frame of Bruno's vision. "He's got a point. Now, you have my attention. Did you have something you wanted to tell me?"

He snorted, choking on his own snot, eyes blood red and narrowed.

"I can't hear you." I put my hand behind my ear. "Was it my number you wanted? Maybe call me and ask me on a date?"

He shook his head. Snorted.

"Liar." I pinched his cheeks until his mouth opened, then I jammed the shoe back in, sole-side down. "Did you want to say hello? Join my crew? I need someone to clean the floors. They're filthy. People walk in with dirty shoes. It's disgusting. No? You're shaking your head, so all right, if you didn't want to ask me on a date and you don't want to work for me, then I'm going to assume you didn't want to send me a message. I'm going to assume you wanted to fuck Theresa Drazen. Is that correct?"

He shook his head as much as he could.

"Now you're lying. Everyone wants to fuck her. I want you to lie to my face, you piece of shit." I pulled the shoe out of his mouth. A trail of saliva followed. "You were going to do what, once you caught her?"

How he had the energy to spit in my face, I'll never know, but I respected his nerve.

Paulie did not. He took his foot off Bruno long enough to kick him in the cheek.

I yanked Bruno up by the collar and pinned him to the side of the car, then got in his face, daring him to spit again. "You have no manners, Bruno. This a Sicilian thing?"

"Kill me. I dare you."

"Tell me what you thought you were doing."

"I was going to teach you a lesson," he choked out. "Give her a little of what those Neapolitans gave Nella. In honor of the last one you killed."

He said it through his teeth, biting back tears. He wanted to beg for his life. I could smell it on him, yet he was pushing me.

I was ready to be pushed. I'd killed a man the day before, and there was an inertia to violence. Once set in motion, it tended to stay in motion.

But vengeance didn't have the same inertia. I was filled. I should have been enraged by what he said. Insulted. Offended to the core. But I felt none of that. As I squeezed my fingers tighter around his neck, what I felt was fear that by staying away from Theresa, I was creating a vacuum where other men would go, and they would use her to take action on their own vendettas. She wasn't one of us, so they wouldn't suffer any consequences. I was leaving her wide open, and the thought of something happening to her drove me insane.

Nothing seemed more natural and right than standing over Bruno Uvoli and taking his life. Because he was an animal, an affront, and mostly because he'd tried to hurt her.

In that moment, I decided to have her. To protect her. To satisfy the longing in my heart. For my own salvation. Once that was decided, I couldn't kill the man. I had to earn her.

I pushed him against the car. "Get in."

Paulie flicked his cigarette to the ground. "Where we going?"

"Sequoia," I said. "I know a doctor who can take care of this little shit's hand."

"What the fuck?" Paulie exclaimed.

Bruno looked at me suspiciously.

"He's going to send a message back to his people." I dropped my cigarette and stamped it. "This vendetta is done. And unless you want to see more blood shed, stay away from Theresa Drazen."

Chapter 7

First Street Precinct

THERESA

Daniel put his key into the service elevator. I hadn't been in it before, as it was used to transport suspects and convicts from the precinct offices to the prisons and courts.

Antonio looked at our escape route, at me, at the elevator, then back at me.

Daniel held the door open.

"If I didn't know you better," Antonio said, "I'd think you were setting us up."

"You, I'd set up," he replied. "If I could figure out how to bring you down without taking her with you." He tilted his head toward me.

There seemed to be a sort of brutal honesty I hadn't been aware of between the two men. As if they had a shared history.

"She stays here," Antonio said. "I'll come up with you. I'll answer any question you have. But she goes to see her brother."

Daniel appeared to consider something. He made all the right signs, gave all the right clues. A pause. A breath. Eyes slightly elsewhere but still present. A tap of the finger. As if he was checking things off a list I'd provided him, years ago.

I had no idea if he was faking or not. He'd gotten that good.

"Fine," he said.

"No, absolutely not." I walked up to Daniel until I was practically in the elevator. "You have nothing on him, or you'd have a rear flank of police and he'd be Mirandized already."

"I never said I was arresting anyone. I said I wanted to ask questions. And his confession's inadmissible considering the evidence hasn't even been gathered yet and, thanks to him, my reputation in this town is shot to hell. So you can come, or I can force you. And I'm at the point where I've got fuckall to lose, so if I were you, I'd just come along for the ride."

"She goes," Antonio said, stepping past Daniel into the elevator. Daniel held the doors open. "He's right. You should go."

Antonio leaned against the back wall and folded his hands in front of him. He knew the law. He'd let Daniel spin while I saw Jonathan. It was the smartest thing to do. But with Daniel between us and my lover boxed in, a little empty spot opened up. A spot that told me I was alone, adrift, not enough.

"No," I whispered.

"You need to see Jonathan. You don't have time for this," Daniel said.

My sinuses suddenly pinched and tingled. "Is he all right?"

"No..." He drifted off as if trying to formulate the right way to say what needed saying, and unless he'd taken serious acting lessons, he wasn't faking the distress in his voice. "He's really fucked up. Bad. You have to see him by tonight, or it might be too late."

"Too late? What kind of too late?"

He shook his head, and my chest tightened. "The worst kind. I'm sorry."

"It was routine stuff when I saw him," I protested.

"It happened fast. Look, I'm going to question you, I promise you that, but I like Jonathan, and you need to see him."

"Go, Contessa," Antonio said from behind Daniel. "I have this."

I couldn't save Antonio, but maybe I could. I wasn't powerless. But if I told the truth, that I'd shot Paulie, I wouldn't see my brother. I could admit to the murder at any time. Tomorrow. The next day. No amount of time would change the facts, but in that time, Jonathan could be dead.

Daniel moved out of the way, and the door started to shut. Antonio was cut into a straight line by the edge, then bisected, then almost gone behind the scratched metal door. He'd be gone in another fraction of a second, cut off from me by rebar and concrete, floors and ceilings, men and women who would become obstacles to my wholeness and safety.

I stuck my hand in the elevator door before it closed, and it bounced back with a rattle. "I'm coming up."

"Theresa..."

"Contessa..."

I stepped in.

"I was trying to save you from grief," Daniel said as the door slid shut again.

"Too late," I said, standing next to Antonio. I watched the red numbers flip as we went upstairs into the belly of the LAPD.

Chapter 8

THERESA

"Who is this?" Margie asked.

I was hunched in the corner of the precinct bathroom with Daniel's phone. The first thing they'd done was take Antonio away and put him behind a door, and my sense of orientation went with him, as if I'd been airlifted and dropped into a foreign nation. My ex gave me his phone and told me to call my sister, whose first reaction to my voice had been silence. Her second had been disbelief.

"It's Theresa, I swear. I—"

"We're all going through five stages of a loss, here. Mom is still on denial and Sheila's on anger, and you're calling me like it's hey-how-do-you-do time."

"You're in the same stage as Sheila."

"What was Fiona put away for?" she asked.

"What?"

"Prove you're you. And tell me who she was in with."

"Oh, please, Margie, we don't have time."

The lights buzzed above me, casting the bathroom in a light that seemed to suck away brightness rather than add it. I'd put my family through hell. Avoidance was futile.

"She was put away twice," I said, resigned to doing this. "Which time?"

"The first time."

I couldn't hear her tapping her foot, but I knew she was.

"Fiona went to Westonwood for stabbing her boyfriend. Jonathan was there for suicide. Both were caused by a girl named Rachel, who was my friend. Who Daddy seduced. Enough?"

She paused then spoke quietly. "Thank God. Thank thank thank God a million times you're not dead. Where are you?"

"I'm at the First Street Station, on the bathroom floor."

"You know what? I have no idea what's happening with you, and I'll care about it tomorrow. You need to be here."

"I know. I'll be there, I promise."

"I'm not trying to be graphic. Just blunt," she said. "Jon has irreparable damage to his heart. It's not going to go well without a transplant. And maybe you don't care. Maybe this new life you have is more important than the old one. That's fine. But—and this is not for me, it's for Jonathan—see him. Okay? Just see him. Then go back to whatever it was you were doing."

"Okay."

"Don't make me come after you."

"I'll be there. I swear."

"All right. Then you can tell me why you're not dead."

My bitter laugh bounced off the green tiles as I hung up. I had to be a big girl and leave the building without Antonio.

After washing my hands, I looked down and did what I always did since the night Antonio and I met. I checked my shoes. A little square of toilet paper was stuck to my right heel, still white and flat, hanging on for dear life, hoping for rescue from the trash.

Come on, Theresa.

I picked it off. I should have thrown it away. But it reminded me of meeting Antonio, of those months and years before, when I felt incomplete, and how that had changed with him. I knew a piece of paper couldn't bring that back. Only I could. But I couldn't toss it without tossing the feeling away, so I put it in my pocket.

I took a deep breath and went into the hall. It was full of cops and lawyers, little metal carts with file boxes stacked high. Linoleum floors scuffed in the middle and shiny where they met the walls. I knew this place. I'd met Daniel here a hundred times, back when the doors didn't mean a thing to me. Nothing behind them had been of interest.

"Daniel!" I said when I saw him opening one of the nondescript doors.

"Can you go to the waiting room?" he asked.

"No. I need to see Antonio, then I have to go to Jonathan. Then after that, you and I are going to talk about what happened at the Gate Club."

"You don't call the shots, Theresa." He said it without reproach or vindictiveness. A man with toes everyone seemed to step on regularly, he said it so gently, I wondered if he was trying to ease me into a new reality.

"Phrase everything I just said as a question."

"Mister Spinelli is occupied," he said.

His insistence irked me, but I didn't feel in a position to argue further. But I couldn't just walk without talking to my Capo. If Antonio was occupied, it was probably Daniel who was occupying him, and there was a good chance he was behind the door Daniel was about to enter.

I stepped back. "Fine."

"Don't go far, Tinkerbell."

I turned and walked away slowly. As soon as I heard the door squeak open, I spun on my heel and pushed past Daniel, through the door, and into an empty room with two folding chairs.

It was dark. The only light was from a window looking onto the adjacent interview room. Antonio sat alone at a metal table, in a beat-up wooden chair. If he knew the wall to his left was a two-way mirror, he didn't show it by moving a muscle.

Daniel closed the door behind him. "You should go."

"I'm going to bang on the window and shout."

"No, you're not. The room is soundproofed and it doesn't look like a mirror on the other side, first of all, and second of all, you're leaving."

He reached for my wrist, but I pulled myself away before he could get a good grip. A door opened, and at first, I thought it was the door to the room I was in, but it wasn't. It was the door to Antonio's room.

Daniel muttered, "I didn't want it to go like this."

I glanced at him, his shoulders slouched, his eyes closed. I turned back to the interview room. Antonio was standing. In the doorway was a woman about my age and a boy of about ten. She had a cascade of black hair and olive skin. Her lips were full and sexual, and her limbs were lanky and long.

The boy.

Well.

The boy was a young version of the man I loved.

I lost the ability to swallow. Once I saw them, I couldn't keep my eyes off Antonio. He could be stoic with the world, but he'd always shown his emotions to me. When he saw who entered the room, his face betrayed his heart. His joy was unmistakable as he said something in Italian.

"She heard he was dead and came here."

Nella. It must be his sister. She was just stunning. A heartbreaking beauty with brown eyes that had seen too much and a quiet confidence that I tried to embody over the feeling of being incomplete.

"She's been in Sorrento," Daniel said compassionately. "In hiding. She wanted to get her son away from the mob."

The woman ran into Antonio's arms, and I stared as he embraced her, pressing his nose to her hair. They spoke in Italian, rushing through words I couldn't understand. He touched her face and kissed her cheek.

"I went looking for you and found two Spinellis on a manifest from Naples. I thought it was a ruse you'd set up. But it wasn't. Obviously. It makes me kind of almost believe your story."

Antonio got on one knee to speak to the boy, his nephew. I'd never seen a man so happy. Even in that gritty box of a room, he shone with contentment, as if he was where he belonged and with the people he was meant for. His family. I knew then that I had to go back to Italy with him. If I was in jail twenty years, thirty for shooting Paulie, I'd meet him under the olive trees at sixty. He needed to be home with his family, and I'd be with him, no questions asked.

"The only thing was the names were so close," Daniel said, leaning on the mirror, watching me. "Are you all right?"

"I'm fine." Why wouldn't I be? I was witnessing Antonio speaking softly to his nephew as if the child was his own son. "Close to what? The names?"

"To you. Antonin and Tina Spinelli. It seemed like a ridiculous subterfuge."

Wait.

Something was wrong.

"Tina?" I asked.

"Short for Valentina."

I rummaged around the dark corners of my mind, looking under memories and details. I was snapped out of it when the little boy slapped Antonio's face and screamed at him in Italian. Valentina pulled the boy back and held him, her eyes welling up with an apology.

"Valentina shortens to Nella?"

Daniel didn't answer right away. He waited until I'd turned from the scene to look at him leaning against the mirror, eyes cast down. He fidgeted with his fingernail, gave it a quick bite. Stopped himself.

"Daniel. What is it?"

"Tink, I don't know how to say this."

"Don't call me that." Before the sentence was even out of my mouth, I uncovered the name from a mental file box of things that were precious to Antonio in the past.

Daniel let me know that what was written in that file was right. "Valentina is his wife."

I thought, in that moment, Daniel would be a vindictive dick. But he wasn't. Not with my hand covering my mouth and my eyes filling up.

Over.

Everything was over.

"Theresa. I'm sorry."

His apology was a backdrop to the scene in the interview room. Antonio spoke softly to her, Valentina…his wife…as she held her…. no…*their* son. He put his arm around her. What was her scent? Did he remember it? Even with his eyes closed, he looked as though everything was coming back to him.

He was home, and I was on the other side of a wall

Chapter 9

ANTONIO

I'd had a life once. I was a family lawyer. I practiced keeping families together because I'd never had one. Valentina had married that man. She married an optimist with a future who had escaped a life in the shadows. She married endless potential, strength, contentment.

The man she was married to the day before she died was a monster. She'd watched me become everything she loathed, everything my mother had tried to save me from. Valentina watched me fail and drew away away away. I didn't even realize she was a stranger until her car exploded over the hills of Naples and I didn't know where she was driving to.

The despair. There was nothing like it. No experience in my imaginings. No anguish so great I could kill man after man to eradicate it. But I dampened it. I buried that optimistic man and all his possibilities and I steeped myself in what I was to become.

An animal. A hell-bound murderer.

And...

And before Valentina was brought in, Daniel Brower had asked me questions that didn't make sense, about Italy, about my whereabouts ten years ago. My relationship with Paulie took up no more than three minutes. I couldn't turn the questions on him because there were two cops in the room, and my personal history with the district attorney was dangerous territory.

I knew he was hiding something. I knew he was beating around a bush. I knew he was playing a game of his own making when he dismissed the cops and said the interview was over. They shut off the camera and started out.

"And Theresa?" I'd asked as Brower was the last one out the door.

"Don't worry about her."

"Don't dismiss me."

"I'm not dismissing you." Brower held the door ajar. "Believe me. You fucked me royally. I'd never dismiss you again. But you're about to hurt her, and I thought I could stand that. I was wrong."

Before I could tell him he was wrong about that too, he closed the door, and my denials died on my lips. I'd never hurt Theresa. I'd take death for her. Eat it with a spoon. Embrace my damnation to save her. She was my hope, the call to that earlier self I thought had died.

In the minutes between the door closing and opening again, I unraveled the components of our predicament and tried to find a way through. She'd confess to shooting Paulie even if I swore I'd done it. The evidence might back her up. I had no idea what forensics would find. Hopefully the Carriage House had been such a mess nothing could be proven. Hopefully there had been so many criminals in such a small space that doubts would arise. But mostly, I hoped that the district attorney loved Theresa enough to protect her from what she'd done.

What simple worries. What facile hopes.

I forgot all of them. They imploded. A windshield—smooth, simple—cracked into an unpredictable web of joy, horror, confusion, completion.

And disbelief.

In the first second of seeing Valentina, I thought I was looking at a ghost. Or a different woman. Or a trick of the light. She was older but the same. She was...my God. My heart went up and down at the same time. It went to the heavens with joy and dropped out of me like a stone, because my grief was for naught, and my anger had been misdirected.

And still, even with her hand on the shoulder of a boy who looked exactly like my father, I didn't believe it until I held her and smelled the grass in her hair. It was her. I felt nothing but confirmation, a clicking into place of a memory with a fact.

I had questions. Too many. Where? How? Why? And they were drowned out by the sound of a windshield cracking slowly into a million complex shapes that would never fit together again.

She'd done to me what Theresa and I had attempted to do to everyone else. She'd faked her death. Her resurfacing was the perfect vengeance for the wrong we'd done.

"Antonio," she said, the Italian lilt a hymn from her lips.

Her voice brought me back ten years, to the rustling olive trees, the trickle of the fountain in the *piazza*, the thick smell of soil. She ran into my arms, and I had to catch her or she would fall.

"Valentina? Is it you?" Her cheek felt the same when my lips touched it; the smell and taste were the same. Though I felt all the tenderness in my heart for her and all the joy in the world that she was alive, another crack appeared where my love should have been. I pulled away, more confused than I thought possible.

"It's me, *amore*," she said.

"I know, it's just...how?"

"We have forever to talk."

Did we? Forever? Another crack. Another discomfort lodged in my gut where I thought I couldn't be less comfortable. I held her face and called for the old feelings and found only happiness. An overwhelming yet generic pleasure that she still existed.

She cast her eyes down. "This is your son, Antonin."

Her voice was cool and distrustful, and it hitched, as if she spoke through her own pane of broken glass.

I had to look at him. *Dolore.* That was the only word for it. Pain. In him, and in me, and between us. I didn't know children. All I saw was a little man and missed opportunities. Misused lives. Broken promises. And maybe the hope that they could be fixed. Maybe some wrongs could be undone. Maybe even a man like me could get a second chance to do something right.

That must have been what my father felt when he saw me for the first time in eleven years. That was why he'd brought me into his world and tried to keep me from it at the same time. In that crack of realization, that I would do the same with my son as my father had done with me, Antonin let me know it wouldn't be easy. He hit me. I deserved it.

"Antonin!" Valentina cried, taking the boy and looking at me. "I'm so sorry. He's confused."

The blow hurt my face but cracked that moment of hope that he needed me to fix him. Little Antonin was perfectly fine without me. I'd only undo the good work his mother had done.

"We're all confused," I replied. *Andati in pallone.* I could only feel this confusion in Italian. As soon as I put eyes on her, I knew what she was feeling.

"No," she said defiantly, her Italian as cutting as it was musical. "No, we are not all confused."

Chapter 10

THERESA

had to do something. I had to walk. Think. Speak. I had to see my brother. I had to plan the next few days.

I had to do a lot of things. But what I wouldn't do was have the same complete mental breakdown I did when I found out Daniel was cheating on me. So I dedicated myself to shutting out the image of Antonio looking at his wife as if he'd finally come home. Blot out the way he touched her cheek. Erase the sound of them speaking to each other in a common language. I had to focus.

I sat in Daniel's empty office with my hands in my lap and recited a litany of prime numbers, focusing my energy completely on three numbers ahead, imagining the shape of the digits, occupying the lowest parts of my mind on garbage so the higher parts of my mind could attend to the important things. I had returned alive. I was all right. He was all right. And maybe this crazy screwed-up situation was the best thing for him.

Daniel entered with a glass of water. "How are you doing?"

I took it and put it on the desk. "Thank you. I'm fine."

19. 23. 29. 31.

He sat across from me in an old green chair. The leather squeaked from his weight when he shifted forward. "I'm kind of relieved. I thought he'd killed her. I thought your judgment had gone fully out the window."

"And now you think I was being reasonable?"

"No. But at least I don't think he's in the habit of murdering his wives. Just his business partners."

"He didn't. I did." I tried to swallow the admission back. It wasn't necessary to confess just yet, but in my weakened state, the truth was a powerful balm.

"Yeah," he said. "Sure. You did it."

He didn't believe me. Or he didn't want to. I tried to care, but I was broken, split apart, an incomplete measure of a person.

I couldn't come up with a reply, because all of my energy went into remembering Antonio's reunion with his wife.

Focus.

Wife.

An unbreakable bond under God. I'd been bedded, repeatedly, by a married man. I was the other woman. The whore. The one left behind. Big words, explosive ideas, hurtful phrases pushed into my consciousness like a TV left on to a bad show I couldn't stop watching.

37. 41. 43. 47.

"Theresa?"

"I'm fine. I think I should go to the hospital."

"I can take you."

"Sure." What had he smelled when he put his nose in her hair? Hope? Togetherness? Completion? "I'm just a little…" I spun my hand at the wrist. There was a word, but I couldn't think of it because I was trying to get to the primes over a hundred, where it got complex enough to sustain me. I had to shut off the TV in my head. *She stayed gentle. She stayed gentle and died.* "He told me she was dead."

"He thought she was."

He thought she was. Why was it taking me so long to process things? Why couldn't I turn the TV down? *He thought she was dead.* Right. Okay. So I wasn't half the whore, and he wasn't a liar. He'd asked me to marry him.

Don't cry.

Meaning Daniel was telling it right. Antonio wouldn't have asked for my hand if he thought he had a living wife.

Don't.

Cry.
Focus.
53. 59. 61.

"She's been in hiding. She wasn't in the car when it exploded. It was a setup. She and her mother-in-law set it up. She'd disappear until he finished and came home."

I shook my head. The prime numbers clattered around. "Why?"

"They hate the mob, his mother and his sister. Valentina's no different. From what she says, they were fighting a lot about his new line of work. So his mother convinced her Antonio would get clean and return. Told her he knew she was alive. So she waited until she found out he'd died in an explosion in downtown LA."

"And she was pregnant when he left."

"Yes."

"It's an Italian opera, isn't it?"

"Except you're not fat, and you can't sing."

I felt my face stretch into a smile, but my mind was still working on the TV. The tuning had changed, but the volume was the same. Antonio hadn't known. He must be as confused as I was. I worried about what he felt. What he would do. About him as a person who had resigned himself to losing someone he loved and then found her in a police station.

"I don't understand what you have to do with this," I said. "Why I'm not being questioned by the police. Why you know. Any of it."

"Everyone knows Spinelli shot Patalano. That's first. You'll be questioned, trust me, but you're not a suspect. Not as long as I'm the district attorney. And the way the mayor's race is going since the wedding, I'm going to be DA long enough to put him in jail and keep you from throwing yourself to the wolves for him."

I nodded. I'd do what I had to, but I couldn't put it together right then.

"Theresa?"

"Yes?"

"Did you look like this when I hurt you?"

I shrugged. "I'm going to do better this time."

When I said "this time" as if it was a done deal and I had no hope of feeling whole again, I took a sharp, involuntary breath. I cleared my throat. *101. 103. 107. 113.* No. One was missing.

Daniel put something in my hand. "This is yours. It's the only thing I gave you of any value."

I looked down at a soot-covered engagement ring.

"You're too good for me," he said, closing my hand around it. "I had no business asking you to marry me. And he had no business being with you, whether he knew about Valentina or not. I don't want you to settle."

107. 109. 113. 127.

"You're a real fuckup," I said.

"Yeah. But I'm a good DA."

That was the truth. He was even a great DA.

I put the ring at the top of my thumb and let it rest there. Stupid thing. I'd been so excited to get it. I'd felt completed. I'd thought Daniel and I looking up at the solar system together was what it meant to be fulfilled. But it had been precarious, and I was a different woman now. Bone to flesh, I was different. I'd run away, shot a man, been shot at, died, come back to life. I'd gone nose to nose with danger and walked away stronger. I didn't have to make common choices anymore. Antonio had freed me of my own expectations of myself, and I could be whomever I wanted.

"You know Donna Maria's after him," I said. "He has a price on his head."

"There's not much I can do until they try to kill you."

"Is his wife safe?"

"Probably not. Why?"

My tears had dried up, and the rote repetition of numbers that kept me from thinking of Antonio and Valentina in that room dissolved into sense.

"I'm glad you have him," I said. "He's safer with you."

He pressed his lips together. "I can't much longer. I have nothing yet."

"You can't throw him to the wolves."

"I can't keep him in custody. Believe me, I'd love to lock him up, away from you."

I imagined Antonio getting gunned down on First Street, two steps out of the building, cars screeching away, return shots fired, a movie in three dimensions. A man dying, bleeding out, his wife and son finally reunited with him. The drama was epic, and I didn't see how it could happen differently. "You need to protect him. They're after him. He was supposed to marry Irene, and they killed the last guy who tried to get out of it."

"I know."

"We almost got killed in Mexico."

"He's a big boy."

He wasn't budging.

"What about her? The wife? And the boy? Are you going to be responsible if something happens to them?"

"They're staying with me."

"That's a little off book, isn't it?" I said.

"There's no rulebook for any of this. And like I said, my reputation barely matters anymore. The election is a formality."

"So keeping a beautiful, vulnerable woman at your place…"

"A married woman and her child," he said.

"You really hate him."

"Hate's a very strong word."

"Protect him, Daniel. If only to keep my heart from breaking again."

He gave every appearance of considering it. His gaze drifted to the half distance with a little tilt of his head, a lowering of his eyelids, half a swallow. *Tick, tick, tick.* I had no idea what was going on in his mind, except I did. There was a veracity about him. An honesty that you could see on people who'd had an epiphany. Those who had taken a hard look at themselves and made choices based on what they saw.

He'd never be a politician, but he'd become a man.

Chapter 11

ANTONIO

loved Valentina. She never gave up on anything. She fought endlessly for things that were destined to die. Her grandmother's rotting crochet tablecloth. A bird with a broken foot left at the door by our cat. Her Fiat.

We'd met on a rainy day in Napoli because she wouldn't let that hunk of metal go.

Some cars needed to be put out of their misery. The little ones that didn't go far enough on a liter of gas. The big ones that didn't go fast. The cars so dented and bruised they hurt the eyes. I could keep a car running a long time. Slow, inefficient, or ugly, I'd fix it even if I wanted to kill it. We had that in common. We let things live too long.

"Take this one, Tonio!" Imbruzio had shouted from his office.

He was fighting with his mistress over money. I could hear them through the door every first and third Monday of the month. She cooed. He excused. She scolded. He got defensive. She whined. He comforted. She cried. He cried. She shouted. He put his foot down. Then either she stormed out or the desk legs started creaking. The putting down of his foot was the critical juncture, and when Imbruzio told me to take the little Fiat cutting a turn from the narrow cobblestone street into our tiny lot, he and his mistress were in the comfort/cry stage.

I put down my lunch and stepped out of the office into the rain. It had been drizzling all morning and had just increased to a light rain. A thunderstorm was imminent, and she looked like a bird with a broken wing.

The Fiat was smoking like a Turkish cigarette, rattling and clanking up to the garage. The car itself had a rust problem, a dent problem, needed a paint job, and shook so hard I thought the carburetor's idling pin might not just be screwed too loose but was probably missing entirely. When she got out of the car, the little sheets of water turned into a deluge, and the sky lit up as if it were on fire.

I'd gotten the car running again. Cars and vengeance, I didn't let either go. *La vendetta di cent'anni ha I denti da latte.*

Yes, we had that in common. We held onto things.

***

Valentina was pissed. Before she even opened her mouth, I knew she was about to start crying. Antonin had been pulled out by Zia, my aunt. Who knew the whole time. And my mother. And my wife.

I was holding a chest full of anger, but held it back. Too many things were moving. Theresa. Paulie. Daniel, that fuck. Losing control would do nothing.

She felt out of place. Awkward. Angry. Sitting primly on the bench at First Street Precinct, she was a tightly wound coil of unhappy confusion.

"You don't look happy to see me," I said once she and I had sat down. Being able to speak about things in my language was a relief, but of course, I couldn't talk to her about anything real.

A Los Angeles police woman came in with bottles of water. I opened Valentina's and put it in front of her, then I gave myself a moment to think as I drank from mine. Valentina didn't even look at hers, and I needed much more than a moment.

"And you?" she asked.

"I'm happy to see you. You have no idea. I mourned you for a long time."

"I mourned you for a day."

I twisted on the bench so she and I faced each other. I needed to see her to read her.

"Somewhat smaller investment."

"Oh, shut up." She rubbed her eyes. "This lawyer met me at the airport and told us he was taking me to see you, and I didn't believe him. I said I didn't trust lawyers."

"I'm a lawyer."

"I waited too long. I got comfortable where I was, doing what I was doing. I work in a fabric factory. I do the books and operations. And it's good. I manage a little team. I never would have left the house if things hadn't happened the way they did."

"Happened?" As if she had no hand in it. As if she hadn't disappeared of her own free will. As if her love hadn't been a rose with thorns.

"Years just went and went," she said.

"And then I was dead."

"I was going to stay home. But Antonin wanted to see your face, even if it was at a funeral. I couldn't tell him there was no body, so what was I supposed to do? Refuse him? And your mother, she's broken a hundred times. She couldn't leave. So between the two of us, we decided Antonin and I would come."

"My mother *knew*?"

"For Antonin, she thought it—"

I slammed my hand on the table. "Damn you!"

"This!" She pointed at me. "This is what I'm talking about. This craziness. Yes. She hid me. She hates what you became."

"You could have just left me."

Her eyes, huge and almond-shaped, pouted at me. "You would have found me and dragged me back. Me and the baby. I didn't want that for him."

She was right. I would have hunted her, and when I found out she was carrying a child, that would have been it. I would have had her watched, and another opportunity to leave never would have presented itself. She would have been stuck with a man she loved and hated, but mostly hated.

"You're right," I said.

She raised an eyebrow. "I'm right?"

"You hate me. But I wouldn't have let you leave."

"I don't hate you, Antonio. I never hated you." She touched my hand gingerly, then laid hers flat over mine. "Seeing you—" She shook her head.

And there I was, thinking I'd had fake death sorted out. Theresa and I had caved to the temptation to come back to life in less than twenty-four hours. Yet for ten years, Valentina had resisted the temptation to find me.

She was good.

Where did I find these iron-spined women?

As if summoned by my thoughts of Theresa, the door opened, and Brower came in. "Valentina."

Calling her by her first name like that, he irked me, twisting the edges of my discomfort. It was too familiar.

"You're required down the hall," Brower said.

"*Scusi,*" she whispered before she spun on the bench and slipped out. I imagined it was her son, *our son*, she needed to attend to.

Brower was left. I stood. I wouldn't straddle a bench with this fucker in the room. I would break his head open with it. He closed the door and stepped toward me until we were nose to nose. I was in his territory. His building. I couldn't touch him, and he knew it.

He sat down and indicated the bench across from him.

"What did you think you were doing?" I asked.

"Can you sit?"

I didn't move. I could sit, but I didn't want to be across from him. Didn't want to be on an equal footing.

"There was no easy way to tell you," he said. "It was going to suck no matter what."

"So you tried to spare my feelings?"

"Your *feelings*? I couldn't give a shit. Are you going to sit? Or do you think standing puts you in some kind of position of power?"

He sat with both elbows on the table, palms up. I assumed he was going to tell me about Valentina. How he found her, what he intended to do with her.

I sat.

He tapped his fingertips together. "I know you guys. I know how you operate, and you know why."

"Because you pick the olives and uproot the tree at the same time?"

He smirked. "Spoken like an Italian."

"Spoken like a man who can keep two conflicting ideas in his mind."

"The skill of criminals and priests."

"Which are you?" I asked, because in a way, he was both.

He stopped tapping his fingertips and folded his hands together. He took a long time to answer—too long, as if he was searching in a file for what he wanted to say and couldn't find the paperwork for it.

"You know what I think of you," he said.

I nodded. I didn't need a list.

"But that aside, I'm conceding defeat. You win," he said.

"I don't believe you."

"I thought Theresa was dead, and I died with her. Everything died. Even my desire to hurt you for it. When I realized she was alive, I swore I wouldn't make her life difficult any more. Which means I'm not taking revenge on you for hurting her, or stealing her, and I'm not coming after you for fucking me up. I don't care if you think I'm a coward for that."

"Not for that."

"Touché. But I'm not done. We have conflicting intel regarding the price on your head for bailing on Irene Carloni[9]. As low as half a million for your corpse. Alive, we've heard up to two million."

"Alive is nice. They get to torture me." I smiled at him. I wasn't afraid of torture or death. I'd been hurt before, and I'd be hurt again.

"I assumed it was because if the murder is witnessed and documented, she gets your territory."

"Money is a great motivator."

"They also want Theresa. Quarter million."

My hair stood on end. My fists balled tightly enough to stretch the skin over the knuckles to white. I put my hands under the table.

---

9 *On the off chance this doesn't ring a bell...Antonio was sold into marriage to Irene Carloni, granddaughter of the head of the Sicilian mafia in Los Angeles. It was a union meant to answer another wedding between the Sicilian mafia and the Neapolitan camorra. The first Neapolitan who was meant for her refused, and he and his girlfriend ended up dead. So this shit is real.*

"Who told you this?" I asked.

"Fuck you."

"No. Fuck you."

We regarded each other over the table. It didn't matter who the mole was. What mattered was that the life I'd promised Theresa wouldn't happen.

"And your wife and child?" Daniel said as if reading my mind. "Once they find out they're here, she'll be a target. Never mind the fact that if you'd married Irene, you'd be a bigamist. Let's focus on this. You're going to be followed everywhere. You're going to be in constant danger. Even if I wanted to cut you down, I wouldn't. All I'd have to do is step back and watch. Except for Theresa, who's so upset you're married, I don't think she's absorbed that she's going to get killed."

"You told her? That's for me—"

"Do you even know her? Do you even know what you made her? She doesn't hear the word 'no.' I told her to stay in the hall, but she was in the room before I could close the door."

He jerked his finger at a wood panel on the wall. I hadn't given it a second look until that moment, but when I trained my eye directly on it, I saw the translucence. Theresa had seen the whole thing. I tried to piece together my reaction to Valentina. Had I kissed her? Held her? Spoken a tender word in English?

"The safest thing to do would be to keep you here," he said. "But I can't. I don't have enough on you." He stood. "And you need to protect Theresa, because I can't do that either. I've tried, and I have no resources. Not like I did before the wedding."

The facts were damning. If I hadn't made that last unnecessary volley against him, he'd have the power to protect the woman we both loved. The result of my vengeance was vulnerability.

Daniel opened the door. "I'm sorry to say, you're free to go."

"And Valentina?"

"She'll be in touch."

Chapter 12

THERESA

finally left Daniel's office drained, wrung out, a shell of hard skin around an empty core. I'd have to get to the hospital in a cab. That was all I had to do. That was what I'd come back for. After seeing Jonathan, I could let my world crumble. I could make decisions, run, stay, thrive, die. But this thing with my brother had to be done first.

I felt pressure on my elbow, then at the base of my spine, and lost control of my direction and will just as I caught the scent of burned pine. I couldn't spin around to face him until the door was shut and he was pushing me against the wall of an empty room.

"Antonio," I said firmly, "stop it."

"Stop what?" A lock of his hair dropped in front of his eye, and his lips parted with the tick of the last T. "You can't leave without me."

I pressed my hands to his chest and pushed him away, but I couldn't move him. "I know." I paused to see if he could tell what I meant. "About Valentina." I watched the flick in his eyes as they moved across my face, looking for my feelings on the subject. Feelings I was desperate to hide. "I'm happy for you."

"Are you?" He took my wrists and snapped them over my head before I could resist. He pressed his body into me and spoke so close to me that his lips brushed my cheek. "Why?"

"Don't be stupid." I tried to wrench away, but he held my hands fast and immobilized my hips with his. My body didn't care about wedding vows or another woman. My body wasn't worried about moral complexities. My body surged with lust at the feel of his dick against me.

"Men are dead because of her," he said through his teeth.

"She's alive, Antonio. And you have a child. This is your chance at life. It's staring you in the face. Don't you see? You go back to her. Tell Donna Maria that was why you couldn't marry Irene, that you knew. She'll forgive you, and you can go home."

He bent his knees until our eyes were level. "And you?"

I looked him in the eye. If I obfuscated even a little, he'd think I didn't mean it. "I cop to shooting Paulie. I tell the police, not the DA. I convince them. I can do it. You walk back into the life you lost. It's perfect."

He let my hands go but left his hips against me. "Perfect?"

"It's like a puzzle clicking into place. This is your only chance. It's a gift that she's back. Just make your life what you want."

I was a weakling. When he cupped my chin and brushed his finger along my cheek, I turned enough to trick myself into thinking I was resisting, and I put my gaze on the floor, because I couldn't look at him.

"I saw her, and it was shocking. I'm only a man. I thought all the things you think I did. That I could go back. That I could have another chance. I admit it. But the truth? It's more frightening. I kissed her cheek and felt nothing. Like kissing my sister. Or a stranger. I'm not that boy anymore. I'm a man. I'm made of everything I've done and everything I want, and I don't want a life in Napoli with her. That's the idea of who I am. I want a life with you, because you accept me. All of me. I am whole with you. Only you."

I could have fallen into him so easily. I could have broken myself apart and fit the pieces into a shape resembling sanity and morality. When he leaned in to kiss me and I felt his breath on my lips, my body bent to fit him, whoever he was and whatever he wanted.

The door snapped open, and he turned quickly to address what might be a threat. But it was Margie, looking unusually nonjudgmental. I guessed she got sick of waiting for me to get a cab to the hospital.

"Are you coming?" She looked at Antonio as she passed us. "Or do you want to stay here until they find enough to Mirandize?"

He laughed and took my hand, following Margie's brisk pace down the stairs. They spoke another language as they walked. Not Italian, or even English. They spoke lawyer.

We got into Margie's silver Mercedes without her or Antonio breaking the constant stream of jargon regarding Daniel's ability to hold him.

"I wish he'd kept you," I said, sliding into the front seat.

"Why?" Margie asked as she closed her door.

"They want to kill him. As soon as he gets out of this car, they can shoot him. Then when he leaves the hospital. And it's not like he can go home."

Antonio sat in the back, his shoulder against the door. Light slid over his face when Margie reversed, then it fell back into shade, then light again. Gorgeous in the light. Magnificent in the dark. Light. Dark. Light. Magnificent. Gorgeous. His lips relaxed to speak. Those full, soft, married lips.

"Don't worry," he said.

"I want to trust you on this, Antonio, I really do. But you can't stop bullets with bossiness or good looks."

"They would have killed you too."

"I wish you guys would talk about something normal." Margie snapped the ticket out of the parking machine and made a right. "Like cancer."

"It's hard to be normal with this guy."

"I know how you feel," she replied. "Listen, I know the director of neurology at Sequoia. I defended him on a thing. We can get his parking spot. It's secure. I'll coordinate with Antonio to get you both out of the hospital. Do you have a place to stay?"

"Not yet," Antonio said.

"I got that. You have a phone?"

"No."

"Let me take care of you tonight. I'll get you a burner, and you can call him. But please, don't leave fucking town until we know

what's happening with Jonathan. Please. I know it's risky for you."
She looked at him in the rearview.

It didn't matter if he liked her. He wouldn't refuse her. No one
could.

"It's fine," he said. "We came back for him."

"You're all right for a reprobate thug, you know that?"

"You can be a character witness at my sentencing."

They went on like brother and sister the whole way to the hospital, while I looked out the window and reminded myself that my
relationship with him was coming to a close.

We parked deep in the underground lot, past a separate gate,
in a spot right next to the elevator. Antonio held the car door open
for me, but I couldn't look at him, even when we stood in front of
the elevator doors.

"Mom's medicated," Margie said as the doors slid open with a
ding. "Sheila's managing her anger. Deirdre's sleeping on a chair.
Dad turns up in the halls sometimes. Jon's girlfriend is the emaci-
ated specter on the verge of tears."

"Three short?" I asked.

"At the moment."

Chapter 13

THERESA

Returning to Los Angeles had been dangerous and stupid. Our journey back had the potential to ruin our lives. If we'd continued with our plans in Mexico, Antonio would never have reconnected with Valentina. I wouldn't be considering admitting to shooting Paulie. We would have gotten married, bought a house, had children.

But we came back for Jonathan, a fool's errand that wouldn't do anyone any good. When I saw my rake of a brother in that bed—tubes sticking out of him, hair a mess, skin battered in flour—I was glad I had come.

I sat in the chair beside him. "If you're up, I'm over here."

"I'm up," he said, slowly turning toward me. Machines beeped incessantly, and a hiss of a medical apparatus underscored every other sound in the room. "You look like hell."

"You look great. I saw your girlfriend on the way in."

"She's beautiful, isn't she?"

"Yes."

I thought he slipped out of consciousness, or maybe he was gathering strength to speak. But his eyes closed, then opened halfway.

"She won't marry me. I asked, and she ran off."

"Why?"

He held up his hand, or he attempted to. He had too many tubes sticking out of him to do it properly. I held it down and squeezed it.

"Pledge open," I said.

"Dad's making trades with her. He bought her house to keep it from foreclosure."

A seemingly kind gesture in my father's hands always required a payment. You might not see it. You might not understand the depth of it, but no favor went unsettled.

"And I'm stuck in this damned bed," he said. "She doesn't know what she's getting into. I don't know how else to protect her."

"I don't blame her for saying no," I said. "No one wants to be asked out of desperation."

"I'm not desperate," he protested. "I'm pressed for time. And Dad…" He took a few deep breaths. "I'll kill him."

"You need to get better first," I said, as if that might give him some hope and strength. Looking at him, the very idea of recovery was as ridiculous as the idea of him dying.

"What if I don't get better?"

"She'd be a widow."

He swallowed, leaving a long gap between the word "widow" and our next words. I smiled to myself. If Antonio died, he'd have a widow, and it wouldn't be me.

"I realized something today," I said. "I realized what I thought of marriage. I think I took it all for granted, with Daniel. I just said yes because I did. Because I could, and it seemed like the next stage of life. But it's sacred. It's holy. Let no man tear asunder. We have to mean it when we say it. No one should rip up a contract God wrote. I'll go to hell for plenty I did without thinking, but I won't go for a crime I chose while knowing better."

He didn't answer. His eyes were closed, then he tightened them and looked at the ceiling. "What's today?"

I counted days from the Bortolusi wedding. "The nineteenth."

"Merry Christmas."

That was Jonathan, naturally deflecting from his seconds-span of unconsciousness with glib sarcasm. I'd miss him if he were gone. Even if I lived far away under a different name. The world would feel less sardonic and far too serious without him in it. "What do you want under the tree? Besides a 'yes'?"

"I want her," he whispered. "I asked for the wrong reasons, but I want her."

"It's forever, Jonathan." I put my elbows on the bed and my hand on his shoulder. "Do it for the right reasons. Don't do it because it's convenient. Don't do it because you're scared. Marry her because you love her and your life wouldn't add up without her. Can you do that? Can you promise me you're not forcing it? It would break my heart to see you propose because you wanted to give yourself a reason to live."

"What's wrong, Tee?"

"I don't think love should be taken for granted, and I don't think you should keep on a path of least resistance."

"This is hardly...the Italian guy. What's happening? You're acting strange."

"Can you honestly say that if you were healthy, you'd marry her?"

"Yes. But we'd have a proper engagement."

He was sure. Through hid glassy eyes, I saw a rock-solid surety. Antonio must have been that sure when he'd asked Valentina, but me? I wasn't beating myself up, but the circumstances had brought his proposal on too quickly, and after seeing his wife alive and well, I couldn't assume his feelings for me would withstand her return. Even if he'd meant it when he asked me to marry him, everything had changed...

Jonathan meant it. He did. Daniel had meant it. But Antonio couldn't.

I fished in my pocket and came up with my soot-stained ring. I pressed it into his palm. "Try again, and use this. Give it back when you can buy her her own."

His hand didn't close around it at first. God, he was so messed up. Was he even conscious?

"The last time I saw you," I said, "you were killing oranges for sport and making jokes in Italian. This is...I don't know. A wake-up call."

I had to spend the rest of my life doing right. If I had to answer for my actions, I wanted to be able to stand up and say that I had definitively and consciously decided to be better, do better, be a person I could be proud of.

"I never joke in Italian."

"Sorry to make it about me," I whispered.

He smiled a little then held up the ring so he could see it. "I'm boring right now. And all anyone talks about is me. Where did you get this? They said you went on the run? Did you start robbing jewelry stores?" He lowered his hand as if he were too weak to hold it up.

I didn't know how much of this conversation he'd remember, if any of it. "Someone really wanted me for a while. You've met him."

"Daniel won't be happy. He still wants you."

"How do you know?"

"I know regret when I see it," he said.

"He'll tell himself he cares, but we cancel each other out. We add up to nothing. Trust me when I say I'd rather break up for the right reasons than get married for the wrong ones. With him, or anyone else. I'm either first in line, or I walk."

"You're not the uptight priss I thought you were. You're a priss with a purpose. I'm proud of you."

"You thought I was an uptight priss?" I said with a smile. I'd never thought of myself that way, but maybe I was.

"I think I underestimated you. I'm sorry."

"Don't be. I can't explain why I feel okay about it, but I do."

"Thank you." He held the ring in his fist as if he were afraid to lose it. "Pledge closed."

"Pledge closed." I kissed his forehead. It was cold, and my heart ached for him. "I'll try to come back, but you might not see me for a while."

Chapter 14

THERESA

I left in tears. My family was in the waiting room two doors down, and I craved them. Margie and Sheila, even Mom, whose hugs felt like being loosely wrapped in chicken wire. I wanted them. A week ago, I'd wanted to get away from them, but on that day, all I wanted was to be a pack animal. Surround myself in them. Drown out thoughts of Valentina and soak in family love.

I touched my St. Christopher medal before I got in their sights. I'd avoided facing my family on the way in because I needed strength for Jonathan.

Mom sat by the window, face slack with medication. She's been on the worst of them, then gotten off them, then on again. Her expression was as deadened as it had been during her Thorazine years. Margie and Sheila talked with their arms crossed, and the singer stood to the side as if she didn't belong. We'd have to fix that. I'd hold her first, then hug Mom, then Sheila, and I would apologize for running away. I wouldn't explain the unexplainable, but I would go deep into my gut for the regret and gratitude they deserved.

Except I never got to the waiting area. One minute I was walking down an empty hall wide enough for two lanes of traffic, the linoleum shining in vertical stripes where the lights were reflected, and the next, my feet didn't feel the pressure of my body. I was pulled out of the hall so fast I didn't have time to scream, even if a sweaty hand hadn't been covering my mouth. My shoes slipped on the floor, and my knees dragged. I no longer had control of my body.

A door slammed, then there were steps. I clawed at my attacker. Male. Huge. Not Antonio. As I got thrown down a flight of concrete steps, I knew, even as my vision swam and my stomach flip-flopped, that I was alone. As alone as I'd ever been. No one was coming.

The man looked like the guy Antonio didn't shoot in Tijuana. The one behind the rock. Domenico. Bruno Uvoli's brother. I remembered it when my lungs emptied as he grabbed me and, as if he just couldn't be bothered to carry me down the stairs, tried to thrust me down the next flight.

At the last second, I grabbed his ankle. My weight, which already had significant torque, pulled him down with me.

Bodies in motion tend to stay in motion, and we did exactly that. Elbows, knees, hips, the corners of the stairs, and gravity all battled for space. In those two turns, the civilized parts of me peeled off as if by centrifugal force, whipping away, leaving the basest, coarsest version of myself. The raw rage and adrenaline. All action and forward thrust. I considered nothing but action.

When we got to the next landing, I twisted until my hand was free, and I reached between his legs, grabbing for the soft flesh there. I squeezed, twisted, and pulled all at the same time.

Domenico's howl woke me from my fog. He reached for me, and I couldn't get away without letting his balls go, so he got my hair and jerked me around.

"You fucking mick bitch." He went for my throat with one hand and pulled his other fist back.

I kept squeezing the flesh between his legs. His hand tightened on my throat. The edges of my vision dotted black as he cut off my circulation. I kicked at him but hit nothing, and fight turned to flight as I waited for him to smash my face.

But the blow never came.

Domenico was pulled away from me, mouth half open, eyes popping as if I was still twisting his balls.

In the whoosh of air as he was drawn away from me was the scent of campfires in a pine forest. Choking on my bruised esophagus and hurting everywhere, in a stairwell that should have been guarded but obviously wasn't, I felt safe again. I got my legs under me.

"Theresa." His voice, unflustered by anything but simple rage, cut through my pain and disorientation.

"I'm fine."

I wasn't. I was beat to hell, more shattered than I ever had been in my life. Yet I was fine the second I heard his voice.

Antonio held Domenico against the railing with his left hand while he pounded his face with his right. His knee was wedged between the man's legs, immobilizing him into a back-arched position. His face was red.

"Chi ti ha mandato?"

I scanned the stairwell. Why was no one coming? How had this even gone on so long? The camera hung in the corner like a wasps' nest, but it was turned all the way around.

"Chi ti ha mandato?" Antonio insisted, glancing at me quickly. "I'm going to fucking kill him if he doesn't answer."

Domenico made gacking noises in his throat.

"I don't think he speaks Italian," I said through a throat full of sand.

Antonio tightened his grip. "Too bad he can't pray in God's language." He got up in Domenico's face, jabbing his knee between his legs, and whispered, "Who sent you?"

Domenico puckered his lips as if to speak through layers of spit, and Antonio turned his head a quarter to hear.

"What? *Che?* I can't hear you?"

Since Antonio hadn't loosened his chokehold one iota, there was nothing to hear. My lover was being unnecessarily brutal. Cruelty wasn't necessary. I should have been horrified, but I wasn't any more dismayed by this than when Antonio had made Paulie recite the Hail Mary with a gun to his head.

"Antonio," I said, "we don't have time. I don't know why no one's here, but it won't last."

He looked me over, lingering on my throat, which must have been a shade of red that was about to go black and blue.

I turned to Domenico and said calmly, "Who sent you?"

Antonio loosened his grip a little.

I continued. "I've seen him kill people. And I'm no angel either."

How could I revel in it? How could I align myself with the most savage part of the man I loved? And how could I feel so right about it? So empowered by murder?

"P-P-P..." the man sputtered.

Antonio and I exchanged a look and understood each other very clearly. Antonio removed his hand.

"Patalano," he croaked. Domenico looked at Antonio expectantly, then me, breathing hard.

A beat passed before Antonio spoke low and with forceful intent. "Liar."

In one fell motion, Antonio bent and scooped Domenico's knees and pulled them up. The railing became a fulcrum and the man's body a plane, and he tumbled down the space between the stairs. I heard banging and grunting, but I didn't look. I only had eyes for Antonio.

Then it stopped.

Antonio wasn't breathing heavily, as if he'd expended zero energy, physical or otherwise. His gaze burned my skin, peeling it off and looking through me. I felt vulnerable and soaked in desire, bare before him and still safe.

"You're made for this life," he said.

"I'm made for you."

Below, someone screamed, and the camera behind me whirred to life. He took my hand and pulled me upstairs. He took the steps two at a time, not as if he was rushing but as if the steps were simply too small for him, and I kept up. I didn't know how, and I didn't know why, because he hadn't told me where we were going. But hand in hand, step for step, in a pine-scented breeze, I made it to the top landing.

"We don't have time," he said without breaking his pace. "There are no cameras here, so we could get out. Paulie's here. The place is crawling with his family, but it looks like Donna Maria found me."

Antonio turned back to me as he shouldered the door, checking on me. Admiring. Connecting. Yanking that spiritual tether between us.

Before the door clacked open, I noticed the floor and walls shaking in a consistent rhythm. Not an earthquake.

He yanked me forward, pushing the door all the way open and drawing me onto the roof where a helicopter waited. The pressure of the air almost slammed the door on me, but he held it. The rotors spun against the orange haze of the setting sun, and a man crawled out of the cabin to hand Antonio his headset.

"You got clearance to Montecito," he shouted over the whip of the rotors. "Maintain at two thousand. Call in at squawk oh-three-five-one."

"Got it."

Antonio motioned to me and headed for the cockpit. I ran after him.

"Are you joking?" I tried to gather my whipping hair together and failed.

"Get in."

"We can't run away!" Even as I said it, I knew how ridiculous I sounded. Of course we were running away. "And you can't fly this thing!"

"Yes, we can, and yes, I can."

"You didn't tell me you had a pilot's license!" I yelled over the wind.

"I don't. Now get in before I pick you up and belt you in like a child."

I hesitated, and Antonio didn't have time for that. He picked me up by the waist and tossed me into the helicopter. I dropped into the bucket seat just as he reached for the belt.

"I have it." I tugged the belt. "Just promise me you've done this before."

"It's the only way to get around Capri."

He went around to the left side and slid in, buckled in, and put his headphones on as if he knew what he was doing. I put on mine. He reached over to my headset and snapped the broadcast function off.

"If you kill us, that's fine," I said. "Do not kill anyone else."

He turned to me and raised an eyebrow before pulling the helicopter off the roof. The bottom dropped out of my gut, and I gripped the edge of my seat.

"I think the word in English is 'ironic,'" he said once we were airborne. "You don't want to kill anyone by accident?"

"You want to discuss this now?"

"Yes."

I lost my train of thought when he swerved east and my stomach twisted.

"I can drive anything," he said. "They all work the same. This just has forward and backward plus up and down." He dipped again, high over Hollywood. "Like this."

We swerved across Wilshire, north toward the hills and the Observatory.

He leveled it and took out a pack of cigarettes. He offered me one and I refused. He bit the end of one and slid it out.

"I hope Domenico's dead," he said, clicking open his lighter as if he wasn't flying a helicopter at the same time. "I told you once, I'll kill anyone who touches you."

He was dead serious, almost bored. As if stating the date a war ended or began. As if vengeance was no more than a mathematical equation that needed to be solved. And it was the sexiest thing I'd ever seen. Almost as sexy as the knowledge that I'd kill for him with the same seriousness.

"Capo," I said to get his attention.

He shifted his attention while keeping the helicopter at a steady level.

"I don't know who I am with you, but I like me better now than I ever have. I'm scared. And elated. But the wife. Your wife—"

"Stop. We are not discussing her."

"We have to," I said.

We crossed the twisting thread of the LA River, which actually had water in it from the recent rains.

"You are my life. It doesn't matter what I am, or what I've done, as long as you're mine. Nothing in the past matters. There is you, and nothing else." He didn't look at me but kept his eyes on his work. A cluster of taller buildings appeared ahead, and he headed for them. "My one job," he said, holding up a finger, "is to make sure you know how to protect yourself when they finally kill me."

"Stop it."

"It's very clear to me. Do you know why I didn't confess to doing Paulie? Because if they send me to jail, I can't protect you. And yes, I have to protect Valentina too, because I made a promise to her. But it's not the same. Do not make the mistake of thinking it's the same."

He looked at me, a world of confidence and confusion churning in his eyes. Both and neither. I read him like a book and understood that he knew what he had to do, even if he didn't like or understand it.

I wasn't as sure. I didn't know what I had to do. I wasn't as confident that I could keep him alive or as comfortable with the moral ambiguity of the past week.

I gripped the seat on our descent, but he landed the helicopter smoothly.

He winked at me. "Easier than the beach."

"You'll have to tell me how you managed this," I said.

"I'm surprised you don't know already." He snapped off his headset. I unbuckled as he got out and crossed the front of the craft to my side.

"I'd just like a straight answer," I said.

He held out his hand, and I took it. "You come from a very powerful family, Contessa. They are no less organized than mine."

I should have been insulted. Shocked. Confused and curious. But I wasn't. I was frozen in place as I remembered everything I knew and had been told. My father's way of moving mountains to get what he wanted. Margie's way of making things happen with a phone call. The way people who hurt us wound up ruined or dead.

Was I made for Antonio by dint of my genetics?

Was I an animal from birth? Had the real me been dormant all this time?

I took Antonio's hand and slid down into the whipping wind of the landing pad. I felt a twinge of guilt for even touching a married man, but I stifled it. We had too much to do.

He paused for a moment as the rotors wound down. His head keened a little, peering inside me. "Some things are in the stars. I was meant to protect you. And you were meant to rule."

Chapter 15

THERESA

Antonio hustled me down the stairs, waving to the pilot who was waiting for the craft. Montecito Hospital was less luxurious than Sequoia, but it spanned four city blocks.

Antonio seemed to have planned everything in the half an hour I'd spent giving Jonathan my ring. We careened down two flights of stairs before cutting through a bridge across Pacific Boulevard and catching an elevator. Everyone faced the door, and he pulled me into him until my shoulder blades touched his chest. He put his finger on the back of my neck, drawing on it from my hairline to the place where my spine disappeared under my shirt. I shuddered, and his dick got hard before we made it to the lobby.

I had no idea what to do about that beautiful erection, or what it did for me.

Or what it made me. The interloper. The other woman. The siren call to a taken man's filthiest desires. Not a speechwriter in sensible shoes, but an accountant and a killer with the grime of Tijuana still in her hair.

I was all those things, and more. And less.

I followed Antonio to the parking lot, listing them in no particular order.

Tramp.

Trash.

Fool.

"My god, Spin," Zo said when we got to the deepest level of the parking lot.

I hadn't said a word, because I didn't know what role to speak from.

"You look like shit," he said, hugging Antonio and kissing each cheek, left then right. He pointed at me and apparently chose courtesy over truth. "You look nice, of course."

Whore.

Slut.

Mistress.

"It's about a mile away," Antonio said with no preamble. He opened the back door for me and sat in the front with Zo.

I didn't mind being his whore, his one and only plaything. The shoe fit, and I wore it with pleasure. But being his mistress, his second, ate at me. He had a wife, and I wouldn't be the one to break that, nor would I become what destroyed my own life, no matter the circumstances. I wasn't exonerated because we hadn't known she was alive.

"Where are we going?" I asked in the car, feeling like I didn't belong there or anywhere.

"Up a hill." Antonio twisted in his seat to face me. "You're taken care of. Don't worry."

I'd made a concerted decision not to think about Valentina while we were getting out of the precinct, but in the backseat of the car, with him unintentionally using a phrase for the whores of married men, I lost the battle for my own composure.

"Stop looking at me," I said. I couldn't do this in front of Zo. I couldn't break down. I had resources. I'd kept myself from falling apart in worse situations. Goddamnit. My chin wiggled, and my sinuses filled up. I couldn't recall a prime number over two.

Antonio put his hand on my knee. I let my fingers slip around his, and I closed my eyes, just feeling his hand around mine. A deep breath. His presence in the car. The glue that held my mind together.

"Don't," he said.

I nodded, squeezing my eyes shut against tears.

"You are first," he said, reading my mind.

I didn't want him there. His left hand was on mine, with its bare ring finger. I pulled my hand away. "You're married. I can't touch you. It's not right."

He snapped his seat belt off and thrust himself over the front seat, extending his body back to me and leveraging himself against my knees. His body bridged the front and back. His face was an inch from mine, and his smell of the forest after a fire consumed me.

"Sit down," Zo said a hundred miles away. "You're gonna get us pulled over!"

"*Sei mia*," he whispered.

"Don't kiss me," I said. "Just don't, I'm—"

But he did, and so gently that the kiss itself was a request for a kiss. I squeaked involuntarily, because I didn't want to kiss him. I didn't want to do what I'd said I wouldn't do. I wanted to stay strong in my conviction that until we worked out what was happening with his wife, there would be no touching, no kissing, no nothing.

And he ripped all of that away. In the first microsecond of the kiss, when his parted lips brushed the length of mine as if introducing themselves for the first time, I lost every ounce of will I had against him. I needed him. I wouldn't make it through this without some part of his body against some part of mine. I was going mad, surely. Mad with violence or mad with need, but mad mad mad.

I opened my mouth, and his tongue greeted mine. It wasn't a lusty kiss but a joining. A reassurance. A nod to our connected destinies.

I put my hands on his cheeks, and he pulled back ever so slightly.

"I'm scared," I said. "And I love you."

"She admits it," he said, smiling. "*Amore mio*, you may have to carry our love alone, but it won't be heavy."

"It will be, and I don't have the strength."

He pulled back to kneel on the front seat. Before turning toward the windshield, with his left hand on the back of his seat and his right on Zo's headrest, he said, "Then it's agreed. We live. We live, and we share the load. *Dimmi di sii?*"

His confidence was infectious, and I let myself believe him for a second before spiraling back into doubt. "*Si, Capo. Si.*"

"Great," Zo said. "I don't know what you're talking about, but there's a cop two car lengths behind."

Antonio slapped Zo in the back of the head and twisted back into his seat.

Zo stopped at the end of a twisted path, at a modern little house with no windows in front, and we all got out of the car.

"What's the plan?" Zo asked, rubbing his forehead.

"Tonight we sleep." Antonio clapped Zo on the shoulder. "Tomorrow we plan. Give me your piece."

Zo unbuckled his shoulder holster and gave it to Antonio.

"*Grazie,*" Antonio said, then motioned at the car. "You have one in there for Theresa?"

The crickets creaked, the wind crackled through the palm trees, and Zo looked at Antonio as if he'd lost his mind.

But Antonio just stood straight with his hand out. "They took everything on the way up."

Zo reached into the glove compartment and took out a small gun. He checked for bullets and slapped it into his boss's palm. "She know how to use it?"

"Blow your left nut off from ten meters."

"All right." He shrugged, resigned. They shook hands, and Zo drove away.

Antonio punched a code in the door, and we entered. He dropped the weapons on the counter with a clatter. The back of the house overlooked the San Gabriel Valley. I saw the barest of furnishings. A couch. A table and three chairs. Blinds, not curtains. Not a single painting, picture, or scuff mark broke the white expanse of the walls.

"This your house?" I asked.

"It's your sister's. I've never met a fixer like her."

"Margie? God, I "

He crushed me in a bruising kiss, and I responded by accepting it, yielding to what was right, what fit, what made sense. His hands yanked up my shirt, his tongue owning mine.

I pushed him away. "Stop."

Whatever agility he used to hurt people, he used on me, twisting me around, pushing me against the window overlooking the valley and tying my shirt until the tension held my hands behind me. *"Cosa c'è?"*

"I just..." His scent distracted me. His breath in my ear. The hard-on pushing into me. My body made excuses, but damn it, I had a long explanation planned, one that was well-suited to a sane and civil dinner or a car ride. "I can't. I...we need to talk about—"

He clamped his hand over my mouth and pulled my head to his shoulder. "I don't want to talk," he hissed into my ear. "I want to fuck."

I couldn't make more than an *mmm* into his palm. He pulled off my shirt, freeing my hands, while keeping my head stable against him.

"Pull your pants down, Contessa."

I grunted a *no* and tried to shake my head. I was sweating and spit covered his hand, but he held me.

"You're going to pull your pants down right in front of this window. And you're going to be quiet when I fuck your pussy. Not a word. No talking. No yelling. Then I'm taking your mouth, and you're going to swallow all those words."

I begged with my eyes, but we'd done it rough so many times.

He was so serious, squeezing until he dented my cheeks. "Pull your pants down. Let me see it."

He pulled me back until I could see us in the window. He was hidden behind me except for the hand covering my mouth and the face growling into my ear. I swallowed. I saw my hard nipples in the window's reflection, and if I took my pants down, he'd feel how wet I was.

"Don't make me take my belt to your ass before I fuck it."

I heard and felt him undo his belt with his free hand. I made a sound in my throat. He looked at me in the darkened window. I wasn't allowed to protest.

"Look at us, Contessa. Watch when you give yourself to me." He locked my head forward, and I watched him put his hands down my pants. *"Adesso"*—his wrist disappeared below my waistband— "put your hands on the glass. Let's see how much you want to fuck."

I shook my head, but he pushed me forward, and I had to hold my hands against the glass to keep from falling. Cruel. He was so cruel. And my body was lit from within by his brutality.

He slid his hand to where I was soaked for him and put two fingers inside me as if he had every right to. My knees nearly buckled.

"No!" I said it behind his hand and knotted my brows, rattling my vocal cords.

If this wasn't serious enough for him, if he didn't hear this cry of mind over body, we were over. I swore it. My better self needed to be heard.

Chapter 16

ANTONIO

She always resisted when she was tense, and I always forced my way through. This was us. This was how we were. I felt better afterward, no matter how I felt before, and our ferocity always lapsed into tenderness.

But she was crying, and she meant it. She wasn't playing. I was about to hurt her, or I'd done it already.

Had I lost her?

My pain was almost physical. I took my hand off her mouth.

"Let me go," she gasped.

"Why?"

I didn't know why I asked. To fill the space, maybe. I stepped back with a heavy heart. I'd done something wrong. Maybe too rough? I didn't have a minute to ask what exactly had gone over the line in the sand for her. I didn't have a second to make it up to her. She buttoned her pants and walked out of the room.

I didn't know the layout of the house, so I followed because I didn't want to lose her. I didn't fear much, but I did fear having her too far from me, and if she went outside, I thought I'd never see her again. That was a reality to me. Her disappearing into a puff of smoke, or getting shot or taken when my back was turned. I'd let her see her brother for thirty minutes while I met with her sister, and she wound up getting dragged down a stairwell by Domenico Uvoli.

I turned a corner in time to hear a door slam. She'd gone into a bathroom and closed the door without even turning on the light.

I knocked. "Contessa? Open this now."

"Pounding on the door is not helpful."

Had I been pounding? I realized my fist hurt. "Let me in."

"No, please. Just leave me alone."

"I will break this door down."

"Go to hell. I'll climb out the window."

A window? Was she *botz*? Was she trying to drive me to the edge of a cliff? Because jumping out the window and rolling down the scrub-brushed hill half naked was not all right. My blood got hot with the thought. My skin tingled and curled on itself. If she knew that I was sure she'd be picked up by some *stronzo* as soon as she was out of my reach, she would have come out of that fucking bathroom right then.

"This is your last chance to come fucking *out*!"

No answer, just the sound of her weeping on the other side.

Fine. At least I knew she was in there.

I checked the objects in the room. Nothing. Carpet. Blinds. Electrical outlets. Enough. That was enough.

I tore down the blinds with my bare hands. She must have thought I was having a temper tantrum, and maybe I was. She'd separated herself from me by not telling me what I'd done, then again with that door that I could have torn off the hinges.

The crossbar that held the blinds separated from the wall, tearing plaster. I yanked off a vertical blind, cracking it. I used the edge of a piece to start unscrewing the plate from an outlet.

"Are you in there, Contessa?"

I needed to keep her in the bathroom. If she crawled out the window, I would rip the mountains off the earth and fling them at heaven.

"Are you there?" I shouted.

She sniffed.

"I don't like too much talking," I said. "Too much can get misunderstood. So if you say straight what I did, I can apologize and we can finish fucking. But you sit there behind that door, then we're fighting, not fucking. That, I do not like." I finally got the plate off.

She mumbled something.

"I can't hear through the door."

I got the plate off the outlet. It left a nice hole in the wall that would work for leverage.

I pulled up the blinds by the crossbar, extending them to their full length. I jammed one end in the hole in the wall the plate had covered, bending the outlet until I had room, then put the other end against the doorknob.

"It's too much. It's just too much. I can't...we can't...this is wrong."

I bent the crossbar so it wouldn't slide closed. Adjusted. "What's wrong?"

I felt a little less angry knowing she was inside and staying there.

"You're married. I can't get past that."

I didn't even address that concern. It was ridiculous. I went outside. The vegetation at the side of the house was overgrown, and I walked through the brush like a bulldozer, breaking any branch in my way, angry as the floodlights at the back of the house. The rear wall was five feet from a near-sheer drop into the oblivion of the canyon, and at the back wall, the bottom of the bathroom window was six inches over my head.

I tucked my thumbs under the window. It was locked.

"Open this window," I shouted.

"Are you nuts?"

I could see the top of the bathroom door. Saw the geometry of it change then snap back into place. She was trying to open it.

So eager to get away from me. Oh, this would not continue. Not for another second. I was going to make her understand that she was not to hide from me. Not to run. Not because of Valentina or anything. She was mine, and what was mine stayed in my sight until I decided it was safe to leave it.

I knew how to break a window. I'd broken a few dozen. I didn't want to scare her or cut her, but that window was getting broken or opened, and I was getting in there to explain to her what all this meant.

Of course, no rocks in Los Angeles. You had to buy fucking rocks. Sick place, this, where you couldn't find a rock to break a window. I lifted a flat flagstone from the path, exposing fat white grubs and a sprinkling of ants.

I tapped the stone. I loved that woman. She was as much mine as a part of my body, and she was upset about Valentina. I understood that. Sure, who wouldn't be upset? But my wife had nothing to do with her. With us. With the fact that I couldn't think about what to do about Valentina, or the son I hadn't known I had, or anything, with Theresa on the other side of a wall

"Theresa," I called as I put the stone on the windowsill and climbed up. I heard the shower running, and Theresa was nowhere to be seen. Good. I wouldn't have to ask her to move to the back wall. Clinging to the siding and the wood window frame, I touched the rock to the top edge of the bottom window. *Tap. Tap.* Then something stronger, until the window cracked. I pressed the stone to the glass, and the crack widened into a poorly-defined web. A chunk popped onto the bathroom floor.

She poked her head past the curtain. Her eyes were red and swollen, and her hair stuck to her face. "Antonio, just leave me alone."

I reached up and in, twisting the lock. "No. I'm not leaving you alone. Never."

I slid the window up and crawled into the bathroom. My shoes hit the floor when she turned off the water, and I snapped the curtain open. She faced me, skin textured in drops of water, and she covered herself, ashamed of her nakedness.

"Put your hands down."

"I need space."

"You do not. You need to come back to me naked. That body you cover? It's mine. Every centimeter of it."

She shook her head and looked down into the middle distance. "I saw her. When she came into the room. I was behind the mirror."

I took mental inventory again. The moment when I saw Valentina...what had I done? Had I kissed my wife? I didn't think so. Had I held her? What had my expression been in that moment when all my grief and vengeance came to nothing?

"I know. Did Brower do this? Did he make you watch? Because I'll kill him."

"No," she said. "I forced my way in. He tried to get me away. But I'm glad I saw. I wouldn't have believed it otherwise."

"Believed what?"

"Can I get dressed?"

"No."

"She's your fate. I'm just a distraction." Her face dropped, fell apart, and she started crying. Her hands left her breasts and the space between her legs and covered her face.

I wanted to punch whoever had made her cry. I wanted to avenge her every pain, but how could I take vengeance on myself?

"Contessa..." I put my arms out for her.

"Don't touch me!" she shouted as if I were a scorpion in her bed. "You don't get it. You don't belong to me. You never did. We didn't know. All right, that's fine. But I won't be the one to break a marriage. That's forever, Antonio. Forever. Until death. You really need to think about that."

"There's nothing to think about."

She stepped out of the tub, and I stopped her.

"*Aspetta,*" I said, looking around the floor. I pulled up the blue glass-coated rug and flipped it. The underside was safe. I put it in front of the tub and moved out of her way when everything in my body told me to get in her way. "Step on that."

"Don't tell me what to do."

"Your feet are bare. There's glass all over."

Her jaw jutted out, but she stepped on the upside-down bath mat. "You old world guys...you think it's fine to have a wife and fuck a mistress. Don't think I haven't been on the other side." She held up her hand. "And before you even speak, I know this situation is different." She dried herself off, apparently unaware of what her naked body did to me. "It's crazy. Your dead wife shows up because she thinks you're dead. There's no precedent for this, I know. And its irony isn't lost on me. But you're not seeing this situation for what it is because you figure you can keep on sleeping with me while you figure out what the whole 'Valentina and a son' thing means. Well, I don't figure it that way."

She poked her feet through her pants, and I watched her beautiful legs disappear into the fabric. My balls ached. My thoughts were disorganized. All I could think about was getting inside her, like an adolescent.

"The way I figure it," she continued, wrestling on her shirt, "you just had a priority shift, and you have to shift back to your wife." Her head stretched through the neck of the shirt, and her red hair left wet splotches on it. "You belong with her. You speak the same language. Same country. Same community. Your dream to go back to Naples and live in peace? You can't have it with me. You'll never have it with me."

She tried to open the door to end the conversation but couldn't. She pushed, but I'd wedged it closed very effectively. She yanked the door back and forth. "Damn it, Antonio!" She smacked the door so hard she had to cradle her aching hand.

I took her injured hand and turned her back to the door. She had defiance in her face, and I wanted to wipe it away with a fuck so hard we'd both break.

"You listen to me," I said, getting close to her and putting up my finger so she knew I meant what I said. "I want what I love, and I love what I want. What I want is you. You came to me as a lady and now you are a queen. I've never met a woman like you. I don't even deserve you, but I have you. And having you, I'm not giving you up. Not for an old promise I made when I was a boy. Not for a place that rejects me. Not for a family that won't have you. Your world is my world. Our world."

"You have a child."

Her eyes blazed, and her words were the end to a story. She was right. I had a son who was a stranger. I would never shirk my responsibility to him, but I needed a minute's peace to get my head around what that meant.

"I'll take care of him. Don't worry. That's outside all this."

She shook her head slowly. "It's not enough."

"I don't have anything else."

"I love you. But I won't share you."

"I'm not asking you to share."

"In the eyes of God?"

I pushed myself away from her. "You choose your sins like a woman."

"I'll kill for you again, because I love you still. I'll kill for you a hundred times. But I'm not touching you. Not like a lover."

I saw white hot. Did she think she was going to walk away from me? She was wrong.

"No other man will lay his hands on you as long as you live."

She looked as if I'd slapped her, and I had a moment of regret. I'd only spoken the truth, but maybe I spoke it too soon. Or too hard.

"Capo," she said softly, "there will never be another. I'm ruined."

She blinked, and a tear fell. Then another. I wanted to kill the man who'd hurt her.

Chapter 17

I'd made every effort to keep Valentina in a little compartment in my head. To stick her in a box, mark it "LATER," and keep it on the shelf. But when Antonio tried to fuck me in the safe house, the box rattled off the shelf and fell to the floor, breaking apart in a spray of unwanted news.

He is taken.

He has a son.

He will never be happy with you.

He made a promise.

There was more, some more hurtful than others. Some had a comma and the phrase "and you love him," following, as if to drive home the point that not only was all this true, all this mattered. In the bathroom, I stabbed myself with those phrases and tried to wash them from me in the shower.

I knew he loved me. There was simply no question. I'd never been loved the way he loved me. With him, I felt important and whole. Without him, I was a piece of a person.

How pathetic. How old world.

"I'm ruined," I repeated with my back to the door, not to sound pitiable but to shine another light on it. He'd ruined me with his love, branded me with an outmoded way of loving that I wanted more than anything in the world.

"No." He laid a hand on each side of my head and stretched his arms, looking at the floor between his feet. "I'm the one who's ruined. I was left a widower of a wife I loved, and I fell in love again. I can't leave the wife; we have a child together. And I can't leave the woman I love. I can't be with either."

"You can go back to her. It's best for your family."

"No. I cannot."

"Why not? Because you feel sorry for me? That's just—"

"No!" He spoke so sharply I jumped. "No one should feel sorry for you. I pity the man who feels sorry for you. Do you feel sorry for a starving tiger today? Or the animal she rips apart tomorrow?" He stood straight and sliced the air with his hands. "No. You can't get rid of me so easily. I'm not turning my back on you. You're mine. You'll always be mine. We live together, or we die together. There is nothing in between."

I shook my head, pressing my lips together as if tightening them against the words that wanted to come.

"There isn't a good end to this," I said.

"It's decided."

He was out of his mind, but I didn't know how to talk him back to reality. We didn't both have to be miserable. A measure of happiness could be meted out if he'd just accept that he couldn't, and shouldn't, have me.

But he seemed determined to let me drag him down. Then fine, he'd have his damned way. I'd be present at his side, and I'd protect him from harm, but no more.

"There is no sex," I said. "No kissing. No touching. I do not have affairs with married men, and I don't play second fiddle. We're partners. Business partners. Which means if you're up shit's creek with the Sicilians, I am too. It means however we decide to remedy that, I'm right there with you. You can't put me in a box and lock it until it's safe for me to come out. That's not what this is."

"Nothing will happen to you," he said, softening.

"Well then"—I put my hands on my hips, feeling taller and more powerful than I had even ten minutes before—"nothing will happen to you either."

His lips were on me so fast, I didn't have a second to turn away. He smelled so right, and the arches of his body on mine were such a tight fit, I forgot they were a wrong answer brought on by a flawed assumption.

I pushed him away. "I mean it. Do not test me. The next time, I bite. Your tongue will go back in your mouth a bloody piece of meat."

He smirked, the asshole, and slinked closer without touching me. "I'll die before I kiss you again."

In contrast to my voice, his was silken, as if he was saying the exact opposite, that he would kiss me. Maybe not today. Maybe not tomorrow, but he would kiss me.

My heart sank right into that thought. I wanted that kiss. Wanted it ready to be given when I was ready to take it. I turned my face a quarter of an inch, just enough to feel the heat of his cheek on my own.

Did it matter? Since we were doomed anyway, did it matter if I kissed him or not? Logic cut both ways. If I couldn't see further than the length of my arms, what was the difference? I had no future with him and no future without him. No future. What had I sold myself for? For this? A guy with a wife? Of all the ridiculous, irritating, miserable, shitty choices in men.

"You know what?" I said. "Go to hell. You're a piece of shit. And that's not foreplay. I hate this. I hate everything about it. I hate feeling committed to you, because everything about it is wrong. I hate loving you. I hate myself for standing here right now, wanting you to fuck me." I felt the muscles of his face change. He was smiling. I pushed him back. "That was not an invitation. I hate you for turning me into your side piece, and I don't care if you meant it or not. I don't care if you knew. You know what I care about? The damned facts. You made me a mistress, and I made myself a whore for loving you. And shut the hell up. Don't defend yourself or what's happening here. I'm mad, and I'm staying that way."

I took the doorknob in both hands and shook the door. It was wedged shut by something on the other side. I punched it, which was the very definition of ineffective, and it hurt my hand. I pressed my face against the painted wood.

"Theresa," Antonio whispered, putting his hand on my shoulder.

I leaned into it, because I was soothed wherever we connected. "Don't touch me."

"Get away from the door then."

He dropped his hands, and I stepped back onto the upside-down bath mat.

Antonio kicked the doorknob once then again. It bent. One more kick, and it hung by half a screw. On the other side, something *thupped* to the carpet. He opened the door.

I walked through the bedroom and swept up his phone, wielding it like a sword. "I'm using this."

"To do what?"

"To call my sister."

His shirttail hung in fangs at his thighs. Hair stuck up in a sexy disaster. Pant cuffs an ombre of dirt. I'd never seen him look so helpless. I wanted to hug him and tell him everything would be all right.

"Get out," I said.

He stood stock still. I didn't know what to expect. He'd drag me to my knees and put his cock in my mouth, or he'd leave me alone. I half wished he'd take control of my body, force me to bend to him, so I didn't have to be responsible for choosing him.

He spun and strode out of the bedroom, snapping the door closed behind him.

Chapter 18

THERESA

The closet was dark as sin and hot as hell. I'd been there an hour and had just gotten through to Margie five minutes before.

"He needs a heart," Margie said. "That's all there is to it. He's got a shredded valve, and there's not enough blood in the world to make up for the leaking."

"We're really going to lose him." I huddled in the corner. My eyes had gotten used to the light from under the door. Two wire hangers hung above me, and under me were dust bunnies and nylon carpet.

"Change the subject," Margie said. "I can't talk about this anymore. It's making me want to punch someone." She entered a crowded space. I heard voices and a whoosh of white noise. "You're alive. That's the good news. Everyone's happy, but you ducked out without saying a word, and they're scared you're going to do something stupid. Or disappear again. Or die like you mean it."

"I want to." That was the wrong thing to say. I was heartbroken, but Margie was on the front lines of real tragedy. "Not really," I said quickly. "I'm sorry, I'm being—"

"Please. Be dramatic. Talk about small things that seem big. Is he getting a divorce or what?"

"I don't think so," I said, hugging my bare knees. "He can get an annulment."

"And make his kid a bastard? Sure. Good thinking."

"Maybe she'll divorce him?"

"She waited for him a long time," Margie said.

"I'll talk to her. I'll explain that he's different. Maybe I can convince her to leave him, because he won't do it. Out of guilt or shame or some kind of feeling of responsibility." I was grasping for control, looking for something I could do, some action I could take to bring his body and soul back to me. "Maybe she'll tell him to fuck off if she knows he loves me. If I tell her."

"Mom wants to talk to you."

"Can I not?"

But she never answered.

"Theresa?" That voice. So flat and patrician. Jonathan called it *haute vox*.

"Mom."

She didn't say anything, but she sounded wet. I heard a half a breath and a ladylike sniff. Mom didn't cry, so she tried to hide her hitched breaths and clear the mucous out of her throat with a rattle instead of a snuffle. I'd never heard much emotion from her, but what I was barely hearing was a soft sob from most people. For my mother, it was blubbering.

I could have been mistaken, confusing tears with allergies, until she spoke through lungs that wouldn't stay still and a nose full of snot.

"I thought I was losing two in one day."

"I'm sorry, I...we had to disappear," I said.

"You didn't see us on the way out today, and I was scared you were leaving again. Theresa, my baby. Don't...please don't do this."

"Do what, Mom? I'm back. I'm here."

"I wanted you. Did you know? You and your brother surprised me, but you were my special gifts." She broke down into sniffles and hics.

I was frozen. I didn't know how to react. I'd never heard this sappy story of her feelings about her last two children. "Mom..."

"And I'm losing the two of you."

I touched my St. Christopher medal to protect against hating myself for what I'd done. "I'm here. I'm not going anywhere."

Why did I say that? Would I have to stick to it? Was I cursing any chance I had of working things out with Antonio? I wasn't ready to make that bargain. Not yet. Other deals with the universe were still pending, but this was no time to take it back.

"Where are you?" said a voice that wasn't Mom's. The new voice was bent with rage at the same time it was lilting like a singsong meant for a child's ears. Only my sister Sheila could do that.

I opened my mouth to tell her then realized I didn't really know.

"Where are you?" Sheila growled and sang.

On a closet floor, feeling like an ass for getting upset over a man when my whole family is falling apart. "I'm fine," was the only lie I could articulate.

"Oh, bully for you. Really? Did you do this on purpose?"

"Do what?"

"Fall off the face of the earth? Let us all think you were dead?" Her phrases made hairpin turns around razorblades.

I wanted to tell the truth, spill everything. I was sure I'd get lacerated on a lie. "Sheila, I can't answer that."

"Oh, for the love of fuck, how could you? How could you do that to people who love you?"

She said everything I'd feared hearing when I came back, but I thought it would come from Margie or Mom. Instead it was Sheila, who had always had too many children to focus on me.

"I'm sorry to inconvenience you," I said. "I've been a piece of furniture in this family my whole life. I haven't asked any of you for a thing, and I promise you, I never will."

It was the perfect time to hang up, but I couldn't. I'd done enough walking away.

"Don't pull that," she growled. No one got away with anything as far as Sheila was concerned. "Any one of us would have jumped in front of a bullet for you."

I was a pathetic woman crouched in a dark closet, but when she said that, and I heard the love behind her anger, I felt worthy in a way I hadn't ever before.

"Maybe I didn't want you to," I said. "And I promise you the whole situation is more complicated than I can explain over the phone."

"I'm so pissed off, I can't even swallow." But she wasn't. She'd said her piece, and she was on her way down from her rage high.

"Well, get used to it. I'm not a piece of furniture anymore."

"You were always the one we could count on to not change."

"I'm sorry."

"Don't be. Not for that. The other stuff, yeah. I'm still mad. When are you coming?"

"Soon," I said, lying again. It was possible I could be with my family some time before my brother's funeral, but my own funeral was the likeliest event.

"I'm going to corner you, and you're going to talk to me."

"Okay."

"Okay. Good." She seemed fully calmed. "I have to go."

She hung up. I dropped the phone as if it had turned into lead.

I stayed in the dark, hunched over and paralyzed with conflicting emotions. The shower turned on. I waited for Antonio to finish. Then waited a few minutes more before I couldn't wait another second. I opened the door and padded into the living room. The kitchen island separated the two rooms, and Antonio stood under the island lamps, hair still wet, cigarette dangling from his lips, with the guts of his gun all over the counter. He clicked pieces together, *snap clap snap.*

His hands stopped moving when he saw me. I'd seen him magnificently tired, exhaustion making him look more feral and beautiful, but in that cone of light, he looked as if he'd been unzipped and emptied.

"Hi," I said.

"*Buona sera.*" He slapped the last piece into the pistol. "I've been trying to find the right words to tell you. I keep choosing then unchoosing."

I'm a wreck, everything is fucked up, I love you, I can't have you. You could get shot any minute, my brother is dying, and I can't see him. I feel like a half-played game of Jenga. Pieces of me keep getting pulled away and added to the load.

"I don't want to talk," I said.

He didn't say anything. Didn't even look at me in that way that made me feel eaten alive. He just put his gun down carefully and held out his hand. I took it, and he led me to the couch. He lay flat, and I crawled on top of him, lying thigh to thigh, cheek to chest. When he put his arm around my back, the weight of it secured me in place, pressed the anxiety from my ribs, and I slept with his heartbeat in my ear.

Chapter 19

THERESA

I dreamed I was chasing something through the halls of WDE, but I didn't know what. I only knew I wanted it very badly. My father stood behind Arnie Sanderson's wooden desk, knocking on it while saying *it's in here it's in here*. His voice wasn't his voice but a hive of bees in his throat.

I woke with a stiff neck to Antonio's cheap burner phone buzzing.

"Be still," whispered Antonio when I tried to raise my head. He wiggled until he got his phone out of his pocket. *"Pronto?"*

I opened my eyes and rested on him, letting my vision clear. How long had we slept? Longer than I thought I could. The light outside was dull grey, and the birds made a racket. Zo was on the other end. I heard his choppy Italian. I wondered if Antonio's voice would still sound like music if I could understand what he was saying. Maybe if we got out of this and made a life, I'd learn Italian and find out the answer, or maybe I'd just go on loving the way he sounded, listening to what he was feeling instead of what he was saying.

He tapped his thumb to two of his fingers, making a list for Zo. He swallowed and added a third thing. Zo laughed. Antonio did not.

"Bene. A dopo. He tapped off.

I got up, and he sat on the edge of the couch.

"You look beautiful," he said.

"What did Zo want?"

"Marching orders. I don't know what they did without me for two days."

"I want to see Jonathan," I said.

His silence was too heavy. Too obvious.

"You can pick the time if we have other things to do first. Or..."

I realized he had a set of concerns he wasn't sharing, and the look on his face told me he wasn't just going to tell me what he was thinking. He was calculating his next move.

"Say it, Antonio. What are you going to do when Zo gets here?"

"I need you to wait for my call before you leave for the hospital," he said. "I'll send Otto or come myself."

Ah. That was it.

"We need to stay together," I said.

I knew he wouldn't agree. I knew my demand was the first salvo in a series of shots meant to keep us together, and I knew there would be a fight. When he just smiled at me as if I'd not alarmed him but charmed him, I knew something was wrong.

A car pulled up outside.

"That's Zo," Antonio said without even looking out the window.

Antonio leaned into me. I wasn't supposed to touch him. I was supposed to shun his body, but I already failed when I slept on top of him and let the pace of his breathing soothe me to sleep. So there was no harm in letting him put his arms around me. I could pretend nothing had changed. Valentina was dead, and she'd stayed gentle forever. A memory of some past time, some past love of a man who didn't exist anymore. I let him kiss my neck because she was gone and he was mine alone.

The hug lasted two seconds before Zo knocked.

Antonio peeked out the window and opened the door immediately.

Zo stood there with a white plastic bag. "Good morning."

"*Boun giorno,*" Antonio replied, taking the bag and giving it to me. "Your wish for a toothbrush has been granted."

"Lorenzo, I think I love you." I hugged him hard.

He patted my back noncommittally, and when I looked at Antonio, I knew why.

"I'm going to give these roses a rest," I said and dashed to the bathroom to run the brush over my teeth.

There was still glass all over the floor. I stepped carefully onto the overturned rug.

"I'll have to pay your sister for the window," Antonio said as he closed the door behind him.

I ripped open the packaging on two toothbrushes. "Better do it before she sends a collections agency for you. Oh, he got the cinnamon flavor. I like that." I handed him the blue brush and loaded it.

"I want you to consider something," he said before putting the toothbrush in his mouth.

I'd never seen him do a simple cosmetic chore. He'd always been this effortlessly perfect man. Invulnerable. Capable. He could solve anything. Even during the ridiculous ritual of tooth-brushing, he looked as though nothing could touch him. I think I stared at him too long, brushing the enamel off my teeth.

He spit. I spit. Like normal, whole people, neither of whom was committed to anyone else. I got that nagging feeling of incompleteness, and I chased it away when I wiped my mouth. I had no time to feel sorry for myself.

"What am I considering?" I took the brushes and wrapped them back in the plastic bag.

"Staying here for a few hours. Maybe until tonight."

"I'm sorry?"

"I'll have a TV sent. Books. Anything you want. And someone will come to watch you."

My initial reaction was rage, then insult, then a stew of annoyance, sadness, dismissal, and disgust. I ran my fingers through my hair, making sure the mirror showed nothing of my messy emotions and all the neat and proper thoughtfulness I wanted to project. He caught my stare in the mirror, and I smiled at him.

"Well?" he said. "I won't be too long. I can take care of this today. In and out. Easy. Then I'm going to get Valentina and send her home."

"What about your son?"

"I won't turn my back on him, but he's not safe here."

"He might need a father." I kept my face completely straight when Antonio broke our gaze. I wasn't even half done. "And I mean, you know, one who's alive. One who can teach him to stay out of trouble in Naples."

"Like my father did? I'd do more harm to that child than you know."

"You're wrong, but you'll never know if you're dead. And her? Well, it's going to have zero net impact on her life if you die. She goes home and picks up where she left off. But me? Selfish me? I get to sit here and wait to hear you got killed." I turned from the mirror and looked at him. "I know you're inaccessible, maybe forever. I know I'm all wrong in the head to think I need you, but I'll never feel right without you. So I'm going with you. If you die, I die. If there's a miracle and you live, then fine. You take your wife and your family, and you move on. But me? Sit here and have my life preserved in a jar while you do this? So I can what? Be destroyed when the news comes that they killed you?"

"I have nothing if you're hurt."

"You have a wife and a family. Do you not get it? You have something to lose."

He balled his hands into fists and held them up. "You make me fucking crazy."

I pressed my lips together. I had to consider if I was simply irked that Valentina was probably going to enjoy his company today while I was not. Or was I annoyed at having to put off a trip to Jonathan? We were on our way out of the bathroom before I realized he'd said something I'd missed. He was at the bedroom door when I stopped.

"Antonio."

He turned, hand on the doorframe, pointer finger bent just so in a way that made me want to put it in my mouth. "Yes?"

"You said you were going to do something quick before you see Valentina."

"Yes."

"What was it?"

"Do you need the day's itinerary every day? Do we need to hire a secretary?"

Oh, no. That wouldn't do. Not at all. We'd come too far together for defensive nonsense.

"Today. I need your itinerary today," I said.

"I am not going back to my wife, if that's what you're worried about. I may see her for practical matters but—"

"Do not treat me like a toy."

"Theresa," he said softly, "let me take care of business."

"No. Not when I don't know how far you can go without getting shot at. Not when Otto might come back and tell me you're dead. I won't get in the way, but I won't be left behind."

He held up his hands in surrender. "I tell you what. Wait for Otto. He'll take you to your brother. We meet up after."

"After what?"

He shook his head just a little and strode out to the living area where Zo waited.

"I'm not some bored housewife you have to keep occupied."

He said something to Zo in Italian. A command, because I'd never seen one of his men do anything other than exactly what they were told.

Zo reached into his back pocket. I must have been moved by some form of trust, because my attention wavered enough for me to wonder what Zo had, what time it was, if we were going to get picked up by the Sicilians before we even got out the door, then I was airborne.

"What—?"

Antonio had slung me over his shoulder and carried me into the open kitchen. I fought him tooth and nail, though I didn't know why. I only knew he was forcing me onto the counter, trying to get control of my left wrist.

"Calm down!"

I clawed his face.

"Spin, really..." Zo's voice drifted off when the handcuff was slapped on my wrist.

"Little help here, Lorenzo!" Antonio cried.

I kicked Antonio, and he moved about three inches before wrapping his arm around me. I wiggled and wrenched myself away, but he was strong and vicious, slapping the other cuff around the drawer handle. I was trapped.

Zo held up his hands, muttering, as if he wanted nothing to do with anything about anything.

Antonio stepped back, breathing heavily. "You are a piece of work, woman."

"Where are you going?" I pointed at the stove. "I'm going to burn this house down if you don't tell me right now."

He gathered his gun. "I am the boss, Theresa. I go where I need to, when I need to. If I tell you, it's not for your approval. It's for your information."

He glanced at Lorenzo then turned back to me as he stuck his gun in his waistband. Of course, if he didn't tell me, it would look as if he had to hide things from his woman. I'd put him in a position.

"I'm going to meet Donna Maria Carloni. Right now," Antonio said. "I need to clear it up. I need to tell her I was already married and show her the trouble I saved her. Present it like a favor. It's easily done, and this all gets done."

"And what if it's your territory she really wants?" I yanked against the drawer. It opened but didn't come out. "You're delivering yourself into her hands. She kills you, and she gets it? Is that right? It's as good as a marriage, but she doesn't have to share."

"If she wanted my territory so badly, she would have done it already."

"Bullshit. She wasn't threatened before. There was no Bortolusi union. You know how people act when they're cornered."

"I am not taking you to a den of snakes!" he shouted. "End. No more. You brought this on yourself by insisting you can do things you shouldn't. Otto's gonna knock first. If anyone else comes in here, shoot them in the fucking head. If I'm not back in two hours"—he dropped a phone and gun on the counter—"call somebody."

"I'm calling someone as soon as you turn your back," I spit out.

"That's enough of a head start." He strode out.

Zo gave me an apologetic look before following. I yanked the drawer hard. It didn't budge. By the time I figured out how to get it out of the counter, Antonio would be long gone into the den of snakes.

Chapter 20

ANTONIO

When she'd lain on top of me and fallen asleep, I stayed awake for hours. Her chest rising and falling, her legs on mine, her breath on my neck, the blossom smell of her—I was trapped inside her. In the lack of movement, the absence of logistical puzzles, the only thing I heard in my head was:

A quarter million.

The amount was serious, and it floated over her head and under her feet, weightless because of her ignorance of it. She knew she was in danger but didn't seem to understand what the price tag meant. The Carlonis were not messing around. Word would get out in less than a week, less than another day even, and she would be hunted worse than me, because she was a woman, and vulnerable, and if I was out of the picture, they'd get her. As ferocious as she was, they'd get her. I'd be too dead to stand in front of it.

My first thought was to attack. Go into the Carloni compound guns blazing. But the odds of winning that battle were small, and Theresa would be left alone. She had a vengeful heart and would get herself killed trying to get to the Carlonis.

She was the priority. Her long life. Her health. The price on my head was manageable. As soon as I'd started making money in Los Angeles, I became more valuable dead than alive, as my business would transfer to my murderer.

I had to extricate her.

Meet Donna Maria in a neutral place. Tell her about Valentina and trade my territory for Theresa's safety. I would be free, Theresa would be safe, and maybe I'd be out of the business. Maybe if they let me live, I'd walk. More likely, she'd make up a debt. A term to serve as her consigliere again. Which I'd do, if I could just have Theresa.

It seemed so easy. But with the list of things that could go wrong as long as a man's arm, I had to leave Theresa behind. By promise or force, she couldn't join me.

When it became force, I decided I was at peace with it. I'd make it up to her. I walked out of Margie Drazen's safe house relieved.

"I need to get Donna on the phone," I said to Zo. "I need a neutral place."

"Got it, boss." He plucked his phone out of his pocket.

"We're ending this without blood."

I heard the gunshots as I was about to get into the car. If I'd just gotten in and driven away, she would have been safer, but she was fast. She came out of the door with a wrecked kitchen drawer in her left hand and a smoking gun in her right. She put the gun in her waistband and yanked the handle off the drawer front. It clanked to the ground, and she looked at me expectantly.

"We should take the 210 to the 5. Should be clear at this hour. You can unlock the bracelets on the way." She got into the backseat.

Zo stood by the driver's door with his phone in his hand. "What should I do?"

I was supposed to know. I was supposed to control my woman. I was supposed to be the boss and bark orders that were obeyed. "Don't call yet. Take us to Zia's and have the crew meet us there."

I'd have the whole car ride to think about how to do this as painlessly as possible.

Chapter 21

THERESA

had a sense that something would happen, some idea that the culmination of my life was upon me. Anticipation overtook me on the way to San Pedro. My heart fluttered, and my skin felt the touch of my clothing. My fingertips felt kindled, as if I could touch inanimate objects and set them afire.

I looked at them to make sure they weren't reddened from heat or crackling with the future, but I found that though they looked the same, my way of seeing them had changed. They were no longer just fingers but kinetic devices designed for a fate they leapt to fulfill. They wanted to quicken finally. They wanted to lock into the network of life and vitality they'd only gingerly caressed. *Use me*, they said. *Take me. Make me an instrument for your heart's purpose.*

I was distant from the city around me. The lights of South Central, Compton, Torrance were a projected screen showing a fairy-tale reality of hell-on-earth that I was distanced from, yet intrinsically a part of. There was no middle ground, only the peaceful coexistence of extremes.

I was here. And not here. I was the breakneck pace between who I was and who I was to become. I couldn't breathe from the force of my own velocity.

Even when we stopped in front of Zia's, I was a vibrating buzz of connection and purpose, still in my seat, moving toward a new version of myself. Antonio opened the door for me, and I stepped out of the car as a new thing. An as-yet-unseen and undefined creature.

I felt, as I stepped into the parking lot, that the ground was fitted to me and carried me. When he held my hand, I gathered the power of all the stars in heaven and let him pull me to the earth.

Nothing could touch me. Not death, not hurt, not a fear that I was incomplete. Only he could get near me.

I was a wave form of potential, vibrating upward to suffocation and dissolution. I held his hand as tightly as I dared, because I didn't want him to catch fire.

Chapter 22

ANTONIO

I rode in the front because I didn't want to be next to her. I didn't want to touch her or hear her. Not even her breathing. I didn't want to catch her olive blossom scent. I wanted to be as far away from her as possible. Mostly because I wanted to fuck her and protect her, and she wanted neither.

Well, no. The fucking she wanted but refused. The protection, she needed.

I got angrier and angrier in that front seat. Up. Down. Sideways. I couldn't move in any direction because of her. I couldn't run, and I couldn't attack. She was being impossible and unrealistic. A fool of a woman. Chaos. She was fucking chaos. From the minute she walked into my life with toilet paper on her shoe, she had been a wrecking ball.

I got out of the car intending to tell her to stop this. I needed to say it in a way she could hear. I needed to be more clear. I opened her door, thinking I'd get in and explain it in the backseat, maybe get my fingers inside her to make the point.

Yes. That was the way.

But when I opened the door, I knew I had to rethink my strategy. Beautiful and strong. The weight of life on her. Every muscle meant for survival. An instrument of death and life. She was a bird who'd molted into a deadly carrion, sleek and lethal. How then? Had it happened when she chose to shoot a kitchen apart rather than be left behind? Was it her commitment to me even though she thought I was unavailable? Was that it? What had changed except for the way she fit into the world?

The puzzle of the air and space around her had always clicked to meet the way she walked and spoke. But when she got out of that car, the world changed to meet her on her terms.

I got in front of her, stopping her. She would be impossible to control. She scared the hell out of me. Since the day I met her, she had been frightening, and it had only gotten worse. My life was spinning out of control, and it was her, all her.

She stood on the curb, chin up, with a face that asked what could possibly be the problem? What on earth was unusual about her demanding a part in a negotiation with a Sicilian family to get the quarter million death-price off her head?

"What's here?" she asked. "This isn't some mob boss's compound."

"It's a restaurant. I'm meeting with my crew."

"And then?"

"I'm handcuffing you to something you can't shoot, and I'm taking care of business."

"Handcuff me to you."

"I don't know what to do with you," I said.

"Feeling's mutual."

I felt the shake of rage. I had to hold it back. What did I want to say? I wanted to explain the rules and expectations, because if she was going to be by my side, we had to be of one mind. Yet that was crazy. It wasn't allowed, and it could get her hurt.

"You insist on this course. Repeatedly," I said. "We should be in bed right now. My only problem should be how many times I can get my dick in you in a day."

"Grieve for that dream," she said. "Because it died."

Chapter 23

THERESA

Once I said the words, the juices started twirling in my own heart. Our dream of a quiet little life was dead. Deal with it.

Behind me, Zo took off to get the crew, and it was just Antonio and me on the sidewalk.

The little chained sign in the glass door of Zia's was flipped to the CLOSED side even though, behind the print curtains, the lights were on. I tried to walk toward it, but Antonio blocked the way.

"Listen. They won't want to accept you. Do I need to tell you the reasons?" he asked.

"I'm a woman, and I'm from the right side of the tracks. That cover it?"

"Yes. But I ask only that you hide what you're made of for now. Until you need to show it."

"What am I made of?" I asked.

Antonio put his thumb and forefinger on either side of my chin. It would be hard to remember he was married. "I haven't figured it out yet."

"*Bene,*" I said.

Antonio backed up and let me in, then followed. The door slapped closed behind us.

The restaurant smelled of bleach and tomato sauce, and it sounded like the buzz of fluorescent lights and tension. The lunch crowd hadn't shown up yet; neither had the waitstaff. Only the smell of food drifting from the kitchen gave any indication that the captain was at the helm.

Antonio reached back and drew the bolt on the door. As if summoned by the *clack*, Zia came to the kitchen doorway, wiping her hands with a white towel. The space between her and Antonio was tight with strain.

"Tonio," she said.

"Aunt."

Zia's chin wrinkled then straightened. *"Mea culpa. Per Tina. Per Antonin."* Her voice cracked, and fat tears dropped down her cheek. *"Per tutti."*

Antonio didn't move. No one moved. Forgiveness hung in the air, refusing to touch down. People couldn't die from tension in a room, but if they could, we would have at least passed out from the toxins.

"I'm sorry too," Antonio said finally, in a tone that had no room for apology, only an accusation.

Zia snapped her towel and draped it over her arm. *"Tina è per strada. Stu venedo qui."* She sniffed once then spun on her heel and walked back into the kitchen.

Antonio looked stricken.

"What did she say?"

"I'll take you home," he replied, taking my arm.

"Wait, where's home?" I shook him off. "And in what car? What did she say?"

He was still trying to guide me out. "Let's just go."

"Stop it!" I folded my arms. "What did she say?"

He looked at the ceiling as if asking God for help, just for once, a little help.

Outside, a car door slammed. Zia's was on a short block, adjacent to a real estate agent and an optometrist, so there wasn't much street traffic. The car door got Antonio's attention.

"Let's go out the back," he said.

"What's happening? You're scaring me." I followed his gaze outside. Through the curtains, I saw a man in a suit open the passenger door of a new Honda and a woman got out.

Not just a woman. Valentina Spinelli.

And the man in the suit turned around. Daniel.

Antonio took my hand and pulled me toward the kitchen. I yanked him back.

"Do you see?" he said, indicating the two people coming toward the door as if the situation were obvious. To him, they were a speeding tornado and we had to seek shelter.

"You're as white as a sheet," I said, tugging him back. "You're not afraid of death or torture…but your wife and me in the same room terrifies you. What do you think is going to happen? We're all adults." I brushed by him and took three big steps toward the front door.

"You can't be here," he said.

"You have to deal with this. It won't go away by denial."

He went rigid and lowered his head so he looked me in the eye. "We. Are. Leaving."

My eyes locked on his. I reached behind me, stretching, and turned the bolt on the front door. *Clack.*

A whoosh of cool air blew in as Daniel opened the door, and there was Valentina, in the same room as me. Breathing the same air. Haughty and righteous, wearing her skin as if it were a suit of armor, straight where I curved, long where I was short, she clutched a little bag in front of her and tilted her chin up.

"Antonio," she said.

"Valentina," he said.

"You won't call me Tina, all of a sudden?"

"Come stai, Tina?"

"I learned a little English."

"Fantastico. Mi dai il cappotto?"

"Don't make your girlfriend feel left out," she crooned.

"Can I take your coat?"

"I have it," Daniel interjected.

Was I wrong to find the whole thing delicious? All of the emotional upheaval of the last few days had inured me to the threat of his wife. I'd already surrendered to her. I'd already accepted what her existence meant. I was already crushed under the weight of it. Her presence in the same room as us couldn't hurt me.

Daniel slipped off her coat, and I felt not an ounce of jealousy for that either. I doubted Valentina Spinelli would let Daniel get one over on her.

"Aren't you going to introduce us?" Valentina asked, one eyebrow raised. She didn't move but comported herself perfectly. She reminded me of me.

So that was it.

That had been the initial attraction. She and I couldn't have been more physically opposite, but Antonio had seen both deeper than that and less deep. Because her comportment wasn't courteous. She attacked by staying still and asking a question designed to make her husband feel ill-mannered and to draw attention to discomfort.

I didn't like it, but I understood it.

"My name is Theresa," I said, holding out my hand.

She waited a half a beat then shook gently. "I am Valentina. Valentina Spinelli."

"Nice to meet you."

She was far away, taking her own counsel. She had no intention of giving an inch. I'd seen that look in press agents and lobbyists who knew they had the upper hand and had no intention of budging.

"Zia!" Antonio called. "Let's get something to eat out here!"

Zia came out and, seeing Valentina, said a greeting in Italian and kissed her on both cheeks, twice. They chattered in Italian for a minute while Daniel fidgeted. Poor guy.

"*Si, del vin rosso per favore,*" Valentina said.

"No," Antonio cut in as if putting his foot down for the benefit of a defiant child. "No wine."

I thought he would get his way, as strange as it was.

"You are still bossy," Valentina said in choppy but quick English before addressing Zia. "A chianti."

"No! And that is the final word."

Zia looked from Valentina to Antonio, not knowing what to do. I didn't know what his objection was about. Did he find it unbecoming? Was it too early in the day? I'd had a drink or two in front of him, and it had never warranted this level of protest.

"I could use a glass myself," I said.

I went to the sideboard. It was lined in clean white cloth napkins. The grey tray was loaded with silverware, and the empty water pitchers were stacked neatly. Above, wine glasses hung. I snapped up five, wedging the stems between my fingers.

I put the glasses on the counter then flipped up the end of the bar and walked behind it. The floor was coated in a black rubber honeycomb mesh half an inch high. My feet bounced when I walked. I'd never been behind a bar before, and everything seemed neat and compartmentalized. I located the fridge immediately.

I stared at it. I was nuts. I couldn't diffuse the tension in the room with a little wine. I was an outsider.

To hell with it. I opened the fridge door and resolved to choose a damned bottle and do what I was supposed to do. Serve wine and celebrate the continued and uninterrupted life of Antonio Spinelli.

As if I'd called him forth with my mind, his scent filled me. The knowledge that he was close melted the skin right off me.

"You'll never make a good Italian wife unless you learn to obey," he said in my ear.

He said it in good humor, trying to relieve his own part of the tension, but it was a stupid, hurtful, wicked thing to say, especially with a fuckable growl that acted as a whisk for my arousal and anger. I didn't know whether to spread my legs or spit in his eye.

I put a random bottle on the bar with a smack, trying to look casual. As if I didn't want to kill him for saying that stupid thing. Though I wanted to eviscerate Antonio with a steak knife right then, I didn't want to undermine him. I didn't want any of them to think he'd shown poor judgment in being with me. I didn't want them to think I was a liability or that his wife was more refined and mature. I wanted to leave, walk out the front door as if it just happened to be what I was doing at the moment. No more, no less.

I didn't know where I was going. I just had to get out of that cramped restaurant. The December air hit me full in the face, and I wished for a jacket. But more than that, when I got outside, I immediately calculated the width of the street, the movement of the cars, the foot traffic, the rooftops. I was completely exposed. I'd never felt that while walking across the street before. But every window was a gun perch, and every car was a moving crime scene.

I wasn't concerned for myself but the fact that I was drawing Antonio out into the open.

Antonio came out of the restaurant, dinging the bell, and our eyes met across the seven-foot expanse of the street. Miles between us, and close enough to kiss. He could take one leap and be on me in the most pleasing agony.

"Get out of the street," he said, pointing into the restaurant. "Anyone can take a shot at you here."

I tore my eyes from his and went to the covered driveway that led to the parking lot behind the restaurant. Jesus. I was backing myself into a corner. I wondered if I could hop a fence, then I felt him behind me, and before I even got to the back lot, his hand was on my neck.

Time stopped. I didn't know how much longer I could do this.

Chapter 24

ANTONIO

The back of her neck, bare except for the stray hair that got out of the rubber band, was warm under my fingers. When I touched her there, getting my finger under the gold chain that held the St. Christopher medal, she stopped, like an animal with an instinctive reaction not to obey but to listen.

"I want you," I whispered in her ear. "Only you."

"I know," she said. "But am I what you need?"

The scent of the food in the restaurant and the idea that any man knows what he needs triggered the memory that had haunted me for years.

My mother never made risotto, but Valentina had been raised in the north, so she'd brought the dish with her. It had to be stirred constantly. If the spatula stopped moving, the grains could get hard in places. For a consistent texture, not one grain could be still for one second. Nor could the temperature fluctuate. Hot broth went in to increase the moisture without cooling the pan. If she put in cold broth, the rice grains would crack into mush. It was a balancing act she did without even thinking.

She had no family to speak of, so she made mine into hers. My mother and aunt loved her, and she loved them. We'd lived in a small house in the outskirts of Napoli. Two bedrooms, a barely finished kitchen, and a backyard big enough to farm in. The winters were mild, and in summer, we buried our trash twice a day in a hole by the back fence because of the humidity. An apple tree took root where we put the garbage, so we moved our digging spot.

She had been making dinner when I saw her last. I was leaving for the night in an hour, and I hoped for a fuck before I went. But she was making risotto for dinner, and I couldn't stop the process, nor could I skip eating entirely for the sake of the pressure on my dick. She was cooking, and that was all there was to it.

I couldn't tell her where I was going. That was a given. When I was a mechanic, then a law student, then a lawyer, she didn't have to ask where I was going, because I wasn't going anywhere. Work-school-work-study-work.

I'd told her I would take care of the men who had hurt my sister, then I was done. *Stupidi*. She and I both. I hadn't cleared my desk of all of them while she lived, and there was no "done." Ever.

"I have to go," I said. "I'm sorry. I have to miss supper."

"Antonio!" She indicated the risotto as if it were its own reason. And it was. It couldn't be stored or refrigerated.

"I'm sorry, it's business."

She slapped the spoon on the edge of the pot and put it down. Watched it bubble for a second before starting to stir again. She'd never ruin a risotto just because she was angry at me.

"Business. You do mental Olympics to make excuses for yourself," she said, twirling the arm that wasn't stirring the rice. Her nails were trimmed but unpolished. Her hair was thrown up in a quick pile on her head that I wanted to take down and pull from behind.

But no. There was no hair pulling, and there was no "from behind." That had been agreed, but I could still imagine her on her hands and knees. My mind was my own.

"Oh, you think?" I snapped up a spoon. "Maybe I'll leave tomorrow and show you Olympian stamina tonight."

"Stop with your filth." I wedged a little risotto onto the edge of the spoon, and she swatted me away. "I'm serious. Do not dismiss me."

She was always serious. Her mother said it was because she had a heart condition. Even a misunderstanding could start the pains.

I'd never seen any such thing until the night of our wedding, when I'd pulled her hair and she had palpitations.

I popped the bite of risotto into my mouth. It was delicious. Perfect. I remembered that bite of risotto for years after that day. The layers of flavor coated my mouth no matter how much bile I walked around Los Angeles with.

I'd dropped the spoon into the ceramic sink and clasped her at the rib cage. My hands went nearly all the way around her. I could ask her to keep stirring while I fucked her. That would be fun. But not only was that position off-limits, the kitchen was as well.

"Tell me about my excuses then."

"I won't tell a man what to do," she lied, and I smiled. She was so bossy. "But, Antonio, I cannot do this anymore. I cannot watch you go away overnight and not know if you're coming home."

"There's no safer job in Napoli." I brushed loose strands of hair from her neck. "Consigliere is a protected position. If anything happened to me, every capo would make sure I was avenged."

She slapped the spoon on the edge of the pot. "And you'd be in hell." She turned her back to the stove, letting the risotto sit. "I can't live like this anymore. What you do is wrong. It's against God. I won't be a part of it anymore. I won't raise children like this."

I took the wooden spoon and reached around her waist to stir the rice. "You don't like the nice things I buy you?"

"I don't care about them."

She must have forgotten how unhappy she had been when we had nothing. She nagged me to change jobs, work harder, go back to fixing cars.

"And the children? When they come, you're going to want things for them? We can buy a bigger house with what we've saved. Public lawyers don't make shit."

"I mean it, Antonio. Stop now. Today. Stay home tonight."

"And?"

"And what?"

"What do I get if I stay home tonight?"

She stared at me with her almond eyes, lips pressed together, and all the filthiest things she might let me do went through my mind.

"You get to go to confession and have your sins removed."

"And then?" I was such a hopeful bastard.

She put her hands on my chest. "You go to heaven."

"In the bed? Or maybe against this counter?"

She nudged me away and turned back around. "The kitchen isn't for that." She snapped the spoon away, grumbling, "Dirty boy."

I was suddenly very, very angry. She didn't have to promise me anything. She didn't have to give me any part of her body she didn't want to. But she pushed and pushed, and I was expected to do as she asked for the love of the same shit.

I put my hand on the back of her head and curled my fingers, grabbing a handful of bunched up hair. I yanked her head back. I was playing with fire, but I didn't know how to stop myself.

"Ow! Stop!"

I spoke right into her ear. I wanted my words to be so tight between us, the air didn't even know what I said. "I'll tell you when I'll quit this job. When I come home and you've got your palms on the counter and your skirt around your waist. When I spread your sweet cheeks apart, and you say, 'Yes, Antonio baby, fuck my ass.' And I stick a finger in your cunt and you're wet."

"Stop it," she said, crying.

I pulled her head back harder. I was so fucking mad, I didn't care if her arrhythmia went crazy and I spent the night apologizing in a hospital. I was on some kind of track and I couldn't get off. "When I take your juice to wet your asshole, and when it's wet, my cock goes one, two, three, right inside. And you sit the fuck still and take it." I let her hair go with a jerk. "That's when I'll stop doing what puts food on the table."

I left before I did something stupid. I had a panino from the street cart for dinner, and I never saw her in Italy again.

Chapter 25

THERESA

His hand rested on the back of my neck with just enough pressure to let me know he was there. I didn't need the reminder. I knew he was present. Knew he loved me. I'd just needed a moment to breathe.

"You have to stop touching me," I said.

He swung in front of me. The sunlight hit the edge of his face. The rest was veiled in shadow. I could still read him clearly, as if the light was his lust and the shade was his rage. All he had to do was turn his head slightly to be either bathed in brilliance or drowned in shadow.

"I don't know how many times I have to say this—"

He stopped talking when I pulled away from him, backing into the brick wall. "I know. You can touch me any time you want. I've heard it."

"Don't take this lightly."

"Lightly? I'm the only one taking your life seriously." I touched his lapel. It was bent a sixteenth of an inch and needed straightening.

His shoulders dropped an amount equal to the bend of his lapel. Enough for me to notice. It was a half measure of resignation, another half measure of vulnerability. My fingers trailed the edge of the jacket seam, as if they were caught in a groove. He looked down at their journey, his eyelashes the length of black widow legs, lips parted just enough to emphasize their fullness.

cd reiss

"I'm only a man," he said. "I'm not a saint."

"Not a devil either."

He flicked a speck of something off my shoulder, smoothing the fabric. "I don't know what to do. And that alone is uncomfortable. I always know what to do."

I pressed my hands to his chest but didn't push him away. "I can't reassure you. I can't say we'll figure it out. I can't see the way through it."

"We don't divorce. It's not done."

"I know."

"I could kill my mother for doing this."

"She was protecting a life she knew you'd want back," I said. "And before you protest, you want it back. I know you do. It's exactly the life you described to me in TJ. It's a good life. I get it. I want it with you, but I don't know how to get there."

I expected him to resist and tell me I was his life. That was the script. He was supposed to reassure me in no uncertain terms. But he wouldn't look at me.

"This is what it means to get older," he said. "Your choices get less and less."

"You can get there. You can do it. You can have it all. If you manage to get forgiveness from Donna Maria, you need to step back and think about it."

"I should leave you behind?"

"Yes. I think if we can unravel this, then that's how it has to go." A hairline crack appeared in my heart. I knew I was right. This was solvable if I gave him up. If I didn't, it was a mess.

"It's decided then?" he said gently, and the hairline crack deepened.

"Yes."

"You'll be safer that way." He put his lips to my cheek, and my body trembled.

"I will," I lied. I could never go back to who I had been. Never. "I'll live a long, safe life."

"Without me." He kissed my neck, and the shimmering arousal that ran though my body seemed not hindered by the flood of melancholy but abetted by it.

"Without you." My hips found their way to him as if by magnetism. His every kiss to my neck, his every breath in my ear, was a contradiction to the words he spoke.

"And I'll go back home with my wife and fuck her sweetly for the rest of my days?"

I couldn't give him more than *mmm* from deep in my chest because his hand brushed over my hardened nipple, coming back for a second pass with the backs of his fingers. I thought I should push him away, but my body wasn't taking instructions.

"I'll be happy," he whispered in my ear then kissed it. "We'll buy a little stone house, and I'll spend the rest of my life with a sweet, useless little pet."

"Don't bad-mouth her."

He pulled back until we were nose to nose. "She fucks like a plucked chicken."

I had to bite back a laugh, and Antonio smiled so wide, I fell in love with his face all over again.

"Don't—" I said.

"Don't what? Don't change? Don't look back at my past and see clearly?"

"Don't smile like that. You melt me. I can barely stand straight."

"Let me catch you."

He put his lips on mine. I bent under him, yielding completely to his mouth, the rhythm of his lips, the force of his tongue. I allowed myself to hope that there was a way out, and at the same time, the hope lived with resignation.

I didn't want that kiss to end. It shouted down my confusion. I wanted to drown in it. Take my last breath with him. Die connected in a painless flood of arousal and sorrow. But through the window came the pop of a wine cork, and he straightened.

"Let me take you back to the house," he said, his voice covered with a thin sheet of urgency. "I swear I'll meet you there."

"Do you not want me to talk to your wife?"

"I don't want her to talk, period."

"This intrigues me." I slipped away from him and strode quickly back to the street. I opened the restaurant door to Daniel filling the glasses. "Don't you have a campaign to run?" I felt my face getting red in the warm dining room. "You've been socializing without talking politics."

"Gerry wants me out of the way until the trick you played at the wedding dies down."

He handed Valentina a glass. She swirled it, avoiding eye contact with me.

"Sorry about that."

He handed me a glass. "No, you're not."

"No. I'm not."

Behind me, Antonio spoke sharply to Valentina. *"Non bere quell vino."*

"Salute." She raised her glass and, in a single open-throated gulp, poured the entire contents down her throat.

Antonio groaned as Valentina clacked her glass on the bar and made a swirling motion above it with her finger. Daniel refilled it.

"Sit down for *primi*," Zia said as she burst through the swinging doors with a tray of manicotti. She set it in the center of a round table, which had already been set for four.

"Grazie, Zia! Bene!" Valentina said with an enthusiasm I hadn't noticed before. She grabbed her glass and the bottle and sat.

I sat across from her, and when Antonio placed himself next to me, I whispered, "Isn't Zia eating?"

He made a *tsk* noise with a shake of the head and placed his napkin in his lap.

"What about Antonin? Where is he?" I realized the question was just on the other side of inappropriate when it was all the way out of my mouth.

Valentina took the half-empty glass from her lips and answered. "I sent him home. It's hell here. I don't know how you stand the smells. Car exhaust. It's everywhere. When I was first married, I had to scrub it out of my husband's clothes every day. I will not have my son smell like street grease."

"He took a plane home alone? To Europe?" Daniel asked, sliding a cheesy tube onto her plate.

"Non-stop flight. We do it all the time. Only Americans circle their children like helicopters. Give me another one please." She indicated the manicotti and brought the wine to her lips again.

"Tina, enough," Antonio said, reaching for the glass.

She slapped him away. Had I thought she was haughty and controlled? Because she didn't seem that way anymore.

"Tell me, Tonio, what have you been doing here? Besides pretending you're dead and letting your girlfriend drink all she wants?"

"Avoiding this guy." He smirked, pointing his fork at Daniel.

I took a slice of manicotti and watched as Valentina shoveled down half of one neatly and efficiently.

"You fail at this," she said after she washed it down. "He's right here."

Daniel smiled and pushed his cheese around the plate, obviously finding this whole thing very amusing. He filled her wine glass, and she graced him with a beatific smile. God, she was stunning. A thoroughbred.

I got Daniel's attention and mouthed, "More wine."

He grinned and got up for another bottle.

"What else?" She swirled her wine around as if she was baiting Antonio.

"Just running my business."

"You mean your criminal empire?" She bobbed her head when she spoke, a graceless gesture and a sign that she'd had a glass too many.

Antonio dropped his fork. *"Basta,* Tina."

She turned her palms down and shook her hands, telling us to be quiet because something important was coming. "I work in a fabric factory, at the desk, and there's a little *salumeria* on the corner. And the little men sit outside it talking like they're so important. Little *mafiosi.* They come into the factory and take their money. Their tribute." She flung her hands around like butterflies. "They try to take me to bed. You know what I say to them? Your little *pistola* matches your stupid bald head. Both in your pants. Both can't shoot."

"More wine?" I asked.

She pushed her glass to me. *"Grazie.* And all of the *mafiosi…"* She held up her pinkie. "Like this. You can't be in the organization unless you have an okra between your legs." She put her thumb and pointer finger two inches apart, then held up her hands to Antonio as if he'd objected, which he hadn't, except to rub his face in embarrassment. "Not Mister Spinelli, of course. With that *cetriolo*."

I almost spit my wine. Daniel pressed his lips together so he wouldn't bust.

She was on a roll, addressing Antonio with a hand cupped as if handing him a golden piece of advice. "My God, you are going to kill someone with that thing one day. This is what I thought." She put her elbow on the table and wagged her finger at him. "I thought you couldn't be *mafiosi* because..." She put her hands up, a foot apart. "But no. Time passed, and you were just like the rest of them."

She poured wine down her throat and turned to me. "You can have that thing."

I think I went red. She was imagining me with that beautiful dick, and I felt my barest lust exposed.

"No one woman can keep up with him. He can manage two," she said.

"Not in America," Antonio said. "Here, it's one woman, one man."

"Sometimes," Daniel mumbled then leaned back.

She stretched her neck and tilted her head as if bringing her ear closer to Antonio. "*Che?*"

"Don't pretend you haven't heard of it," Antonio growled.

We'd been through hell together, but this? This was a million times worse.

"*Monogamia?*" Valentina said with disbelief. "Not for the men in the organization."

"For this man, it is. I'm sorry, but this *cetriolo* is for her only." He took my hand, and though I was proud of that, I also had to shake the feeling that she shouldn't see any affection between us. "I love her. You waited, I know you waited, until I was the man you wanted me to be. But she took me as I am."

"A thief and a killer?"

"Alleged," I said, keenly aware of Daniel's presence.

She bent her head slightly left then right, left then right, pursing her lips. "We don't divorce. We aren't American. I will fight you."

"I don't want to fight."

She huffed as if that was the first time she'd heard him say such a thing. "You won't make our son a bastard either. I will curse you to hell."

"I'm going to hell anyway."

"Can you just fuck her and leave me alone?"

"That's not up to me. It's up to Theresa."

She faced me, full-on, as if expecting me to answer the big questions of her life with a half-eaten manicotti in front of me, my ex on my left, and the love of my life on my right.

"Way to drop it in a girl's lap," I said, taking my hand from Antonio's.

Valentina swooped up the second bottle in one hand and her glass in the other. She came around the table and bent over to whisper, "Let's go, *troia*."

She strode out to the back, ass wagging like a flag, the swinging doors kissing behind her.

"Did she just call me a whore?"

"Worse. Don't follow her," Antonio said. "She's not right in the head when she drinks."

He started to get up, but I put my hand on his shoulder and pushed him down so I could stand. "Stay here and help with the dishes." I snapped up my glass and went out the back.

Chapter 26

THERESA

Zia had something going on in the kitchen that smelled like meat. I was still hungry but didn't pause long enough to ask what was bubbling. Valentina stood in the tiny parking lot, by the dumpster, filling her glass. She had the bottle out to fill me up before I had two feet out the door.

"What do you want?" she asked.

"You're the one who waited around ten years. What do *you* want?"

"I want my life back." She put the bottle on top of a car.

"You gave it up because you didn't like it."

"The life before he was consigliere for his father. This one I'm talking about. He was very nice. He was a sweet man."

Nice. Sweet. Was she talking about someone else? Her eyes were cloudy, and she held on to the edge of the gate to steady herself. Wine was indeed a bad idea.

"Antonio's a lot of things," I said. "Sweet isn't one of them."

"He used to bring me strawberries, in summer, from the fruit vendor on Via Scotto. So expensive. And beautiful. He took the leaves off and fed them to me."

I imagined that was true. Of course he'd bring gifts and tributes. It was the sweet part that tripped me up. He must have had the act down pat. He'd wanted this gentle girl and lied to himself to have her.

"He brushed my hair." She touched it, remembering in a drunken stupor. "Every night. When I had headaches or felt faint, he rubbed my forehead until I fell asleep. If I was tired, he carried me up the steps, and he sang to me. He can't sing a note, did you know? He's terrible."

She smiled to herself and sniffed. She didn't seem stupid or easily fooled. Valentina was heartbroken and drunk, but I didn't think Antonio could lie to her about who he was. It was possible that somewhere in that bossy, demanding, vicious man, there was a gentle, sweet husband who brushed his wife's hair and brought her strawberries.

"I'm sorry, Valentina," I said. "I think that's all in the past now."

She continued as if I hadn't spoken. "And he changed. I drove him away. I threw him away. I thought...I don't know what I thought. I dreamed he'd change and I'd go back to him, but I knew it was crazy, and now it's not so crazy."

She wiped her eyes with the back of her hand. "He's in there." She poked her chest. "And now I take responsibility. You are young. You seem all right. Maybe you don't have to be a *troia*? Maybe you can find your own man? Because I'm going to have my husband again. I waited ten years. I can take as many more as I need." She raised her finger as if making her point, but when she took her hand off the hood of the car, she wobbled and put her hand back.

"He's mine." I spoke as gently as I could. We weren't going to have a catfight. I had no time for it. "I'm sorry. I'm not going to scratch your eyes out or anything like that, but when you sober up, you need to go home. To Naples."

"Napoli," she corrected. "*Naaah*-poh-lee."

She let go of the car again, and when I caught her, she pushed me away and put all her weight on me at the same time.

Daniel rushed out from the restaurant. "Jesus, Tink, what's going on?"

"What do you think? And stop calling me that."

He got himself under Valentina, and she put her arms around his neck.

"I got a call from Gerry," he said once he had Valentina properly balanced. "He put together a fundraiser tonight. I have to go prepare."

"Good luck."

He squinted in the winter sun, hair dropping in front of his forehead in the way I used to love. Valentina rested her head on his chest.

"Spin says she's not a puker," he said.

"So you guys talked."

He nodded. "I had to tell him I wasn't fucking his wife. Guy thing."

"Ah. Well. Good luck tonight. With the fundraiser."

"Yeah." He shook his head. "I think I ran out of juice. Even before that fiasco at the wedding, I lost energy for it. So I don't know. "

"You can't drop out. Ten more weeks."

He laughed to himself, as if I'd misjudged ten weeks as too long or too short, but I'd somehow misjudged everything.

"I parked in front like a dope," he said. "I'm walking out of a storefront for an Italian crime family—"

"Tell them you were looking at the books—"

"Practically carrying a camorra capo's wife."

"Wife!" Valentina interjected loosely, flopping her arm up before pointing at herself and collapsing.

"You're finished in this town," I said to her.

I started away, but Daniel called to me.

"Tink, when we have enough evidence on who shot Paulie, we're taking him in." He indicated Antonio with a jerk of his head.

I faced him fully and took all the defensiveness out of my voice. I wasn't protesting, I was stating a fact. "He didn't do it."

Without waiting for an answer, I went back into the restaurant.

Chapter 27

ANTONIO

Otto and Lorenzo pulled up out front just as Daniel went out the back for the women. He'd told me he wasn't fucking Valentina, which I could have told him. I wasn't giving him permission either. He was still on the other side of the line, and I wanted him to stay there. I reserved the right to break his legs over that or anything.

Otto closed the driver's side door, scanning the street as always. Lorenzo got out of the passenger side. And no one else. They walked away from an empty car.

Could they not find the others? Or were they coming separately? Normally that wouldn't even give me a second's pause, but a bit of doubt crept into my head. Something wasn't right.

Zo came in first. He didn't make eye contact. Otto came in in the middle of lighting a cigarette. I sat at the bar as Zia came out with a tray of something that steamed.

"How many are coming?" she asked, putting the tray in the center of the table.

"Two more," I said. No one disagreed.

"The staff will be here in half an hour. So sit!"

Otto and Zo mumbled thanks and sat for lunch. When Zia passed me again, I put my arm around her. I didn't say a word, just kissed her forehead. She'd been good to me, and I might always be angry at her for hiding Valentina, but I had to forgive her or more than my love for my wife might die. She patted my arm and pushed past the swinging doors.

Otto leaned back in his chair, cigarette between his third and last fingers. Zo sat with his hands folded over his crotch and cleared his throat.

There was a heavy silence I didn't understand.

"Simone and Enzo?" I asked, sitting.

Zo put his hands out then back down. More silence. A pot banged in the kitchen.

"Come on, Zo!" Otto shouted.

"I can't say it."

Otto stamped out his cigarette as if nailing it to the ashtray. Then he clapped twice. "Welcome back!" Otto came at me with both hands out. He planted them on my neck and kissed my cheeks twice. "You look good for a dead guy! *Gagliardo!*" He patted my shoulder and kissed my cheeks again.

"You kiss me again, you're going to have to marry me," I said.

"I have a wife," Otto replied. "This guy"—he indicated Zo—"he's single. Give him a kiss, would you?"

"I think Zo fucked me already," I said. "Where are the others?"

Zo made a noise that was a cross between a groan and an *ah*. "They ain't coming."

"Excuse me?"

"We...uh. The day you was gone, we made a pact with Donna and now...they got families. They don't want another war."

"They're cowards!" Otto shouted, but I didn't hear him.

There were a million reasons to make peace. Strategies within strategies. It depended on who my people thought had killed me. If they thought it was the Bortolusis, which was what we'd intended, then the allegiance would be to partner against them.

"You made a pact? For what purpose?" I asked.

Zo looked stricken. "Business."

"I'm glad you didn't marry that bitch," Otto said, as if trying to pull solidarity from the jaws of anarchy. "I don't want to work with the Sicilians. I never liked it. You ever been to Palermo? It's backward, like they got their own pope. I don't want to answer to a man I never met. Never shook his hand. Nothing."

Otto was talking for the sake of talking, because no one was hearing him. It was Lorenzo and me in the room.

"I'm sorry to speak ill," Otto continued. "But Paulie, he was dangerous. I'm sorry you had to do what you done with him, but I'm glad I don't gotta worry no more."

"Lorenzo," I said, "you didn't tell me this was your plan."

He faced me full-on. He wasn't afraid of me, and that concerned me.

"So?" he said. "This way we didn't have to avenge you. Because I didn't want to avenge a guy who wasn't dead."

He was right. He could have used my death to start a fight that might have brought him millions if he won. But he'd opted for the path of right and found a way to navigate it. Not bad for a baby don. Not bad at all. Except he hadn't maintained the loyalty of the crew. Because they were gone, with a bigger love for peace than their own lives.

"They already tried to kill us," I said. "And the crew, they don't realize it's me today, and it's them tomorrow." I had a finger up, talking to Zo but seeing Enzo and Simone. "If we were in Napoli, that would be a given. You cannot trust Americans. Cannot. They turn on you the minute there's a risk. Nothing gets done alone." I pushed my wine three inches left. Two right. "Americans. All lone guns. Let me tell you something. That fails."

"I'm with you," Zo said. "You was dead, but now you're not and they put a price on your head. It's changed. But some guys don't change so fast."

The wine became offensive to me. Liquid celebration turned bitter by betrayal. I threw it across the room. It hung in the air in a streak of red then splatted everywhere.

Theresa walked in from the kitchen just as the glass landed, and I felt a deep shame at my tantrum. She deserved better. She deserved a man who could solve problems. But my thoughts were like pigeons in the piazza, a sea of cohesive grey scattered to the wind by a running child.

"You got this," Otto said, seemingly unaffected by my tantrum. "I don't know how. But as long as we can get close, we can attack. And that gets the price off your head because if you kill her, you run her business."

That was the last thing I needed. But he'd given me an idea if I could just get my head around the execution.

"No," I said. "There are too many ways to die."

Theresa came up behind me and put her hand on my shoulder. I slid mine over hers and stayed that way for a second. I was surrounded by treachery, but she was behind me, like a balm.

"You guys eat," I said. "I have business to attend to."

Chapter 28

THERESA

When he took my hand and stood, making eye contact, I melted a little. He cut through the business, the violence, the calculation, and took me to the kitchen. My cognizance of the space his body occupied sharpened like a razor. I was nowhere near his dick, but I was aware of it. My body was aware of it. My nipples hardened as if that could get me that much closer to it.

"What happened?" I asked.

"I am being betrayed."

"By who?"

"Possibly all of them."

"What do we do?"

He took my hand, and I let him because I felt no will outside my desire. He led me past Zia scrubbing a pot and greeting the lunch staff, to the office where I'd looked at the restaurant's books a million years before. The same squares of yellow sticky paper covered the wall, and the same beige computer hissed and hummed. He snapped the door closed and pushed me against the shelf that served as a desk.

"Let me have you," he growled. "Today. Now. *Adesso*. I don't care about anything but your body. I can't think without it. I'll get a divorce. An annulment. I'll murder anyone who comes between us. I'll promise not to. Anything. But I want you. Please. Call it a fuck of agreement. Call it a fuck for good-bye. Call it a *che sera, serà*.

I don't care. But don't tell me I'm married to someone else. There is no one else."

I didn't want to believe him, because everything about what he was saying was wrong. But I did believe him. From the soaking arousal between my legs to the tips of my toes, from basest parts of my lizard brain to the intellect in my frontal cortex, I believed him.

I didn't believe the world would cooperate, but I didn't want the world inside me. I wanted him. His...what had Valentina called it?

"What does *cetriolo* mean?" I asked quietly.

His mouth twitched on one side as if he was trying not to smile. "You call it..." He cleared his throat and rubbed his eye as if he were so embarrassed he couldn't even see straight. "A cucumber."

"No, that's not what I call it at all." I spoke only in breath, my eyes on his luscious mouth. Those lips. On me. On my neck. On my body. My resistance slid away, lubricated by Valentina's dismissal and the shape of Antonio's mouth.

With a tilt of his head and a *tsk* of his tongue hitting the roof of his mouth, he had me.

"She doesn't seem to care if you fuck me," I said.

"She said that?"

"More or less. She seems to want every part of you but your eggplant."

His eyes lit up, and his mouth tightened in a smile. I'd given him as good as a "yes."

"It comes with the set," he said into my neck.

"Give it to me. The whole package."

I kissed him, pushing my body up against his. We wrapped our arms around each other, and pressed together, the outline of his erection was tight against me. He pulled back, and I drank in the lines of his face, the texture of stubble on his cheeks, the espresso of his eyes. Our lips came together again in an explosion of shared desire.

He pulled my shirt and bra over my breasts in one move, releasing them. "I missed these," he said, squeezing a nipple. "You are *magnifico*."

I groaned his name when he took my breast in his mouth. "I won't let you go," I said in a gasp. "I know I said I would, but I can't. I'm so confused." He sucked the nipple hard, and my last word came out as a squeak.

"I'm not." He opened my pants. "Fucking is very simple."

I was going to do this. I was going to break my promise to myself into a thousand pieces.

"Your body is mine." He kneeled in front of me, kissing my belly and the triangle where my legs met, slipping my pants down as he went. "I'm going to do what I want with it. Trust that I want what's right for it."

"I trust you, I just..." My words fell into breaths when his hands caressed my ass.

"Trust me. Trust that I won't leave you. Not from being careless or reckless. Not if I can help it. Not for a woman in my past." His eyes became brown disks warm with a pure decency I'd never seen before. "I will never leave you. I need you. Tell me you understand."

I didn't. Not at all. But I believed his intentions. "I trust you."

He lifted my feet from my jeans and kissed inside my legs, my knees, his tongue waking my skin as if from a long sleep. He spread them apart, pushing me back onto the desk. "You're going to let me fuck you so hard, you remember me forever. There is no such word as 'no.'"

My head rested on the wall, and he kissed where I was most vulnerable. The hair on his face scratched my sensitive thighs, but when his tongue reached my center, the discomfort was forgotten.

My feet tingled. My heart went code red. I couldn't see an inch in front of me. His tongue coursed up and down, exploring every inch of me. He put the tip of his tongue to the tip of my clit.

"I'm so close, I'm so close," I breathed.

He sucked on my clit in response, and I went rigid, using my arms to lift myself from the desk, mouth open, eyes shut, thinking nothing more than *oh god oh god oh god*. He slipped two, maybe three fingers in me, and new sensations opened, as if it hadn't been full enough before, and tears streamed down my face.

My hips dropped back to the desk. He stood over me, beautiful and cruel, and took out his cock.

"Wider," he said. "Spread them wider."

I did it, holding my legs open with my hands. I wanted to split myself in two for him. When his dick touched me, I thrust toward him, hungry for it.

"Capo," I prayed.

"Take it. All of it," he growled and thrust into me completely in one stroke.

I was so wet he got in all the way, burying himself inside me. He paused there, eyes half lidded with pleasure, and pulled out slowly.

"All of me," he whispered then slammed back in. "Because you trust me."

I touched his face, and mouthed, "I trust you." as he thrust into me.

My fingers memorized his face, the textures and lines, to the tempo of his rising urgency. *I love you I trust you I love you I trust you.* Warm pleasure spread over my body like spilled milk, until I was covered in it, toes curling, back arching, legs stiffening. I held back a cry and came for him, only him.

When I came down, he gathered me in his arms and kissed my neck while he fucked me until his breathing sounded out in short bursts.

"I'm going to come so hard in you."

"Yes," was all I had. No other word would do.

I felt the pulse at his base as he came with a groan. Antonio the invulnerable became vulnerable, and he opened himself to me in his parted lips and slowing thrusts, emptying his violence inside me where it could do no harm.

He pressed his lips to my cheek for a long time, only moving them away when there was a knock at the door. And though I felt the flood of all my previous concerns, including his estranged wife and the shadow of impending death, they didn't soak through. I trusted him.

He pulled away as if he sensed what was about to happen, the way cats and dogs know when an earthquake is coming. In the restaurant, glass shattered, and Antonio stared into my face, listening. A car screeched away.

"It begins," he said. "Are you ready?"

"No."

"*Bene.* Because I am."

Chapter 29

ANTONIO

"B*ene*," I said into Theresa's neck. Olive trees and fresh air. How she did that in Los Angeles, I didn't know.

She didn't have to go to Napoli to make me happy. She brought it with her wherever she went. I didn't want to leave that room, because I had an idea what the broken window was about, and I knew it meant I might never bury my face in her neck again.

A knock at the door.

"Spin." It was Zo.

"*Due secondi.*" I stroked Theresa's breasts, and her nipples got hard all over again.

She bit her lip and her skin turned into a field of goose bumps. Outside, Zo shuffled away.

"Lean back," I said, and she did without question. I pulled her shirt and bra down, adjusting them so everything went in its place.

"Thank you."

"You're welcome," I replied, kneeling in front of her. "I want to give you an option, because you're a grown woman, and I know you won't take it because you love me." I'd intended to pull up her pants, but I stroked her legs because they were supple and perfect and meant for my hands. "But if you need to go, ever, then I will let you go." I slipped up her pants. "Even right now, if you need to walk out, I won't stop you. When we're in the middle of the storm, if you need to leave, I won't think less of you. Because there is going to be a storm, my love. I think you can handle it. I do. But if you can't, don't even say good-bye. Just turn your back and go."

I meant all of it, and I didn't. If she left, I'd be half a man. No plan I made would ever work without her. But I had to give her the option as much as I needed to hear her say she'd leave if she had to. I needed her full consent.

She didn't say anything at first. She let me fasten her pants and straighten her clothes. She let me put myself back together and button up. Then she answered.

"If I can't hack it, I'll walk," she said. "As an act of loyalty, I'll turn my back on you."

"Is this your wise mouth? It doesn't sound like it, but I need to be clear. I am going to make a deal with the Carlonis. Zo has proven it can be done. But I'm not him. I pose a bigger threat, and I have more to lose. It may go south."

"No sarcasm. I mean it. It's a promise between us."

I believed her, and in doing that, I was free to make any decision I needed to in order to save us. I opened the door feeling like a whole man.

Chapter 30

As we strode out to the dining room, I decided I meant it. If things got too hot to handle, I'd walk because he wanted me to. I'd walk because it was the best way to prove I was loyal. I'd leave him behind if that gave him comfort. I'd do it because he didn't try to force me. Didn't pigeonhole me. Gave me the choice to do it or not based on what I thought, felt, knew, and expected. He didn't try to think for me.

When we got out to the front room, the trouble was obvious. A brick lay inside a spray of broken glass. Zia was screaming at Zo, who was trying to soothe her. A man with a broom waited at the edge of the spray to sweep it up, and the waitstaff set up the room as if the broken window was no more than an obstacle to a final goal.

Otto had gone outside to look down the block with his hand on his waistband. He came back in looking sheepish. "Missed them."

The brick hadn't been touched. They were more worried about the person who threw it, which made sense. But there was a rubber band around it, and that couldn't have been a mistake.

Zia turned her attention to her nephew and rattled off what must have been a litany of southern Italian cusses. I thought he apologized, but after only a few words, she threw up her hands and stormed to the kitchen, giving the guy with the broom the go-ahead.

Antonio hoisted the brick, tossing it up a few inches and catching it. The blue rubber band that looked like it had been taken from a head of broccoli held a piece of paper to the weight. He tossed the brick up and down until he had the attention of everyone in the room.

Otto lit a cigarette. Zo leaned on the booth and crossed his arms.

"Come on," Zo said, flapping his hand. *"Presto."*

Antonio took the paper from the rubber band. I took the brick so he could unfold the note. He let me look over his shoulder, and though that meant a lot to me, and seemed symbolic of a real trust between us, it was useless. The short handwritten note was in Italian. He pressed his lips together, and his face tightened. He was angry. He wanted to vault into action. I knew him at least that well. But he kept it together long enough to read it out loud.

"Shit," Zo said.

Antonio glanced at me. "The Carlonis. They say they're going after Valentina."

"No deal then," Zo mumbled.

"No deal." The note disappeared into Antonio's white-knuckled fist.

"Daniel," I said. "She left with Daniel."

Chapter 31

THERESA

His look went from red hot to ice cold in the time it took for him to pull me to the kitchen. No words were transmitted between us. We weren't telepathic. No. We were something deeper.

"What?"

His tongue flicked over his bottom lip. Almost a nervous tic. The first one I'd ever seen on him.

"I can't," he said as if he'd made a full statement.

"Can't what?"

He ran his fingers through his hair. "They could hurt her. Or kill her."

"What do you want to do?"

He didn't say anything.

"Antonio?"

"I want you to know I love you. I am yours. Only yours."

He was trying to reassure me as if he was about to do something that would hurt my feelings.

How sweet.

How stupid.

"You want to go get her. Just say it."

He said nothing, frozen between his wants and his obligations, or his past and his future, or between his wife and his mistress. I put my hands on his biceps, and regretted it instantly. His body was a warm, automatic friction against mine, and I had to take a deep breath before I spoke.

"We can't let her die," I said. "I won't make you choose."

He breathed. I hadn't realized he'd been holding his breath, but relief poured off him. Somewhere in the kitchen, the door to the fridge clacked open, waitstaff yelled, stoves flamed, and a shovelful of broken glass tinkled into a garbage bin.

"*Grazie.*"

"I am beside you."

He raised an eyebrow. "I can't bring you with me."

So that was his conflict. He knew he had to get Valentina but worried about dragging me back into danger. In that moment, I loved him for his loyalty more than anything else. I was relieved he'd never considered abandoning her, and annoyed that he still considered me an asset to protect rather than use.

"If you leave me behind, I'll follow."

"No."

"We live together or die together, Capo. You said it."

"I lied." He pulled out his gun, clicking it open, then closed it.

I crossed my arms and leaned on one foot. "She was with Daniel last. Do you know how the Sicilians are getting into his place? They can't just stroll in and start shooting."

"Yes, they can. Danny-boy's worked with them for years."

My face got red hot. I was ashamed of my ignorance and my naiveté.

He saw the prickly heat of shame on my skin and flipped the gun around. He handed it to me grip-first, blocking everyone's view of it with his body. "Keep this, and pray for anyone who sneaks up on you."

"I'm going," I said, taking the gun.

"You are not. If you die, if you're hurt, if you so much as cry again—"

"You need me. He's the fucking district attorney. A mayoral candidate. How are you getting in? Because I'll tell you how I'm getting in. He fucked me for seven years. I'm walking in."

When would I stop being surprised at how fast he was? He had an arm carried by electricity, landing at the back of my neck in a fierce grip. "Are you trying to piss me off?" he hissed, his mouth kiss-close, bending my head until my face met his.

He didn't scare me. Not one bit.

"Yes."

"It's not working," he lied, the lead weight of rage heavy on his voice.

"His security detail knows me. From. All. The. Fucking."

The dishwashers chattered in Spanish, and I realized our intensity was a lousy shield.

Antonio let me go. "*Dio mio*, woman. When this is over, I'm going to take you to a place no one knows, and I'm splitting you in two."

"Take me," I whispered, pausing before I finished..."with you. You'll never get past security without me. And they'll just walk in and take Valentina into a field and shoot her, if they haven't already."

He pressed his lips between his teeth as he always did when I was getting to him. "You are to stay with me at all times."

"All right."

"You do not let your attention wander."

"Yes." My god, every command turned me on.

"You do not use your weapon unless we get separated."

"Yes."

"I am your weapon."

"Yes." I was barely breathing.

"Say it. Say I'm your weapon."

"You are my weapon."

He put up his finger. "I don't like this."

"Yes, you do."

Chapter 32

THERESA

When Daniel and I had moved in together, he rented out his tiny condo a block from City Hall. Once the tenant's lease was up, he returned to it. The proximity to the civic center made campaigning easier. He needed security, and he needed a place that was easy to care for. Antonio held the building's brass-and-glass front door open for me. Zo came in after me.

"You sure you don't want to wait in the car?" Zo asked.

"We're going in together," I replied "You don't need to watch me."

The lobby was a stark study in white and wood. Everything was in its place, but nothing was exactly right. I didn't know what I had been prepared for. Nothing and everything. I was prepared to see his wife, alive and beautiful, a cinderblock wall shaped like a supple woman between Antonio and me. I didn't want to meet her and I didn't want to save her, but she was important to him, even if he wouldn't admit it, and I didn't know how he'd bear losing her again because of his actions. He carried things around. He held grudges and pain. I walked into Daniel's building for Antonio, for his health, for his peace of mind. Because I loved him, and it wasn't about me.

That aside, it was too quiet. The security detail I'd promised to get Antonio through was absent.

Zo lumbered behind me like a loyal puppy while Antonio moved like a cat, as if he was only checking territory he already owned. The front desk wasn't manned, so all my talk of getting

Antonio past it was for nothing. I stopped him with a *tsst* sound. He turned, eyes everywhere, and I indicated the closed circuit monitors behind the security desk.

They were off.

He nodded slightly, paused.

"I know what you're thinking, and forget it." I moved my lips but no more sound came out. *Live together. Die together.*

His eyes lingered on my mouth. I didn't know if he understood me, but my thoughts went dirty, and a weight of wetness dropped from my spine to the space between my legs.

"Let's go," I said and went toward the elevator. "We have a nice Italian woman to rescue."

I didn't have the key to Daniel's place, but as we walked down the soft white hall upstairs, I saw a keypad outside his door. Zo checked his watch. Antonio touched his jacket under the arm, where his gun sat in its leather holster.

It was up to me. I didn't know how many digits, and Daniel didn't have a commonly used password for the daily business of getting into the easy stuff.

I put in his birthday.

Red light.

His childhood address in City Terrace.

Red light.

His social security number.

Red light.

His phone number.

Red light.

His mother's phone number.

Red light.

His phone number backward.

Red light.

"Contessa," Antonio said, "let me shoot it."

I held up my hand. If we wanted to get in and out, we had to make as little mess as possible, and I wanted to prove my worth. Had to prove he'd brought me here as more than a burden, and I factored into the situation as more than a dead weight with a murderous streak.

I put in my birthday, just to keep my fingers moving.

Green light.

"Excellent," Antonio said, pushing the door open. "What was it?"

I didn't answer. I didn't want to lie, but I didn't want Antonio to get distracted by the fact that my birthday was the code to Daniel's loft.

Zo pulled out his gun and held it up. Antonio reached into his jacket. I still had the hunk of metal in my waistband, and it was staying there. If this went down the tubes, I didn't want to kill anyone else.

Antonio put his other hand on the knob. "You ready?" His voice was couched in a tenderness I sometimes forgot he was capable of.

"I'm fine, Capo. Let's just get her and go."

He swung the door open.

I smelled gunpowder. Antonio tried to hold me back, but I beat him into the big room. My footsteps echoed. Zo closed the door. Antonio checked the corners then leaned against the doorjamb to the bedroom. I swallowed, wondering if she'd be sleeping or naked. But he shook his head. There was no one.

The kitchen was open to the larger room, with a bar creating a psychological barrier. I touched the shiny marble surface. I heard a creaking sound. I looked around. Didn't know where it came from.

I pressed my fingertips together. There was a white powder on the pads from touching the marble.

The creaking came again.

Antonio came toward me.

Zo checked the bathroom. Nothing.

I rubbed the powder on my fingers and listened to the interminable creak.

Slap. A shoe clonked down onto the counter, and I jumped. I looked up to where it came from, and Antonio followed my gaze.

I screamed.

Daniel was hanging upside down from a beam in the ceiling, ropes around his calves, feet free but squeezed enough that his remaining shoe dangled from his toes, the other foot covered in just a sock. He moved back and forth slightly, the rope creaking against the beam. A silver rectangle of duct tape covered the bottom half of his beet-red face, and his hands were tied behind his back.

"Get him down!" I shouted.

Zo jumped onto the counter, but anyone could see it wasn't high enough. The rope was still six feet above him.

"Antonio!" I shouted his name in supplication. I didn't know what to do, but if I prayed hard enough to the right god, some answer would come. "Get him down!"

Antonio put a barstool on the counter and hopped on it.

No. That was too unstable and wouldn't reach the rope.

I stepped back and yanked the gun out of my waistband.

"*Basta*," Antonio cried. "Wait!" He grabbed Daniel by the chest and steadied himself.

I stepped back and aimed.

"Let me do it," Antonio said, because I could as easily shoot Daniel as get him down.

But I was upset, and it was too late for sense.

I squeezed the trigger before worrying about it too deeply, and the rope that held my ex-fiancé by the ankles cracked. Daniel fell, and Antonio broke his fall. Both tumbled to the floor.

Antonio twisted out from under him, and Daniel rolled onto his back and I saw his face. It was swollen with blood, veins popping.

I didn't think about what I was doing. Daniel had broken my heart. He'd soiled my soul. I thought I'd never trust another man because of him. But he drove me to Antonio. I'd loved Daniel for seven years. I'd given him everything I had, and he'd given as much as he could.

I burst into tears. I cursed through them, unaware of Antonio or Zo. I hated this. Hated what had happened to Daniel. Hated that I'd caused it in some twisted way. I couldn't remember a bad thing about him, though I knew there was plenty to complain about. I only remembered being included, being validated, feeling as if I was part of a team with a larger purpose. I remembered all the good works he'd done, his compassion for the marginalized and underrepresented. I remembered him before he'd thought he had a chance to make anything of himself, and his wide-eyed joy at the thought that he could be polished into a man who could make a difference. All of that unknotted itself from the cheating, the manipulating, the double-dealing, and the strands of my vision of him separated. I saw him for the complex person he was, and appreciated what he was, what he could have been, and how very wrong he was for me despite all that.

"Contessa," Antonio said gently.

"Get that shit off his face!" I clawed at the duct tape.

Antonio took the other side and ripped it off, leaving spots of blood on Daniel's mouth. Daniel coughed as Antonio got his hands untied.

"Oh my god!" I said through tears. "Jesus, Dan! Dan."

He rolled facedown on the floor, holding his head at the base of his neck. I looked at Antonio, who crouched with his elbows to his knees. I must have had a question written all over my face, because he answered it without me speaking.

"Blood's flowing out of his brain. He's got a headache you can't imagine."

"I'm going to kill them," I said. "He could have died."

"He still might, if there's a blood clot. I never told you about my uncle."

"Should he stand up?"

"I don't think so. Give him a minute." Antonio crouched on one knee, without jealousy or rage in his eyes, and slipped his fingers along my jaw. His touch was an embodiment of tenderness and strength, and though the facts remained, it helped me see through the tangle of my emotions.

I couldn't just sit there. Zo was wiping down surfaces we'd touched. Antonio was hovering over Daniel to see if he would survive. I went into the kitchen and snapped open the door over the sink. He'd organized the cabinet the way I had when we lived together. His medicine was boxed by pain killers, cold and flu, skin care, etc., with a little plastic cup for water. I tapped out a headache pill for him. Four came out, I was shaking so hard.

When I'd said I wanted to kill whoever did this, I was serious. My feeling of bright white rage would only be relieved with the death of someone, or their howls of pain. Was that why Antonio felt he needed to right wrongs with murder? I got it. I really did. And if his life was cut short, I knew I would get myself killed avenging that death.

"Don't fucking touch me," Daniel said. He was on his back, hands over his eyes.

Antonio took his hand off Daniel's arm just before I crouched down.

"Here," I said, putting the pills in Daniel's palm.

"This is so past anything I had in the cabinet."

"I know."

"Valentina," he said. "Did you find her?"

Antonio and I exchanged a look.

"No, what happened?" I asked.

He groaned and tried to sit up, wobbled. I snatched a pillow from the couch and put it under his head. It was a bed pillow, I noticed, and the blanket was spread as if someone had slept on the couch the night before.

"They came in, Domenico Uvoli and another guy. I thought they were going to give me a hard time about the Bortolusi wedding, so I hid Valentina. But they were fixing this rig up, and she started screaming. They were really here for her. They kept asking...fuck. We have to get her." Daniel wasn't talking to me. He was talking to Antonio. "She went pale and fainted. She didn't look right."

"Not good. That's not good," Antonio said. He didn't look alarmed as much as he looked as if he was controlling his unease. "You're the DA. You should call the police." His voice didn't mock Daniel, but it had the weight of a rhetorical suggestion.

"I will. And in the time it takes me to explain it all, they'll kill her."

"What do you want me to do about it?" Antonio asked.

I didn't know if he was seething because Daniel had stepped on his territory with me or with his wife, and I didn't care.

"Antonio," I growled. "It's not the time for a pissing match."

Behind me, Zo's phone buzzed. Meekly, he reached into his pocket.

"They have you on speed dial, Lorenzo?" Antonio said.

"Your burner don't hold a number or do shit, so...it's on me." He shrugged and answered then immediately gave the phone to Antonio.

He stood up, straightened himself, and spoke. *"Pronto."*

Daniel stood, wavered, got his bearings.

"*Signora. Buon giorno.*"

That was all I caught. The rest was a tangle of syllables I didn't understand. Zo understood though, and by watching him, I could gauge the level of worry I should feel. Daniel spoke enough Spanish to communicate with his constituency, and Italian wasn't that far off, so his sharp breath worried me as well.

Antonio, however, was very calm up to a point. Then he changed completely. "*Valentina?*"

I couldn't pretend to understand any of what he said after that. The words were just a sharp music, slicing me apart with their song. He was gentle with her, and he was upset, looking at the ceiling while he listened to her voice. I couldn't hear a thing. He turned away from all of us slightly, the angle of his body courteous and inclusive but sending a message that the conversation was not for my ears.

His voice was reassuring, confident. I couldn't help it—I leaned in and caught just enough of her voice to hear hysteria and tears.

He lowered the phone, tapped the glass a few times, and put it back against his ear. "*Shh, Tina, tesoro. Shhh. Cinque secondi. Non dire nulla. Respira.*"

He spoke to her as if she were a child. There was love in it, but not as a husband to his wife. If I'd ever doubted him, I stopped completely when he was gentle but not tender with her. She was silent but for a few sniffs, and he closed his eyes. What was he doing?

A female voice came over the phone and barked in Italian. Antonio put the phone down, and I saw on the screen that the line was dead. He tossed the phone back to Zo, who caught it.

"What did they want?" Zo asked.

"To prove they had her and she is upset. To pull my heart around so I do what they want."

Daniel leaned on the arm of the couch to stand. "We have to get her."

"I'll get her, Brower. Just stay out of it."

"She didn't look good when they pulled her out. I know she was scared, and they had me by the balls."

"Shocking."

"She was white as a sheet. Sweating."

"Do you know where she is?" Antonio asked. "Did they say anything?"

"No. Not that I understood." He looked chastened, and I wanted to slap Antonio.

Antonio gestured to Zo, who gave up his phone as if reading his boss's mind. Antonio laid down the phone.

"You set the recorder?" Zo asked.

"Yes." Antonio tapped the screen. "First, we need to figure out where they have her. Then we discuss the rest."

Antonio fiddled with the phone and came up with his call to Valentina. She was hysterical; I hadn't heard that. I felt sorry for her. She was totally out of her element. I didn't need to understand the language to understand that much.

"*Shh, Tina, tesoro. Shhh. Cinque secondi. Non dire nulla. Respira.*"

She did quiet down, and the background noise became audible. Indoors, yet the sound of a siren came through. And someone talking. Two people. Professionals. But I couldn't hear the words. Then another siren with a different cadence.

And a beep.

An odd beep.

Then more hysterical Italian chatter from her, and my deep, heartbreaking pity for her.

Antonio played the five seconds of silence again. Siren. Talk. Siren. Beep.

"The hospital," I said, leaping forward. "She's in the hospital. The first siren is an ambulance. The second is police. The only time you're getting those two so close is in the hospital. And the beep. It's an ECG monitor. I remember it from my brother."

Antonio pressed the phone to his forehead and closed his eyes, as if thinking hard. "She has an arrhythmia. This is why she looked pale to you. And why she has no business with wine." He spoke to us but seemed deep in his own world. "Zo, get Otto and find out if his daughter still works for the medical supply company. See if she can make some calls. Find out which hospital."

Chapter 33

ANTONIO

I didn't tell Theresa what Donna Maria had said. The details were irrelevant.

She is safe. For now.
You, we will gut.

"She" was Valentina. The gutting was assumed to be literal. Donna Maria had used the word *sbudellarlo*, which had a particular Sicilian connotation. It was used for the most disloyal offenders. The ones who broke *omertà* and gave information to the police, who stole, or who married outside the business.

And if you don't come to us by tomorrow night, we will open her up. Don't think I won't for this shame you visited twice on my family now. My granddaughter still has no husband. It will not go unanswered. You have twenty-four hours to present yourself, or she's dead.

I wasn't afraid of that or anything, but Theresa would go after anyone who hurt me, and she would get herself killed by less talented and more experienced hands.

I held out my hand for Theresa. "We're taking care of this, Mister Brower."

"What are you going to do?"

"We're going to find her first," I said. "Then we're going to send her home."

"What do you need me to do?"

"Keep the police off us," Theresa interjected. "I don't care how."

Daniel nodded. "Today. No problem. I can't guarantee tomorrow."

I held out my hand, and he took it. "Take care of that head," I said.

"Sure, sure." He still looked a little red in the face. "Don't let this asshole get you killed."

She hugged him. "Go to the fundraiser if you can."

When she hugged her ex, and he rubbed her back, I had a sudden sense of wholeness with her. I'd changed. What a fool I'd been. Not a fool but a man in a box. A box I'd been raised in but had had every opportunity to break out of. A man nailed to the ground by tradition and conformity.

When I'd first seen her on the news, next to him, I admired her purity because that was what I thought one admired in a woman. It never occurred to me that she could be more. Though I'd come to respect her ability to do what needed to be done when the air was on fire with bullets, my mind didn't truly expand until I saw her inside her old life and knew she didn't fit. My world unfolded and laid itself before me. I'd loved the wrong reasons inside the right woman and made excuses for the love. But I'd known it the whole time, hadn't I? The way she aligned herself with Daniel. The way you could tell she meant more to him than a docile little wife. She was the power behind him. The fearless, intelligent, fierce lioness.

I didn't know what to do with her or myself. Now, today, she fit with me and I with her. But tomorrow? I'd been a man without a nation for a long time, and now I was a man without friends. She was mine, and she fit me where it counted, but not where it counted with everyone around me. They'd turn on us. As soon as there was a moment's peace, we would be targets, and she wouldn't let me stand in front of her. I'd tried handcuffing her, leaving her, diverting her, yet she bent herself toward death.

I had no answer. I only knew if she died, I was going with her. It was the only way.

Chapter 34

THERESA

I could never predict his moods. He was businesslike and managerial while figuring out the whens and wherefores of the coming twenty-four hours. He called Otto and got us a car. Half an hour later, we were in a nondescript lot in Silver Lake, walking up to a white Porsche. Otto leaned on it, holding up the keys.

"Did you talk to your daughter?" Antonio asked, snapping the keys away.

"She needs time."

"We'll be in Paseo. If she can't, you need to call me." He opened the passenger side of the Porsche, staring at me as if he wanted to eat me alive.

"Does Otto know how you feel about Porsches?"

"His idea of a joke. And the sooner you get in this shit car, the sooner you're out." He pulled out of the lot and threaded through the back alley and out onto Sunset.

"Where are we going?"

"We own a building on Paseo Del Mar. Not a luxury, but I'll be fucking you so hard, you won't even notice." He glanced over with a gaze like a starving cat.

"Before that, I need to know we have a plan," I said as he made a left, using his signal, keeping it under the speed limit. No sharp moves.

"A plan? We're going to find out what hospital she's at and grab her."

"And then?"

"I can't predict the future. No. I can. I'm going to fuck you tonight. I'm going to fuck you until Otto calls or until you're in a thousand pieces on the bed. Whichever comes first."

A thousand pieces on the bed. I knew what that looked like. It looked like me, naked, sated, catching my breath. Sore everywhere. Drenched in sweat and the smell of pine. Barely conscious with not a thought or worry in my head. It sounded so good, I didn't want to derail it. I wanted it to happen as promised.

But as we drove west, I had a nagging question, and I was sick of dancing around it. I needed a plan. *We* needed a plan. I played a game of Whac-a-Mole in my head. Every time the issue popped up, I smacked it down, but it popped up again.

"Antonio, I..." I didn't finish the sentence because he smiled at me and looked at me as if I were the last woman on earth.

"Yes?" He pulled into a narrow alley behind a little house that was packed against its neighbors.

I could press him about his wife, or I could take what was mine and discuss it later, after I was in a thousand pieces on the bed. I was sure there was no right choice. "I hope this place has a washing machine."

He snapped a key off the car's ring and dangled it in front of me. "Go in while I put this in the garage. And get your clothes off. If you're not naked when I get in there, I'm taking my belt to your ass."

I turned red from my cheeks to my chest, where my nipples hardened under my shirt.

"Go," he whispered.

I got out and walked up the wooden steps to the back. The little porch was clean of dust, dirt, and personality. No one lived there, of course. When I unlocked the back and went in, I knew I was right. There was a pot on the stove, but it was spotless. The lights went on, and the kitchen could have been a hotel.

I realized how few times Antonio and I had made love in anything that resembled a permanent home. His unfinished house in the hills. His temporary space in Mount Washington. The loft I shared with Katrina. That was as good as it ever got. And now we were in another generic space, probably owned as a business loss. The likelihood that he and I would ever have a marriage bed was unlikely, and I got sad for a second before I remembered his demand that I be naked.

I felt like hell. Filthy to the core. I took off everything and found a washer/dryer in the closet. I threw everything in, dumped in some soap, and snapped the lid closed.

"What about mine?" Antonio asked from behind me.

"You're fast," I said, opening the lid.

He responded by peeling off his shirt, a fast reveal of the perfection underneath. The hard abs, the straight shoulders, the line of black hair from his navel to the heaven below.

He threw his shirt into the wash then got out of his pants. He was fully erect, and I found my need for a shower turned up a notch.

The rest of his clothes went into the wash with a swoosh. I turned my back to him and snapped the lid closed. I pushed buttons. I didn't even know which ones. The colors were mixed, and I didn't know if I'd put the right amount of detergent. Hot water? Cold? Rinse? His body was against mine while I turned dials and pushed buttons. He grabbed the hair at the back of my head.

"Where do you want it?" he whispered in my ear, his cock at my ass.

I trembled then turned. "I need a shower, Capo."

"All right." He leaned into me and reached behind me to pull the dial. *Click.* The water whooshed as the machine filled.

"Oh, you do laundry?" I cooed.

"Tonight, I do laundry and you."

I kissed him through a smile, and he carried me to the bathroom.

Chapter 35

ANTONIO

I knew what was on her mind. I wasn't stupid. But I didn't know how to soothe her without fucking her. I didn't know what to say that would be practical. She was hiding her worry from me, and that bothered me. I didn't like it. She needed to be completely open.

The bathroom had no towels and only little chips of soap, but we managed to clean each other with what we had.

"You make a lot of bubbles with a little soap, Capo. I admire that in a man."

She was coated in white drifts. I ran my hand down her body, cutting through the glaze to her bare skin. She put her head back and let the water run through her hair, the impossible shade of strawberry blond turning dark brown. We had no shampoo. She just wet it then looked at me with her lashes stuck together and beads of water on her lips. I brushed them away.

"You were going to tell me something in the car," I said.

She looked away. "Yeah." She shut off the water. "I guess we have to air dry."

We found sheets in a drawer under the bed. White flowers on blue with worn spots. But clean. Better than I'd expected.

"Are you worried she's in the hospital?" She was naked still, arms out as she flapped the top sheet over the bed. "I mean, she could be sick."

"It was the arrhythmia. They're lucky they brought her in, or I'd kill them for not taking care of her."

She didn't say anything. Her silence was enough.

"Theresa, she's my responsibility."

"I know. I'm not blaming you. You're honorable. If you felt differently, I'd think less of you. You can't just throw someone away because they're not convenient right now."

She crouched to tuck in the sheet. I'd never seen her do a domestic chore. I knew she couldn't cook, and she hired out the cleaning. I never would have married her in my youth. Wouldn't have even considered it.

"I have no cause to trust any man in the world, but I trust you. I don't know if that says more about you or me," she said.

"It says something about us."

"And I know you're not going to get confused and start fucking her. Or leave me to start over with her. I don't know how I know that. It's just…part of me still thinks you should." She tucked the sheet around the bed, across the foot, and back up to the side I stood on.

She stood and put her hands on her naked hips, and I couldn't take not touching her for another second. I put my arms around her waist and kissed her face.

"We were always complicated," she continued, "but this? I don't even know what this means. I don't want to tell you what to do. It's your culture. Your family. Your values."

"This bed is a disaster. I've never seen a sheet so crooked in my life."

"Don't change the subject."

"I'm not changing the subject."

She pulled her face away to look at me, mouth pursed, head tilted just a little to express disbelief.

"You know who can make a bed? My wife. And fast. She practically had the sheets trained to make themselves." I was a brute, of course, to bring her down before bringing her up "You want the values of my culture? In those sheets were everything. If a woman could cook and care for the house, she was everything a man needed. And I was the luckiest man on earth. But who am I now? Am I the man who values straight sheets? Is that what I want anymore? And if I don't care about the sheets, or the cooking, what do I care about?"

"If you're telling me you love me, I know that. But a plan. I need a plan." She seemed exasperated, as if she wasn't getting through to me.

I pushed her onto the bed. I wanted to rumple those sheets. Shred them. I straddled her and put her hands over her head as if that would shut her up. I was getting to something, and I had to speak it or lose it. "You. There's only you, Theresa. I can't figure it out, and I don't have time to tonight. Who am I anymore? I don't know. I'm a different man now. So you want a plan, but I can't make one because I don't know what I want besides you."

"You have me," she said.

I let her hands go. She was still concerned. It was in her voice, as if she wanted to add something but didn't because I was on top of her naked and only half dried-off.

I rolled onto my back. The ceiling was a popcorn pattern with chips missing in the shapes of islands lost in the sea. "When I was a boy, I knew my side of the piazza. I was the little mayor. Sophia sold cigarettes, Vincenzo sold fruit, and they'd give me some for running errands, though I tell you, Sophia was a hardass. Made me work for it."

Theresa got up on her elbow. "Her product was more expensive. Vincenzo could give you a bruised reject. She couldn't."

"True, true."

"Did Vincenzo have strawberries in summer?"

"When I was a kid? Never. I had him get them for me special later, though. I was a mechanic. I couldn't afford them but..."

But Valentina loved them.

"I like them better than cigarettes," Theresa said.

"Sophia's smokes stank to high heaven anyway." She touched my face, stroking my cheek as if appreciating something seen for the first time. She looked breakable, but I knew otherwise. "I want one now that I mentioned it."

"Is that how you made money? Running errands?" she asked.

"I was fast. You shoulda seen me run. Via Duchessa to Via Concezio in seventeen seconds. I took care of business. Made sure my uncle got to the docks, made a little money where I could. Went to school sometimes. Everything had a place. When I went to work for my father, the places were different, but there was less chaos. Men did what men did, and women did what women did, and it all fit. Who I was as a child still fit in that world. It wasn't what my mother wanted, but it was something I understood. I didn't have to think about it."

I looked at the islands on the ceiling. The longer I looked, the more there were. It was a regular archipelago up there.

"And now it's all different." Her voice came over the popcorn waters as undulating music. "The rug's getting ripped from under you, but not all at once. Piece by piece."

I turned to her and put my hand on her face. "I told you once that you were making me soft."

"At the wrap party."

"That day, Daniel Brower had a press conference. I went to see him because he'd been to that movie with you the night before. I didn't know what I wanted from him, except to keep away from you. He said he wouldn't. I felt powerless. I thought I was going to go insane." Remembering that moment, I felt helpless all over again. The feeling had been new at the time. I would never get used to it. "You've been making me soft since we met. And now I'm lying here telling you this bullshit. I should be fucking you."

"No." She straddled me. I put my hands up, and she held them. "I should be fucking you."

"Oh, really?"

"Yes, Capo."

"Well. Let's see how you do then."

She hitched up a little and guided herself onto me. She felt perfect. Built for my body. I was consumed by her. I took her hands again, and she leveraged herself against them. She leaned down, and I held her, let her be the boat on my sea as the islands above formed and reformed. I closed my eyes and felt her softness in my hands, all warmth and curves. When I felt her stiffen and shake, I released inside her.

We slept in each other's arms, and the last thing I saw was the chipped ceiling, no more than part of a room in need of a paint job.

Chapter 36

THERESA

Los Angeles nights were cold, and if the heat wasn't on in the safe house you happened to be staying at and the stash under the bed wasn't equipped with a blanket, you huddled for warmth. At some point in the night, Antonio and I had unwrapped and rewrapped ourselves around each other, and his heat kept me warm under the flimsy sheet. When I woke, I thought he was asleep, but when I turned and looked at him, hoping to see him in restful peace, his eyes were open.

"Shh," he said. "Someone's outside."

I thought he should be moving, standing, something. It took me a second to feel his arm and an uncomfortable hardness under my pillow. He was holding his gun. He was more alert than he appeared, trying to lure whoever it was into a false sense of security. I reduced the pressure of my head on the pillow, wedging my shoulder under me so he could clear the shot easily if he had to. I stiffened at the knock on the back door.

"He's a polite intruder," I whispered, and Antonio smiled. Who wouldn't be safe with this man in her bed?

"It's one of my guys," he said, throwing off the sheet. "Get dressed."

I'd tossed our stuff in the dryer in the middle of the night, so we unloaded the clean clothes and wiggled into them. Being grunge-free felt good.

"I should have put that toothbrush in my pocket," I grumbled.

"Your mouth tastes like roses." He kissed me on the lips while he tucked in his shirt.

"Blech."

Antonio peeked out the kitchen window then opened the door. Otto stood there with a bag in each hand: one paper, one white plastic.

"Good morning," he said.

"Boun giorno."

"Hi." I took the paper bag from him. It was warm. "Is this food?"

"I got a little breakfast from the place around the corner."

He and Antonio shook hands, and I open tore the bag. I didn't have time for staples and tape. There was hot food to be had. I set out the containers while Antonio looked in the plastic bag. Eggs. Pancakes. Potatoes. Exactly what we needed.

"Otto, I think I love you." I hugged him hard. He patted my back noncommittally, and when I looked at Antonio, I knew why.

"Give me a break, Capo. Sit down and eat."

Properly chastened by the woman of the house, they sat down. Antonio peeled open a coffee and drank it black.

"My daughter got the information about Valentina," Otto said, opening Styrofoam boxes. "She's at Sequoia. They kept her overnight, and they'll probably keep her again. She hasn't said she's a captive or nothing. Hasn't asked for the law. Nothing."

"She understands *omertà*. That'll work in our favor."

Otto pushed away his food. I stayed quiet, but his position and attitude didn't bode well.

"Lorenzo," he said. "I don't want to be the one to tell you, but I'm the last one with a mouth to open."

"Zo? Zo what?"

"When you was gone those days, he was on top of the crew. He was good. But he knew you was alive, right?"

"Yes." Antonio's voice, in one syllable, was all right angles and hard surfaces.

"He barely breathed. Said we could mourn you for a week, then we were back to business." Otto took out his cigarettes and turned to me. "You mind?"

"No, go ahead."

Otto lit up and tossed Antonio the pack. "He put the lid on any ideas about vengeance. He was ready. Took control. Laid out a plan to continue business with no interruptions."

"Make your point." Antonio lit his cigarette, tilting his head a little.

"He likes things organized. He..." Otto dragged on his smoke. "He left. Promised himself to the Carlonis in exchange for peace. I'm sorry, boss. He sends his apologies."

Antonio pushed his chair out with a hard squeak and stood. "Ten minutes."

He stormed out the back door.

Chapter 37

ANTONIO

Those motherfucking sons of whores. Each of them. Fuck all of them. Even Otto. Fuck him too. Fuck all of the little cowardly bastards. If I had the time, I'd stomp them from the face of the earth. Right under my shoe.

I scraped my sole against the pavement. Tomorrow. Once I did what needed doing—retrieving Valentina and sending her home, solidifying my position—they were all going under my shoe. Simone. Enzo. I would save Lorenzo for last. He would cry for his life, that son of a motherfucker. And he had no wife. No kids. No one would miss the little bastard.

And fuck him. He had been too ambitious from the beginning. Ready to jump in my motherfucking grave as soon as I was gone. No wonder he had a sourpuss on the minute we turned up again. He wanted to be boss? Well, he could be boss between now and when I killed his crew.

My crew.

I scraped again and slipped a little on a stone. The sidewalk was troubled with cracks and upended pieces. I heard the water at the end of the block, crashing constantly. I found myself at a railing overlooking the beach, the sky turning bluer, the goddamn ocean in and out same as always. Maybe I'd drown them.

I had a pack of cigarettes that had travelled with me all the way from Tijuana. They stank, but I pulled one out and lit it, then picked a piece of tobacco from the tip of my tongue. An inadequate distraction.

My father would never have tolerated this nonsense. If he let them live, they'd be doing it with one or two limbs less. A crew was a marriage. Worse. Better. It was a blood bond, and they were breaking it.

The thought of it.

I realized my fists were tight when I started pounding the railing and the vibrations rattled my knuckles. I'd lost half my crew after nearly killing Bruno Uvoli. I never knew if I'd lost them because I went off half cocked over Theresa, or because I was too soft to wipe him from the earth. Maybe neither. Maybe both. But I'd been blinded by two things: the fact that my vendetta for my sister's rapists was satisfied, and desire for Theresa filling the place where the desire for revenge had resided.

That moment, looking at Bruno with blood running down his face. He'd tried not to cry. I remembered that, because that was what changed me. I had no need for revenge, only a need for her. And his efforts to be tough and not cry or beg? I'd felt myself feeling pity for him, and if I hadn't known it that night, I knew it standing by the water. She'd been chipping away at my command from day one.

I didn't want to kill my crew, but I felt obligated to. The weight was my anger, yes, but the need to do something about it was the burden. What if I didn't do anything about it? What if I got angry without turning the anger into physical action? What if my anger didn't have consequences?

I'd be killed, for sure. I'd be weak, then dead, because a boss never forgets and only forgives for a price.

I walked back to the house lighter but no wiser. I'd decided nothing but what not to do. The last of my crew was safe from me until I got Valentina.

Theresa and Otto were in the front. He had his phone out, and they watched the screen. Her brow was knotted, and he was rubbing his pinkie space with his thumb. Theresa saw me when I was halfway down the block, and she ran to me, siren hair flying behind her.

"Contessa?"

"They're saying you shot Paulie," she said. "Your face is all over the news."

"Daniel?" I spit the name. "That motherfucker."

I looked at my watch but didn't see the time. How foolish would it be to survive all this and end up in prison? I put my hands to my mouth, imagining being separated from her when we'd worked so hard to be together.

She took my wrists. "Let me see if I can take care of it."

"You? Just you?"

"You can't go anywhere in daylight right now."

"Then neither can you. I never told you, there's a quarter million out for your life."

"That's it? I'm insulted."

"It's not something joke about."

"They don't want me. They have Valentina. It's probably safer for me away from you."

She was wrong. Nothing about this world was safe whenever she was out of my sight.

"She's right," Otto interjected. "They got Tina, and they're all holed up in Sequoia watching her."

"Fuck you, Otto," I said.

He shrugged. Somehow I'd been overruled.

I took her in my arms and held her. My damnation and salvation. My spark of change, dragging me into the light, kicking and screaming. She took my sins and made them her own. If only I could save her before she consigned herself to hell.

"Don't worry," I said. "We'll make it out."

I buried my nose in her hair and breathed her in. I didn't have a plan or a crew. I had nothing. Yet I sat on a throne before a kingdom of possibilities.

Chapter 38

THERESA

I called Dan from Antonio's burner and got him to meet me in a corner booth at the Nickel. At eleven in the morning, most of the red vinyl booths were empty and the tabletop jukeboxes were silent. I slid in next to Daniel, who regarded the menu as if he didn't know he was getting the same thing he always got. BLT. Lightly toasted. Extra mayo.

"Theresa, where have you been?"

I propped the big plastic menu in front of me as if I didn't know what I was ordering. Nothing. I didn't have an appetite. "How did you get the duct tape glue off your face?"

"Nail polish remover. Did you find Valentina?"

"Yes."

"Is she safe?"

"No." I put down the menu. I saw the TV behind the bar, and Antonio's face on it. "We located her. We don't have her."

"Where is she?"

"Why do I see Antonio's face on television?"

"We'd pressured his doctors to declare him dead under the Determination of Death Act, and to be honest, your family pushed it."

"What? Why?"

"He's got a functioning heart and the same rare blood type as your brother. This turned into homicide this morning, and my staff pushed through the indictment while I was busy hanging from a ceiling."

I flipped the songs on the little jukebox, trying to separate my feelings from my strategy. The pink tabs flipped. I knew all the songs yet couldn't place them. "Do you have change? I'm out."

"What's with you?"

I held out my hand. "Ambient noise."

He stretched, reached into his pocket, and came out with a handful of change. I plucked out four quarters.

"You're a wild card, Daniel." I put fifty cents in the jukebox and played some random ballad from the seventies. I rubbed the other two coins together. I liked the way they scraped and slipped at the same time. "One minute I think you're going to do right by me—"

"I told you I'd keep LAPD off you yesterday so you could find Valentina. And I did, but you didn't get her."

"We found her, but no. We didn't get her. Not yet."

"I can only go so far. I have a job and a department full of people with their own minds."

"Right now, he's stuck. If he can't move, he can't get Valentina. And if you think you can get her, forget it. She won't tell you crap, and you know it. She'll swear whoever's holding her are her cousins. You know it's true. He's the best chance she has and the only chance I have. So make it go away."

He leaned forward to make his point and to keep his voice low. "I can't hold back my entire staff. I actually kind of like the guy, but the entire Los Angeles justice system knows Antonio Spinelli shot Paulie Patalano."

"He didn't."

"Well, who did?"

I didn't say a word. I didn't breathe. I just looked the district attorney in the eye until he leaned back.

"Jesus Christ, Theresa." He knew. I didn't have to say it, and he knew. "Jesus, Jesus...why?"

"You understand what'll happen If you allow this to continue. All roads lead to Rome. If you're all right with that, then I have to be."

I didn't wait for an answer. I just slid out of the booth. It wasn't until I reached for the keys to the Porsche that I realized I still had those two quarters between my fingers. I slipped them into my front pocket and drove back to Antonio.

I was a killer. For real and for sure. I couldn't hang on Paulie's working lungs and heart anymore. It was homicide because his death was inevitable. And still, I didn't feel as bad as I thought I would.

Maybe I had been born for this. Maybe it was in my blood. Which gave me an idea. A disturbing idea, but one that might work. I pulled up to the safe house convinced it was our only option.

Antonio met me on the porch.

"You're supposed to stay inside," I said as I stepped up.

"It's too nice a day," he lied. It was clammy and cold.

"Do we know if Valentina's still at the hospital?"

"She is."

"I thought of something," I said. "Remember what you told me about my family? Our history? Who we are?"

"Yes?"

"I think I can get us in. But I don't know if it'll come with a way out."

Chapter 39

THERESA

"No radio," Antonio said, snapping it off. I'd heard his name and turned up the car stereo. It had started pouring on the way to Sequoia, and the *pat pat pat* on the roof and *puh puh puh* on the windows was going to drive me nuts. It was dusk already.

"They might be saying something we can use," I objected but didn't try to turn the radio back on.

What was it like to have your name all over the media in connection with something as evil as murder? I didn't know. I only knew what it was like to be the actual murderer. I put my back to the passenger door and slipped out of my shoes. Antonio had driven, even though it was Otto's car. We'd parked in the outdoor lot across the street from Sequoia and were waiting for Antonio's only loyal friend to appear with the one person who could help us get in.

"Trust me," he said, "I've done this before. Those reports aren't doing anything but worrying you. Half of what they're saying is lies, and the other half are things we already know."

He was right. I'd been intimate with the media and what they fed to the public.

He took out his pack of cigarettes and shook out the last one. I reached for it, slipping it out before his lips got on it. He raised an eyebrow at me.

"Light me up, Capo."

He clacked open his lighter and I dragged on it until it was lit. I handed the cigarette back to him while blew out the smoke. I hadn't smoked since high school, when I wanted to impress Rachel, who was so cool she seemed other worldly.

Antonio took the cigarette, regarding me before putting it in his lips. I liked everything about the way he did it. The placement of the cigarette between his fingers, the shape of his lips as he pulled on it, and the snap as he removed it.

"How can you look so relaxed?" I asked, taking the smoke from him.

"I can ask you the same."

"I'm worried about Otto." I flicked the ashes in the tray.

"He can do more with eight fingers than most men can do with twelve."

I cocked my head at him. He just looked out the window, touching his lower lip before it stretched into a grin. I jabbed his knee with my foot.

"You're better than that joke."

He put his hand on my foot and ran it up as far as my pants would allow. "No, I'm not. Do you think you can live with a man who makes jokes like that for the rest of your life?"

"I think there's a regular comedian in there." I handed him the cigarette, flame side up. "We just have to draw him out."

"I wish I could laugh." He shook his head a little, still smiling slightly. "I met your father a long time ago, while I was consigliere for Donna Maria. He was building something in our territory. There were union issues. He might remember me."

"This should be a fun get-together then." I wasn't surprised my father had worked with the mob. I was pretty sure that wasn't his first business deal with them, or his last.

"I'm wondering, should I ask him for your hand tonight? Or wait until we're both in jail?"

I took the cigarette from him. It had gotten short and hot, like my temper.

"I don't think you can ask while you're legally married to someone else."

He smiled ruefully and rubbed his eyes. "What a mess."

"They're here," I said. I rolled down the window a crack, as if I was still in high school getting caught being a bad girl.

Antonio looked up, hand reaching for the key. Otto and Declan Drazen, each carrying an umbrella, walked out the sliding doors. Dad looked no worse for the wear in a sport jacket and sweater. He barely looked both ways when crossing, as if a car wouldn't dare try to occupy the same space as him because he was entitled to the world at large.

Or at least that was how I saw it. We all saw him differently, and we were all correct. He was an exacting judge, a paymaster, evil incarnate, a master controller, a father whose only concern was the ten people in his family and their legacy. Only Jonathan had failed to disappoint him, and he was the child who hated him the most.

The back door clicked open, and my father slipped in. Otto closed the door behind him, staying outside to watch.

"Hi, Dad," I said.

"Theresa. Mister Spinelli. Good to see you again."

Antonio reached over the front seat, and they shook hands. "Sorry about the circumstances."

"My daughter explained it." He was talking about Margie, who I'd called first. "Quite involved, this whole situation." In the window behind my father, Otto's cigarette smoke drifted by, unaffected by the rain. "Theresa was always the one who caused no trouble at all." He looked at me. "Guess you were saving it up."

"How's Jonathan?" I asked.

"Near death. You might want to stop by."

"I wish I could."

"Indeed. Now." He jerked his head toward where Otto stood outside. "The gentleman tells me you wanted something?"

"There's a woman inside this hospital," I said. "She's probably being discharged right now. She's being watched by a group of people—"

"The Carloni family?" Dad said.

Antonio twisted around to face my father a little more. Was he regarding him more seriously? That was wise.

"How many?" Antonio asked.

"I haven't had cause to count, but if you put them together with the family of Paulie Patalano, it's like an underworld reunion."

"Dad, this is important. I know you have some pull in this hospital. If you could just put her in a room alone for ten minutes, Antonio and I could go in and walk her out. No problem."

"How is it you can do that?"

"She and I have the same name," Antonio said.

I tensed up. We would have to explain.

Antonio, as if sensing that I needed to get it over with, finished the thought. "I'm her husband. They'll let me take her."

Why had that felt like a knife in my heart? As if I didn't know it already. Was it because my father was sitting right there, and my shame was so great, the pain became fresh and raw all over again? Dad seemed to consider all the implications, letting the pause hang.

"They're going to kill her," I said.

"So they brought her to the hospital? Please, Theresa, you've never been one for dramatics. This is disconcerting. Disheartening, even. Mister Spinelli, I am sure you're a man of values, but they're not my family's. And it seems like in addition to losing my son in the next few days, I've already lost my daughter. My goal in life has been keeping this family together, and it's blown apart."

"It hasn't," I said. "I'm here, and this is a bump in the road."

I didn't even believe it, and neither did he.

"Prove it," he said. "If this is a bump, when it's done, you stay. You don't do a Carrie and move away."

I glanced at Antonio, whose eyes stayed on my father.

"I can't promise that," I said.

"Then I can't promise anything either."

"I promise it," Antonio said. "We'll stay within reach."

I wanted to kick him. Was he giving up his dream of going back home, or his dream of being with me? Or was he failing to take my father seriously?

"Hardly something you can promise, Mister Spinelli, seeing as you're already married."

That should have hurt. Should have cut me to the bone, but it didn't. The initial shock of my father knowing I was sleeping with a married man was bad, but once that was done, I felt nothing either way about it. Antonio had promised. That was good enough for me.

"You told me to make one good choice," I said. "One good choice, and you'd release the funds to keep Zia's afloat when Antonio was gone. Well, I made a good choice—I came back to LA to see Jonathan. Here I am. And I don't need the money anymore. So this is the trade I want."

"You're pushing it."

"I could still be gone."

He leaned forward in his seat. I turned.

"You will never leave," he said. "Not for any man. Not for any money. Not for any reason. You belong here. Your blood runs beach water and backwash." He opened the back door. "If there's a woman being held against her will, you need to call the police."

He was out the door before I could formulate an answer. We watched in silence as he strode across the street.

"It's okay," I said. "We'll figure something out. He was a long shot anyway."

Antonio was too quiet, tapping the steering wheel and watching my father cross the street, his umbrella straight. Not a drop got on him.

"We'll go in the hard way." Did I sound desperate?

"We shouldn't go in. I'll take care of it. I'll do the trade. I'll let them take me and figure it out, or not. I'm not afraid to die."

"If they hurt you, Capo, I'll kill them."

He turned to the windshield and took a deep breath, like a man falling under the weight of his burdens.

I took his hand. I hadn't meant to worry him, but I'd said the wrong thing. The same words that made me feel confident when they came from his lips ripped the world out from under him when they came from mine. I was about to take it back, lie and say I'd do nothing. But he gave my hand a quick squeeze and ran out into the night, dodging a car. The car door slammed behind him, and I lost him in the wash of rain on the window. I rolled it down. Antonio caught up to my father on the other side of the street. Otto watched, smoke rising from under his umbrella.

They were talking, and I couldn't hear a word. I saw Antonio's gyrating hands and the bend of his back. He wasn't flinching from the rain; he was imploring my father for something, arm stretched toward the car, where I was. Jesus. What was he saying? What was he trading? Discomfort spiraled from my gut to my throat. Dad wasn't even talking, just Antonio, out in the cold and wet. Supplicating. Begging for what? I didn't even know. But I couldn't take it anymore. I got out and was pelted with rain. Otto tried to cross around the car to give me his umbrella, but I pushed it away and started across the street.

My father nodded.

They shook hands.

No.

No no no.

"Antonio!"

He came to me, hair flattened and face studded with raindrops, lips dripping before he even spoke.

"What did you say to him?"

"Get in the car." His clothes stuck to him, leaving veiny ridges up his arms. I saw the flex in his forearms when he grabbed my biceps and tried to turn me around.

"Capo."

"Get in the fucking car."

"We're in this together. *Together.* Did you forget?"

He shook his head, eyes dark in the night, with only a glint from the streetlights to tell me confusion and pain swirled in them. He put his lips to mine so hard it hurt, and it wasn't until I yielded to his arms and his mouth that they softened on me.

"Trust me," he said between kisses, cradling my head. "Just trust me."

And I did. Through the raindrops and thunder, the groans building in my throat, the warmed space between our bodies, I trusted him, his judgment, his intentions, his actions.

But I didn't.

Chapter 40

THERESA

We passed Margie's car on the way to the elevator. It was still parked in the spot reserved for the neurology guy she'd helped with a "thing." When this was over, I was going to sit Margie down and ask her what she really did for a living.

Otto stayed in the car while Antonio and I stepped into the elevator.

"What's the plan?" I asked, watching the numbers change. The secure lot was four levels down.

"Cardiac wing is on four." He didn't look at me. He looked at the numbers. "There'll be a distraction in fifteen minutes. We will be on two."

"This sounds pretty vague."

"I'm using what I have."

The elevator dinged, and the doors slid open into a back hallway painted a particularly diarrhea shade of mustard.

Antonio walked out, and I followed. He was closed to me, and I didn't know why. No. Forget that. I did know why. The price for whatever this distraction was must have been sky-high if he would rather shut me out than talk to me.

I'd mastered my impulses long ago, covering them with implacable smiles and social maneuvering, but I almost grabbed Antonio and yanked him back to demand an answer because he'd stripped away all my practiced refinement. But did we even have time for that? Did he have a moment to tell me what we were doing? Or were there too many components to explain as we walked down a hall lined with laundry bins and broken gurneys?

I had to trust him, and when he turned to an open door, stopped himself midway, and looked at me with full engagement, I was glad I'd waited. He gestured at the empty staff lunch room. Two vending machines. A wall of lockers. A coffee maker with a crust of sludge. A round tabletop on a single center pedestal and three red chairs with chrome legs.

I stepped inside, and he pushed me through to the "Pump Room," which was no bigger than the smallest of my mother's closets. Meaning, it had room enough for a glider and footrest, a cabinet, and a little table with a half-full paper coffee cup.

He snapped the door closed behind him.

"What's the problem?" I asked. "What's happening?"

He crashed his lips onto mine.

I pushed him away with force. "There couldn't possibly be a worse time for this."

He took my hands, holding them between us. "Please, just do this for me. Don't ask questions." He turned my hands over and kissed my palms. "Don't ask to be hurt. Don't fight. Just love me."

His voice was soft enough to turn stone to putty, and all desire to defy him left me.

"Okay," I said, "but I—"

He pressed his fingers to my lips. "Hush. Trust me. I've worked it out. All you have to do is follow along."

"The bouncing ball."

"Follow the ball." He picked up my shirt and ran his hands over my nipples until they were as hard as stones. "That's it. I need you by my side, and right now, I need you to love me. No more."

"You're scaring me."

He unbuttoned my pants and slid them down my legs. "You wouldn't be scared if you loved me."

"That's not true."

It was hard to concentrate on everything that was happening when he stroked my thighs, kissing them as I stepped out of my clothes.

"It is. There's no fear if there's love."

He guided me to the wooden slider and sat me in it.

"Open your legs," he whispered, gently parting my knees until I was exposed to him. His eyes alone sent shockwaves through me, and he kept them on me when he kissed inside my thigh slowly, from knee up. He brushed his lips against my folds, flicking his tongue.

"Oh!" I cried. I couldn't help it.

"Shh. Quietly."

He opened me with his thumbs, exposing my clit to his tongue. He was good, so good. Skilled, yes, but he loved it. Loved every inch of my body. Loved every place we joined and touched. No one could do what he did without love.

I dug my fingers into his hair and put my legs on the armrests. I pressed my hips into him, whispering, "Yes, yes, yes."

The closer I got, the slower his tongue got. I was engorged, soaked, gasping for breath, and the tip of his tongue barely touched the very edge of my clit.

"Please, Capo, I'm so close."

He said nothing, answering by keeping his movements slow and light. The build, drop by drop, filling an ocean of tension, felt impossibly taut.

But still...he was slow and steady.

"Please, please. Oh, God let me go."

I looked at him. He moved his face from me, smiling. The air touching my clit was going to bring me right to orgasm.

"Stay there," he said, getting his pants down. "Don't move."

He sat on the footrest, his cock a waiting rod. He pulled me up, and I maneuvered myself to straddle him and brought myself onto him. I was so close already, so full of blood, tight as a drum, that when I slid my body onto his length, my body crackled to life. I moved back up and slowly, slowly back down again. The pace left me time to feel every inch, every trickle of pleasure, building at the next perfectly timed stroke.

I exploded, curving against him, biting back a howl. He held me still while he pounded me from below, and I came in a torrent, wiped clean of worry, stress gone, just a flood of love. When I looked at him, his lips were parted and his breath had become ragged. He held my face and pulled me close. I moved along him, still feeling shots of pleasure where we joined. He put his face to mine, his short breaths against my mouth.

"Ti voglio bene, Theresa. Ti amerò sempre. Fino alla fine dei miei giorni."

His eyes closed in utter surrender, and he came inside me, giving me everything.

We panted together for a few minutes, clutching each other, his dick still inside me. We had ten or fewer short breaths together before he pulled back.

"You ready?" he said, looking at his watch.

I got up, dripping. "I could be if I knew what we were doing."

He yanked up his pants. "We're trusting me. We're not being afraid." He tucked in his shirt.

"We're staying together."

He held out his hand. When I took it, he kissed it. "Let me check outside first."

He took me back out into the lunch room.

I let him, because he asked me to. I slid a paper cone from the sleeve and rested my hand on the watercooler lever. I let him walk to the door because I didn't think anything of it. He'd asked me to trust him, which was redundant, because I trusted him already. He'd tried to leave me to protect me four times, and all four times he'd come back to me.

So why would I expect a fifth time?

That would be crazy.

Right?

I released the water lever when the cone was full, watching him in admiration of his grace. He looked out the door, the angle of his body as desirable in my satisfaction as it had been ten minutes earlier in my ache.

He looked back at me, fingers sliding along the edge of the door. "You should never doubt that I love you."

"Neither should you."

"I'm not trying to protect you," he said.

"Thank you for that." I brought the cone to my mouth. The water numbed my upper lip with an icy shock.

He clicked a button on the door's edge. "This is something else."

He stepped outside and closed the door with a resounding click, and I dropped the paper cone, splashing cold water on my feet.

Then the fire alarm started.

What had he promised in exchange for the blaring klaxon alarm that went off? I didn't wonder about that until after I'd tried the knob and found he'd locked it from the outside. I pounded on the door, screaming his name for all of fifteen seconds, calculating what he'd traded with my father.

Our life together. That could be the only thing my father would want. And I knew Antonio's calculations, because we were of one mind. He hadn't lied in saying that he wasn't trying to protect me. He was doing something else entirely. If his plan was to give me up, take Valentina home...then what?

Then something. Maybe he intended to figure it out once Valentina was safe and he'd made peace. Maybe I already knew the answer.

I trusted him. Even as I screamed for him to open the god-damned door, I trusted him.

Then I caught the stink of smoke.

My eyes burned. Was it in here? Would he leave me if the room was on fire?

I turned around. The room was dark but for the illumination from the chai-colored sky and a tiny pinprick of hot orange.

"So," an Italian-lilted voice said. I heard her clearly between the honks of the alarm. "I can finally see you."

Chapter 41

ANTONIO

A*mor regge senza legge.*
Loosely translated…love rules without laws.

Romanticized. A completely painted-pink version of truth. When love swells and all the world seems small in the face of it, the heart feels like the most powerful thing on Earth. Above all worldly things. Money. Laws. Common sense.

One follows the heart to paradise or destruction, but it rules, and it doesn't tell you where you're going. You just go. Laws be damned. Laws of family and country can go to hell, and you can follow.

I'd had no business marrying Valentina, but I loved her. After the first few months, I became dissatisfied in bed, but I stayed faithful. Nothing I did was good enough for her, so I tried to do better. She became an emotional burden, yet I committed myself to her.

Valentina had had no business marrying me, but she did. She was from the north and hated the southern part of the boot. Yet she loved me. She hated the camorra as much as she embraced my family. *Omertà* burned her alive and set her apart from her friends. But she kept silent for me.

As time passed, maybe one of us would have changed enough to make us happy together. Maybe we would have bent toward each other and met. The day I left with the taste of her risotto sliding against my tongue, disappearing behind the growing bite of bitterness, I realized how far we were from each other. She'd become vicious and moody, and no matter what I did, the only thing she wanted to talk about was my walking away from being my father's consigliere.

She was pregnant. She didn't want to bring children into the fold. Saddle them with a father who could be dead or imprisoned. She'd never told me any of that, but I knew it was true. It was obvious.

I didn't owe her anything. We'd failed each other. I was no more responsible for the failures of our marriage up to the point she disappeared than she was. But after that, I blamed her for everything. For keeping my son from me. For letting me grieve for her. For showing up only when she thought I was dead.

I trotted down the hall, running with the *whoop* of the siren. I'd grabbed a white coat and headed against traffic to the cardiac floor. I had a room number. Theresa was locked away. That had been my promise. Declan Drazen would manufacture a way for me to get Valentina if I left Theresa behind. I had to go alone. He was protecting his daughter. I was grateful. At least if I wasn't seeing sense, he was.

I was going to get Valentina and send her home by plane or slow boat. Arrange something with my son she'd agree to. I would apologize to Theresa with the most profound and honest apology I could muster. Then I would end my marriage somehow. I'd do something that was against every tradition in my family and get a divorce. Or get an annulment and make sure my son was taken care of in some other meaningful way. Something more, and something less, than my father had done after my mother annulled their marriage.

I was elated. Walking on air. Everything I wanted was about to come to me. I could settle down and let Zo take the reins of the business without fighting for my crew. Theresa and I had enough money, time, love.

My god, I loved her.

I didn't think it could happen. She and I, together almost normally. But it was going to happen. In the short trip down the hall,

I remembered the scent of olive blossoms on the way up the 5 freeway. I would buy a small orchard between Los Angeles and San Diego, and we would live on it together. Close to her family. Close to Zia, who I forgave in my heart for keeping my wife and child from me. I would run the business legitimately, completely above board, and Theresa would keep the books and numbers. She'd pressure me to be more efficient, and I'd teach her why I couldn't be. We'd fight and make up and fight and make up and make children and make up and—

I got to room 498 mid-smile. The door was closed, probably because Valentina was supposed to have checked out already. I had a moment of concern that she might have tried to escape when the alarms went off two floors below, but I was propelled by my plan, thoughtless in my fantasy of a life with Theresa, and naïve in my belief in her father.

They wore white coats, and I felt a prick in my hip. It was too late to say or do anything. Too late to apologize or to ask where Valentina was. Too late to run, too late to fight. The room went sideways, and the smile left my face.

Chapter 42

THERESA

My eyes adjusted. A woman smoking. Thin as a rail. She sounded old, but I couldn't see her well enough to confirm. She blew a stream of smoke, leaving the last huff for two rings that drifted up in a breaking halo.

"Donna Maria," I said, remembering her from the wedding. The alarm was muffled through the door, but it was a constant that made me raise my voice. "How long have you been here?"

"I've heard people fucking before. Don't worry your pretty head about it."

I let that hang like the layer of smoke collecting at the ceiling. It had been a separate room and a closed door, but still. She stepped forward into the window light. It cast her in blue, revealing her age. I stepped back.

"I wanted to see you," she said. "To get a good look at you. I wanted to see if you have vengeance in you."

"And what if I do?"

"We can't have that."

We regarded each other for too long. I didn't know what I was looking at, but I knew it frightened me. She looked like solid evil. Sin made flesh. As old as she was and as small as she was, she had murder on her hands.

I stepped back again. "How did you know we were here?"

"Why? Are you afraid my consigliere set you up?"

"He didn't." I hadn't considered it because there was no way Antonio or my father would put me in a room with this woman. Lorenzo? Otto? One of them. They would pay.

Donna Maria pointed at my eyes. "And there it is." She shook her head slowly.

"What?"

"Some people are born with a need to make things even. Imbalance is like a stone in their shoe. They need to shake it out. This never changes. It's not even a choice. It's who they are. This is you. I saw it on you just now. For you, there will be an imbalance, and you'll need to correct it, unless I correct you first."

Imbalance?

Vengeance.

Then there must be something to avenge. Oh God.

"Don't." I said one word as a full sentence, begging for Antonio's life as an answer to what was in my head, not what had come from her lips.

She looked at her wrist then at me. "It's probably already done."

I had an excess of physical reactions to quell. My hands got hot. My thighs tingled. My rib cage shrank until all the air was squeezed from my lungs. There might have been more, but I hadn't time to catalog them.

She was on me so fast, she became invisible in the space between us. My feet were lifted from under me, and the floor thwacked the back of my head.

She was so fast. I'd never seen anything like it, even in Antonio. The knife was a streak of blue light against the darkness, and my instincts acted where my mind was too slow, turning my head to avoid the blade. I jerked my hips and threw her off me just as the door opened. A solid wedge of light poured in, and the decibel level of the alarm doubled.

I was alone on the floor, sprawled like a drunk.

"Miss, there's a fire alarm on this floor," said the orderly, turning on the light. "Let's go."

I spun to look for Donna Maria Carloni, scanning every last place she could hide, but she was nowhere to be seen. The door to the pump room was closed. I pointed, but the orderly dragged me out.

Chapter 43

THERESA

Donna Maria had terrified me, but she'd propelled me into action. If she hadn't tried to kill me, I might have poked around for Antonio, trusting that he'd planned our reconnection.

How long did I have? I followed the orderly and the crowd down the hall until he checked the next doorway, then I slipped away.

Donna Maria had to kill Antonio herself, despite what she'd said to freak me out.

Right?

Unless someone else was supposed to inherit Antonio's territory?

I had a moment of doubt when I worried that he'd intended this. That he'd given himself to death to save both of the women in his life, and Donna Maria had come to me to make sure I wouldn't avenge a death he chose.

I couldn't believe that. I trusted him.

I opened the emergency door just as a throng of staff and patients headed toward me. Jesus, a lot of people worked the late shift.

"Turn around," said a ponytailed woman my age, wearing dark blue scrubs and pulling a gurney.

She took my arm, still guiding her supine patient. We were followed by a crowd of professionals acting calm and bored with a sense of urgency to their motions. The doctor let go of my arm, and as the crowd pushed down the hall, I took one step back into the lunch room. She was gone.

Hoping another staffer wouldn't detain me, I got back out into the hall. I acted official, as if I was heading back into the burning hospital for official life-saving business that couldn't wait.

My father was a piece of work. A fire. Did he make sure there was a real fire? Or did he just pay someone five figures to pull the wrong lever somewhere in the guts of the building?

Once in the hall, I grabbed a clipboard and trotted against traffic as if I belonged there. I had to get to the cardiac unit. If I could find Valentina, maybe I could retrace his steps. My family was on that floor with Jonathan.

The hall was mostly empty when I passed a room with the door open. It was the third I passed, but for some reason, I stopped. Inside was a man lying down, eyes taped shut, head in a kind of plastic box. I stepped in. The lights flashed against the patient's skin. Fat tubes came out of his mouth, his bow lips gauzed against friction.

"Paulie," I said, my voice drowned out by the klaxon.

He didn't answer. He never would.

I backed out. I wasn't there to make my soul right. I was there to find Antonio. In the reflection in a chrome tray, I saw a dark-haired woman come from around the corner. I dodged and ran to the stairwell.

I clutched my clipboard and fought the traffic to go to the stairs to find the cardiac unit on the fourth floor. Once I got to the third floor, the mad dash stopped. The alarm stopped.

Up on four, nothing had changed. Had the drill only been on the second floor?

As I approached the waiting room my family was in, a cheer went up from them and my blood rushed with the tingle of adrenaline. There stood a version of my family I'd never seen, because the Drazens didn't huddle in a group hug so tight you couldn't identify every participant. They didn't jump up and down together at this time of night. Not my mother. Not Sheila. My father wasn't inside the hug's circle but stood with his hands pressed together, head bowed over them, eyes closed as if in prayer. A part of my brain became electrified when I saw my father in that pose.

"Dad!" I ran to him.

He didn't move. I knew he'd seen me before he closed his eyes over his hands. "Daddy, what have you done?" I asked.

I smelled Antonio, and a forest, and saw my father with the sounds of a thousand birds behind him.

The memory had been activated by an algorithm of input.

The memory of the boy in the forest. The one who came all over my shirt and slapped me. The one who had been found at the bottom of a ravine with a broken neck. The first boy who kissed me like a man. The first one who got his fingers inside me and shocked me by making me come. That boy. I'd laid his death in my father's lap, because all the facts clicked together, but when Dad folded his hands in prayer because Jonathan was obviously going to live, the whole memory came to me. I'd blamed my father not because he was capable of murder, but because I hadn't been able to deal with the fact that I was.

The ravine, and the boy twisted at the bottom, and Dad next to me with his hands folded and saying, "What have I done?"

Me, looking at my own hands and feeling their power. A brown button sat in the center of my right palm. I'd pulled it off when I'd yanked the boy by the shirt and thrown him over a cliff. It was so clear now. Dad had arranged a meeting to simply threaten him, and I'd shown up. I'd swung him by the shirt, using his weight and surprise against him, and let go. Just let go and watched.

"What have I done?" he'd said. Dad had wanted to know what kind of animal he'd raised.

I'd killed that boy. I'd killed him for leaving a swirl of prematurely released semen on my shirt and slapping me. I'd killed him for our shame. I'd been a murderer way before I met Paulie Patalano.

Antonio hadn't made me a killer. Violence was in my blood, my skin, the sinews of my heart.

Dad put his hands down, and the memory shattered, like a painted window broken to reveal an entire landscape beyond.

He opened his eyes. "They found a heart. He's going to be fine."

I pressed my hand to my chest as if checking for my own heart. "I need to know," I said while no one was listening. "Antonio. Where is he? What deal did you make?"

"Two of my children are saved tonight," he said. "That was the deal I made."

If I stayed to grill him further, I would get sucked into my family's joy, and I didn't have time. Antonio didn't have time.

Chapter 44

THERESA

didn't know where I was running to with my stolen clipboard and nothing but forward momentum. He had to be alive. Had to be. The life would be sucked from my world if he was removed from it. I had hope, and I clung to it like the last dollar to my name. He had to be alive. He had to be. I trusted him to live.

Jonathan would be okay, and my family would be all right. Antonio had to be fine. I was so mad at him for leaving me in that break room, but I would forgive him and let him fuck me like a rag doll.

I hurled myself down the steps and into the waiting room next to the vending machine Antonio had fed a twenty-dollar bill an eternity ago. My face was bathed in sweat and tears. I couldn't breathe from running toward then away from the make-believe fire, and my ears rang from the alarm. I passed the colorful box of shiny plastic food, all screaming for attention. Something about it made me stop in my tracks. All the crinkly packages held upright by black coils were the same. Or not. I didn't remember the food, because Antonio had been so beautiful with two-day scruff on his cheeks and his sparkling eyes. And his hands, breaking open the granola package…the way the fingers had articulated, the sheer power and dignity of them. Later, I'd learned to love the grace with which those hands managed small things because I knew how rough they could be.

The vending machine wasn't interesting. The memory of my resistance to Antonio was, as was the sobbing of the woman next to it as she crumpled a bunch of papers in her hand. That was why I was attracted to the machine. It wasn't the memory of Antonio or the brightly packaged non-food. It was the woman. It was Valentina.

My ribs took on a life of their own, squeezing the air from my lungs as if I couldn't breathe without the help.

She wasn't supposed to be sitting on a blue plastic chair by herself, crying. Antonio wouldn't leave her like that. Not for a minute. Not for as long as it took me to stare at a bunch of snacks.

That only meant one thing.

Donna Maria had been telling the truth. She had him.

"Valentina?" I sat and said her name at the same time, putting my arm around her. "Where's Antonio?"

She looked up and saw me, her eyes at the bottom of deep, salty puddles. She rattled something off in Italian, hands waving, mouth wet with tears and spit. I looked around the room. Sick grandmothers. Wailing babies. One woman so pale I thought she was wearing a mask. No one cared that a beautiful woman was crying her eyes out.

"Valentina, English, please. Antonio? He was coming to get you. Have you seen him?"

She shook her head. Spit out more Italian. All I understood was the name "Tonio" and the emotion, which read something between regret and resignation.

She wasn't functioning, and more than anything, I needed her to function, at least well enough to tell me that Antonio had left us both for a life on the run, or a third woman, or some other attempt at vengeance. I didn't even care what it was. Didn't even worry about "us" but about the worst-case scenario, which I refused to even tell her.

I set her papers aside and took her hands. I tried to remember his voice, his tone, how he broke through her walls of panic and despair.

"Shh, Tina, tesoro. Shhh. Cinque secondi. Non dire nulla. Respira."

She heard me. She must have. She took a breath through her mouth. It hitched, choked, but I saw the concentration in her face.

She looked right at me, as if trying to seek out strength in me she didn't have for herself. I tried to project Antonio-like confidence as I made a show of taking another deep breath. She followed, her second breath hitching that much less.

"*Bene*," I said. "Another."

We breathed together three more times. She swallowed. Breathed. Sniffed. Dug an overused tissue out of her sweater sleeve and wiped her nose. When she looked at me again and sucked her lips between her teeth as if there was something she wanted to say but was now calm enough to be ashamed of, I panicked.

"Okay. Tell me. Do you know where Antonio is?" In my heart, I still hoped she was crying because he'd broken her heart, not because I liked seeing her hurt but because the other option was terrifying.

"I don't know." Her face started melting again.

I squeezed her hands so hard it must have hurt. At least, that was the intention. "Have you seen him?"

"No."

I needed an open-ended question that went away from Antonio and back to what Valentina knew.

"Why are you crying?" I asked.

"I'm scared."

"Of what?"

"First Daniel. Did they kill Daniel?"

Who? Daniel? That had been years ago. I had to shake myself from thoughts of Antonio to remind myself of the last time she'd seen Daniel. He had been hanging upside down from a beam in his ceiling. Then I pictured on the floor, face red, grey strips of duct tape glue on his cheek.

"He's all right. We got to him."

She broke down in fresh tears that didn't have sorrow or desperation in them, only relief. She put her head in her hands, and I stroked her back. I didn't have a second to let her release, but I didn't have a choice but to let her feel it.

"He's fine," I said softly. "He has a headache."

"They took me away. And my heart gave out. It does when I have stress. They didn't know whether to bother letting me live.

They had me in the room." Her arm went straight, pointing at the place she was describing, which may or may not have been in that direction. "They didn't know I have some English. So I just listened. I tried not to give away my face. And they were saying..."

She was going to break down again.

"Stay with me," I said.

"They had him go to the wrong room. They were going to take him away and..." She tilted her head and pivoted her hand around her wrist as if trying to think of a word. "*Sbudellarlo.*"

"I don't know what that means."

She made her fingers into a plane and pointed the edge of it toward herself, moving her hand up and down. "Cut him open. My sweet husband."

She broke apart again, and no amount of breathing was going to get her back. She fell into my arms even though I was in no condition to comfort or soothe her. I just stared at the side of the vending machine, eyes wide and blank. The personality I'd cultivated for thirty years poured out of me, and I was empty. Nothing but a vessel for that other self I'd just discovered. The animal. The huntress. The savage. Though I thought that primitive woman would rend everything in her sight to achieve her ends, she surprised me. A cold calm took the place where panic and uncertainty would have been.

I was a stone. In part, I had to be or I'd break, thinking of Antonio dying. But also, if I was to avenge him, I had no time to turn into Valentina.

I took Valentina by the chin and forced her to look at me. "I'm putting you in a cab to Zia's. You stay with her."

Her head shook as much as my fingers allowed.

I let go of her chin. "You can go somewhere else beside Zia's, but—"

"Where are you going?" she interrupted.

"To find him."

"Where?"

If I said "Wilshire and Western" or "under Santa Monica pier," she wouldn't know what I was talking about. I could have made up anything and at least answered the question to her satisfaction, but she was illuminating a point. I didn't know where I was looking.

And she knew it. The bitch. She looked at me with a smug little face I wanted to crack open.

"You know," I said.

"I want to tell the men. This is not the place for us. You're going to get him killed."

"The men?" I set my voice to a sotto growl. "They abandoned him. They sold him. Every one of them."

Except Otto. Maybe. He was I-didn't-even-know-where at that point.

"They said it though?" I asked. "They said where they were taking him? They said the whole plan?"

"All of them?" she asked by way of an answer. "There isn't one of his men to talk to?"

"No. Did they say it in front of you? Just tell me what they said without the particulars."

"We should call his father then."

Was she serious? She wanted to call a man across the world who may or may not have approved his son's assassination? She needed to go back to the fabric factory.

"I don't have a cell," I said, and the ridiculousness of her idea seemed to hit her.

She looked helpless again, trying to twist her mind around matters that were beyond her scope. She was an innocent. A nag and a righteous poseur, but not evil. And not particularly direct or approachable when sober. She was a traditional girl with traditional ideas about what she could do by herself.

"How far away is Whittier?" she asked.

I didn't react. I didn't let blood flow to my face or shift my posture. Instead, I shrugged.

"We're on the west side of LA, more or less," I said casually. "Whittier's on the east side, over the river. But not too far over."

"Are there trees?"

"The preserve has trees."

"They were arguing about whether to hang him from a tree or do it at the compound? I pretended to be asleep. What they were saying? It was sick. My heart was sick. Even thinking of it now. I want to throw up."

She wasn't alone.

"Whose compound?"

"If I tell you, I want to be sick again. I want to tell someone who can stop it from happening."

"Whose compound?" I repeated, throat dry, ears pounding, adrenaline making it nearlu impossible to stay still.

"The old woman."

That was enough. I had it.

Breathe.

Touch St. Christopher.

Run. Run for the phone like a long-limbed animal on the Serengeti. Run like everything you love is on fire. Break the ground beneath your feet with the power of your steps. Stretch your gait past the length of your entire body. Fold space with your speed. Breath fire. Eat air. Take off. Fly.

I was going so fast, I slammed into a bank of phones on the back side of the Sequoia parking lot. First one broken. Second dead. The third had gum in the change slot. I picked it out. It wasn't quite hard yet. I spit on it. Pulled it off.

I had Daniel's two jukebox quarters. I jammed one in the slot. Pushed it past the sticky residue with the second quarter. They both fell in.

I stopped myself before I touched the keys. I had to dial right because I didn't have more quarters.

Twoonethreesevenfourtwothreethreeohnine.

Ring.

Ring.

"Daniel?"

The sheets rustled. "Theresa. What time is it? Where are you?"

"Late. Early. I need your help. Like, now."

He took a deep, waking-up type breath. "Yes. Okay. I was worried about you."

"Valentina's here."

"You found her?" He jumped at the chance to ask, "Is she all right?"

I caught sight of Antonio's wife scuttling toward me. "She's fine. She asked about you." I didn't know why I felt the need to soothe Daniel's ego. Maybe I needed to feel something positive in the middle of a shit storm, or maybe I needed a coin of goodwill in a pocketful of resentment.

"What do you need?" he asked.

"It's...I mean it's so bad. There are so many moving parts. You just have to trust me. They have Antonio at Donna Maria's. They're going to kill him, or they've killed him already."

A breath. More sheets rustling. "Theresa, I can't do much. My credibility is shot."

"I can't get there. I don't even know where it is."

More sheets. A crisper voice. "She lives in the preserve, past the federal parkland. It's a point of contention, but slow down. How do you know?"

"Valentina overheard them. Please, please, I'll tell you everything. I'll tell you how I know. I'll tell you about Paulie. Just get someone over there."

"That's the problem. It's not accessible to local authorities. It's three miles into Turner Canyon."

"You can't call federal marshals? Are you serious?" Desperation forced my voice a few octaves higher.

"If I send them, anything they find could land him in a courtroom."

"Save his life, Daniel. Please."

"How did it all end up like this?"

"Will you or won't you?" I needed confirmation. I needed it nailed to the wall so I could stare at it and make sure it was real.

"I'll try. I'll make the calls. I'll throw my weight around. What little I have left. Just...she overheard them? What did she overhear? I can't send them without a reason."

"*Sbudellarlo*," I said. The phone clicked. I didn't know why. I'd used a payphone twice in my life.

"Ah, I heard of that when I prosecuted the Taorminas. I'm sorry. I kind of liked him after the other day."

"Don't you ever speak about him in the past tense," I growled, but he said nothing. "Daniel? Daniel?"

The phone was dead. My money had run out.

Chapter 45

THERESA

"I need your car keys," I said.

I had to get somewhere quickly in Los Angeles, and I had no car.

Margie wasn't taking the urgency seriously, arms folded, sensible shoe tapping the hospital linoleum. "Why?"

"Because."

"That car is registered to me. If it's going to be used in the commission of a crime, I could get disbarred."

"Give me the keys and report it stolen. But give me half an hour to get across town."

"You just admitted you're committing a crime."

"I did not. I was trying to make you feel better. I'm going home. I'm going to bed. I'll be back in the morning to visit Jonathan."

She twisted her bag around so she could reach inside and yanked out a string of keys. She popped off a black key fob and put it in my outstretched hand.

"Thank you," I said.

"Leave me some gas."

I walked away.

"Theresa," she called, and I turned. "Your jacket. In the back."

I reached behind me and felt cold metal. My jacket had slipped behind the gun, exposing it. I didn't thank her. I just got into the elevator.

She got in front of the doors. "Theresa."

"It's all right. I'm just tired."

"Be good. As good as you can be. Okay?"

I was about to promise her I'd be good, but the doors closed before I could lie.

Chapter 46

Valentina had been waiting in the lobby like a lost puppy I couldn't get rid of. She'd gotten in step behind me and followed me to Margie's car.

I thought of shaking her but decided against it. She was a grown woman, and I didn't have time. She got in the car as if I'd said it was all right, her sense of entitlement as unshakeable as a holy sacrament.

"He could be already dead," she said from the passenger seat.

I got hot everywhere. My hands. My back. My face must have been a searing shade of purple. I'd never felt so angry in the face of the sheer emptiness of the world.

I was supposed to do something when I felt like that. Breathe. *Respira*. Touch the St. Christopher medal.

Of course, touching the medal did nothing. It did not fix the situation. It did not change the danger Antonio was in or transmit his whereabouts into my head. It only reminded me that I was capable of anything, and that even in my savagery, I was a child of the universe and loved by God.

That's all.

I tapped the GPS on the dash, getting a satellite picture of the slice of wilderness between Whittier and Hacienda Heights. Take the 10 east to the 605 South. Off on Beverly. Left. Right. Left onto a dirt road, along a drive into a nondescript house with no address.

That had to be the one. It was the only structure in the area large enough to be a house and small enough to be hidden.

"What will you do if he is?" she asked. "Dead, that is."

"Kill all of them." I didn't check for her reaction. If she got to ask off-the-cuff questions about what I'd do with my life, then I got to answer in the immediate.

The 10 was empty, but I stayed a little over the speed limit. Getting pulled over wouldn't get me there any quicker, and I had a loaded gun in the glove compartment.

"Do you know how many men he's killed?" she asked. "Would you like to count? How many wives he left crying? How many children he left without fathers? This isn't something we have to like, but maybe it's justice."

"You left your own son without a father. Where's justice for you?"

"Antonin is better off."

I didn't know how to get through to her. I didn't know what to say, because she was right. Antonio had been damned before he ever set eyes on me. He'd made years' worth of choices that were beyond deplorable. He'd let his rage set his mind to murder again and again, trying to set the scales straight and only making the weight of his crimes greater and greater. There would be no forgiveness for him, not in this world or the next.

"You said he was sweet when you met," I said.

"He was so nice," she said wistfully. Had she been like this when they met? Or had he destroyed her too?

"He said you were gentle. He said you were innocent and beautiful. I think he thought you could save him," I said.

"I kept trying."

"And he kept getting worse."

She nodded.

"He's done everything wrong," I said. "I know he has. He was in the life, and he killed...I don't even know how many men inside his organization. Too many. One is too many. I'm not excusing it. But I think he can be saved. I think we can get that man back. The one you married. Maybe not totally. He'll never forget these years. But that man who brought you strawberries and was gentle and kind? He's still in there, and I think he's ready to be free."

"I'm so confused."

"You're right to be."

"Do you think he can come back?"

"I do." I didn't warn her that he wasn't coming back to *her,* and if he did, then she and I would have a deep, long-standing problem. "He was trying to get out of the life. There's nothing he wants more than an end to it."

"I wish he really was dead," she said, staring at the edge of the morning skyline. It wasn't even close to sunrise, and the city was as quiet as it ever was.

"Yeah, I get that."

I did truly understand. She'd come to Los Angeles to pay respects to a husband she hadn't seen in ten years and wound up at the center of a mob war over a bride he'd abandoned for another woman. If he'd been dead, she'd have closure. If he'd been dead, she could grieve and let go. He'd never change. He would be the subject of her prayers for years to come. I saw her so clearly, and I felt nothing but compassion.

"If you want to leave and go home to your son, I think you'll be forgiven. At least by me. Whatever happens will happen without you."

"Everything already happened without me," she said as I turned off the freeway.

More would happen without her, because whatever I was stepping into, she would be a liability if she came along.

I remembered the map and turned down the dark routes and ways without much trouble until I hit a high fence with barbed wire on top. I parked the car to the side of the road and shut off the lights. The moon was diffused by the rainclouds, which had closed the sky to a slight drizzle.

I should have left Valentina at the hospital, or the freeway entrance, or anywhere but in the middle of nowhere.

"You should stay here," I said.

"Yes," she replied with a sharp nod. "I will."

"I'll be back with Antonio."

"Yes, you will."

"If one of us isn't back by the time the sun is up, can you drive?"

"Of course I can drive. I'm not stupid."

"I'll leave the keys in the ignition."

"Go. Please." She pushed my shoulder with one hand and pointed out the door with the other. "Save him."

"Thank you, Valentina. You're all right."

"You may call me Tina." She shook her hand at the door again.

I took a deep breath and got out.

Chapter 47

THERESA

The fence was high enough to be a real obstacle. I'd never climbed a fence, but what I lacked in skill, I made up for in not giving a shit. I was careful, because the chain link was wet from the rain. I got through a gap in the barbed wire right over the entrance hinge while staring into the camera because honestly, I wouldn't trick myself into thinking I knew how to get in without anyone knowing.

I dropped onto the mud and took the gun out of my back waistband. I had no idea how many bullets I had in it. It was heavy, so I knew it wasn't empty, but beyond that, I was at a loss. Yet another place where my instincts highlighted the gaps in my knowledge. If we lived, we were going to laugh about this.

Respira.

The rain had stopped, leaving clear air and good visibility, as little as there was. I took a deep breath and ran. It was dark as hell, and I lifted my feet to clear the mud and tree roots. I was sure I was running in the right direction. I had no cause to be sure, but I was. So I ran faster, and when I saw a dim light ahead, I knew I had been right.

Run. Run like this is the last hour of your life. Run as if there will be nothing left to run to tomorrow. Crush the ground. Pull it off its moorings. Make your mark in this world because it is your last chance. You are about to die. Take off. Fly.

My forward momentum came to an abrupt halt and my thoughts spun on their axis as I hit an obstacle full-on. A yielding obstacle that grunted. A man. I scrambled to a crouch and turned around. Unmoored, I had no idea which direction he was in. I held out my gun as if I could aim at anything but the world at large with my senses scrambled.

My legs went out from under me again, and light and dark went upside down, or right side up, and the ground hit me hard enough to push the air from my lungs.

On my back, I pointed the gun at the cloud-diffused light of the moon.

A form blocked out the light, and I heard a hammer cock.

I squeaked because it was too soon, because I had things I still had to do and I had a tiny bit of air left in my lungs with which to do them. My vocal cords engaged that last breath, and my squeak was audible.

That saved my life.

The form shifted a little, and I kept my gun on him. His face was in shadow, but I didn't need to see the details to shoot him.

He moved his gun away from me, putting up his hands.

"Don't shoot," he croaked. "They'll hear it."

I breathed. It was a hitched inhale made with the very tops of my lungs, but I lived to breathe again. "Antonio?" I kept the gun on him, because I wasn't sure, and the feeling of peril saturated my consciousness.

"Breathe," he said, still struggling to speak.

I scrabbled to my feet without using my gun hand, because I didn't trust that it was him. I didn't trust that the sky was up and the mud was down. My finger was outside the trigger guide. I wouldn't accidentally shoot him, but my brain had short-circuited and I wasn't convinced I shouldn't.

"Prove it," I said.

I expected whoever he was to either kill me or start talking, but he didn't. He pushed my hand out of the way and laid his lips on mine. I tasted him, the sting of burned pine and blood. The arm with the gun went around his shoulders as he owned me with his kiss. Alive. He was alive. In my arms. If we died in the next ten minutes, we would be together. My chest expanded and contracted with relief, and my breaths became short and deep while my eyes fogged with tears.

"Stop," he said.

"How?" I took him in. No shirt. Wet skin against freezing cold. The side of his face was too dark. "What did they do to you?"

"They had no idea how fast I could run. Come on."

He pulled me toward the gate. Behind him, voices. Yelling. Whistling.

"We're going to run?" I said.

"We have to."

I yanked him toward me. "Again?"

"They'll kill you."

"How many bullets are in this gun?"

He let the pressure on my hand go. "You can't—"

"We can end this," I said. "We need to. You can't protect me. I know it's your instinct, but you can't. Face it. The more you try to protect me, the worse it gets."

With everything crashing down on us, time froze. Antonio froze. The kiss he'd left on my mouth tasted like years with him. I'd die with it on me.

The pressure to move toward the gate disappeared as he considered. The line of shouting men from the house got closer. Louder. More intense.

Antonio let me go.

He turned and aimed at them, and I followed suit. I doubted there were enough bullets between us to make any kind of difference. Maybe if every one found a home. Maybe in the event they were all unarmed. Maybe if God was with us, which was unlikely.

Suddenly, they were all cast in bright light. Drowned in shadowless white. Antonio knocked me out of the way a second after I heard the roar of an engine and the creak and scrape of something being dragged.

A car roared past us, pushing a nice length of barbed-wire-topped gate. The men chasing us had to jump over the wire. A couple didn't make it and sprawled away with injuries.

"Margie's going to kill me," I said, getting my feet under me. "That's Valentina. I don't know what she's thinking, but we can't run now."

I stood over Antonio. With his face and chest to the light of the night sky, I saw what they'd done to him, and they were all going to die. I was going to leave a swath of blood across Los Angeles. The decision was calculated. I couldn't detect any emotions in it. Just facts.

He was on his feet like a cat. "With you, I can do anything."

Chapter 48

ANTONIO

'd plucked the gun from Carlo's hand. He'd made the mistake of letting his attention wander while he was alone in the room with me. I'd been ready to die, but there was no reason not to avoid it if I could.

They were clearly interested in my territory and readying to make sure my death at the hands of an old woman was recorded. I would have given every penny to them if there were rules to achieve such a thing. But there weren't, because too many had changed their minds later and brought war.

Kill. Die. Run. Those were the only ways out, and I'd already tried two of the three.

So as much as I'd been running for my life before I crashed into Theresa, I was ready to attack. I had been running because I had no choice. I was attacking because with her, it was possible.

She attacked with me, running in the shadows alongside the car while we could, because they'd assume I was still headed to the gate and they had no idea she was even there.

Get to the house. Attack. Assault. Confront. That much was understood between us. We didn't have a plan any more detailed than that.

The trees opened into the small clearing in front of Donna Maria's house. The light of the car changed behind us, and I turned to look. Valentina had shaken the gate and was making a U-turn. I stopped.

"Jesus," Theresa said.

Valentina headed in the opposite direction. The two men that were left jumped out of her way. They shot at the car, but it kept moving. If she made it out, she'd just keep driving. Theresa and I had no way out of the miles of preserve. I was in no worse position than I had been when I'd crashed into her.

I glanced at her as she watched the car, then she turned back to me.

"No turning back," she said.

She was a cat. A beautiful devil. I feared and admired her. I wished I could fuck her one last time, but I would have to do without. "Let's go."

Chapter 49

THERESA

Even with the crazy circumstances, I had expectations. I thought the head of a mafia family would have a house made of dark wood and fat moldings with crystal and doilies. What I got was a squeaky wooden gate leading to a house with worn furniture and the smell of food deep in the fabrics. I touched Antonio's arm and pointed at a corner piled full of bright plastic and googly eyes. He nodded. There were kids around. I didn't have to say a word.

He leaned down and spoke in my ear. "House in the back. I'm going to take her out."

I didn't know who the men were outside. I only knew they shouted, and their voices got closer. The sound waves bounced off the wetness left in the air, making them seem to be everywhere all at once.

Antonio and I, as if pulled by the same strings, looked back through the open door to see them coming. They were going to follow us to the back and pick us off. We'd be dead before we started.

We didn't have to speak. I didn't have time to process the feeling of connection between us, only to react, skipping the niceties.

"I'll go upstairs." I was already leaning toward the stairway.

He grabbed my arm. "No."

"Let me draw the fire. Split them up."

"No!"

"We're together. I swear it. Dead or alive, you're with me. But we, both of us, won't get out unless I draw fire and you take care of business."

Time compressed again, and he spent minutes, hours even, considering.

He grabbed the back of my head and smashed his lips to mine, then jerked away. "Go, before I change my mind."

I stepped back with the sound of approaching hell through the squeaky gate, getting one last look at Antonio in his shirtless wonder. A warrior. A king. My capo, always always always.

I turned and ran up the stairs to a long dark hallway lined with open doors. I got my bearings. I needed to go left in order to face the back. I went through a door halfway down the hall.

It was a nursery. A girl's. Fluffy things. White crib. Soft colors made grey in the darkness. Across from the hall door, French doors to a balcony overlooking the back. I went out and leaned on the railing. The sky turned blueish with morning, and I saw a field lined with animal hutches. They scratched and wailed in nocturnal frustration.

To the left, a house with the lights on. That must be where Donna Maria was. I had to make sure he got in there.

Antonio ran out. I was ready. I held up the gun, waiting for whoever followed him. I was to distract them and draw fire to myself so Antonio could end this by killing an old woman. I was all right with that. We were both going to hell anyway.

I heard them clamor. Antonio looked back into the house before continuing into the yard.

"You're going to hurt yourself with that thing."

I spun back toward the nursery, gun out. Donna Maria stood there holding a baby. It was sleeping. I lowered my weapon when I saw the child.

Donna Maria Carloni smiled.

Chapter 50

ANTONIO

There were no shots from above. Either she was dead or she'd changed her mind, and there was no way she'd changed her mind. I glanced up along a veranda and saw her with her back to the railing. Someone was with her. I couldn't make them out, but in the moment before Domenico ran out into the yard and I had to react, I regretted leaving her alone. Deeply regretted it.

But regret was a luxury for later. Domenico was followed closely by Zo, who had Enzo and Simone huffing and puffing at his heels. It had been a tough night for those guys, and it was about to get tougher. They were my crew, and to prove their new loyalty, they'd beaten the hell out of me.

I didn't blame them, and I didn't hold it against them. It was business.

I shot Domenico. He fell like a bag of rice.

Then I took aim at Zo, who I'd loved and trusted and who had sold me out at every turn. He stopped long enough to get a clean shot at me.

Chapter 51

THERESA

was confused. I had to clear the way for Antonio to get to Donna Maria, but she was here, right before me, with a baby. I couldn't shoot her, even at close range, with a child in her arms.

The first shot came from below. I spun to look over the railing before the sound was done echoing. A man dropped.

"I'm just an old woman," Donna Maria said, coming up next to me with the baby. "This breaks my heart."

Another man came. And another. The only one I could identify was Antonio. The rest weren't even men but shadows.

"It wasn't supposed to be like this," she continued. "It was supposed to be a business."

There was a dead pause below. A weighted moment when everyone froze.

I had a job. Donna Maria had made me forget it, and if she wanted to kill me for doing it, that was okay. I just had to clear the way for Antonio until he was safe. I could figure out what to do with the misplaced mob boss in a minute.

I held out the gun and took a shot at the last man who came out. It was dark, and the angle was impossible. I think I killed one of the animals, or a dandelion. But the last guy out looked up at us and took aim. I shot at him to draw fire, stepping back when he took aim. I popped off another one, with the *clack clack* of Antonio's shots in the background, and Donna Maria buckled next to me.

Fuck.

The baby dropped headfirst, and some biological instinct made me reach for it, even with the gun still in my hand. I couldn't fight evolution. I got close to Donna Maria as she fell to get my hands under the baby, feeling badly for forgetting to drop the gun, realizing how light the baby was, how smooth its face, how oddly peach.

It was a doll.

And I was close to her. Close enough for a blade to land inside me, releasing pain that shot outward as every cell in my body screamed. Close enough to see the pleasure on her face when she jerked the blade upward so hard my feet came off the floor.

I dropped the doll.

Donna Maria relieved me of my gun. "Thank you, *troia*."

How long would it take to die from a stab wound? Long enough to see Antonio's face below, his mouth a circle of terror as I bent over and blood fell from me.

I'm sorry.

I didn't actually say that. I wanted to. I felt my failure deeply. Antonio put his hands out, and I think he cried out. I think something came from him, but I was suddenly deaf from the rushing in my ears.

Lorenzo turned away from Donna Maria and me and faced Antonio, pointing his gun at him for his territory and his crew. His kingship.

Antonio! Watch out!

I didn't actually have the strength to say that either.

A flash of light and a pop came from Zo's weapon. Antonio spun.

And fell.

And stayed fallen for a millisecond too long.

In the rising light, with his knees bent and his gun two feet from his hand, he stayed down, the ground under his head gelling with mud-pattered blood.

I screamed *Antonio!*

But nothing came out. The scream was sucked back into my gut in the form of pain.

The light in my life had been taken from me, and I wanted only one thing in the world. To die. And to kill. Because inside the pain and the furious rush in my head was a cold place that needed to be taken care of.

I was on all fours. Breathing hurt. Living hurt. My legs shook uncontrollably, and I coughed a stream of blood, heaving air and moisture back in.

I looked up. Donna Maria stood over me. She didn't look old. She looked twenty. Forty tops. She looked like a woman untouched by her own mortality. I grabbed at her, my hand slipping down her corduroy pants. I was pathetic. But I grabbed for her again, and she stepped back.

I had her by the ankle when she stepped back, but I didn't have enough strength to keep my grip. My hands weren't doing what they were supposed to. They were dying, and the life flowing from them did so in waves. I'd caught her on a fisted wave when my hands were grasping and flattening, rigid and slack, completely out of my control. She fell.

My crawl slowed, and my body came closer to the ground. Something scraped.

Donna Maria grumbled and got up on her elbows as if she were lying on the beach, getting the sun. "This is over, my girl. All this foolish nonsense."

The scraping under me. The knife. She'd left it in me. I swiped at it. Missed. My hand had gone flat.

"You don't belong here," she said. "Coulda told you that. Coulda told that *stupido* downstairs with his face in the mud. You till your own soil. What are you going to do with that knife? Anything?"

She had my gun in her hand. She put it against my head. It didn't feel cold. I must have been freezing. I got a grip on the knife and jerked it out.

Pain engulfed me for a second. Stuff started swimming, and I stopped having coherent thoughts. I was going to black out.

Get it together, Theresa.

People came onto the veranda. Men. I didn't know who. I couldn't look at them and finish this job. My fist clamped around the hilt of the knife.

Donna Maria pulled the trigger.
Click.

There were no bullets left.

With my last breath of life, in the interval between milliseconds, where atoms play and thoughts happen so quickly they're lost before they're remembered, I lunged for her throat, knife in front of me. Because I was a killer in my heart, the knife understood what I wanted and lodged itself right below her jaw, where life pulsed.

She didn't even yell. She just sprang forward, blood spurting, mouth open in a soundless scream. I did the impossible and got on my feet. Zo stood in the doorway, meek and boring. Harmless, except when he wasn't. He'd shot Antonio, and I couldn't touch him. His world would continue, and Antonio and I had died together, as promised. I felt a profound loss as my last real emotion, and I understood what drove vengeance all of a sudden.

Envy.

That a wrongdoer would continue with their life while you could not.

That they took something and walked away unscathed.

That they had everything and you had nothing.

Envy. So insidious it could disguise itself as anger or righteousness and travel over seas and mountains to see itself satisfied.

Not having the strength or balance to support myself, I spun around. The edge of the railing bit my side, then nothing nothing nothing as I fell.

The ground.

Hard.

Harder than anything I'd ever felt.

Stuff crunched.

A bag of chips.

The bag was fine.

The chips.

Crushed.

But my name.

Contessa.

The mud hadn't made the ground any softer.

At the bottom of a ravine, a stupid boy twisted.

I'd felt nothing.

Oh my God, Theresa.
Oddly empty.
I'd killed him.
That hard earth under him.
Broken like a bag of chips.
I will kill them.
What had I done?
Wrong.
I'd done wrong.
And Paulie.
Who loved.
Who hurt.
And I felt.
All of them. I will God oh god oh
Regret.
Theresa. Theresatheresatheresa
My family would have to grieve again.
Margie would hate herself for giving me the car.
And Antonio would blame himself forever.
He would kill someone for this.
And that was hell enough.
To be loved so well.
That your death inspires regret.
And envy.
And you die swimming in it.

I opened my eyes. Everything was hard to do. Especially this. Opening my eyes. Breathing. Swallowing blood. But I knew the voice, and I had to see the sweet brown eyes and the lips curved for love one last time.

"Capo," I said. I think.

He had blood over one side of his face, under a gash where the bullet had swiped the side of his head. His mouth was twisted in a rictus of anger and sadness. I wanted to kiss it happy.

"Contessa."

"You're not dead."

"No, no. A scratch."

It was still bleeding. I couldn't see much, but I thought I saw bone.

"Please," I said, guts twisted so tight I could barely get the word out. "Do something for me."

"Anything."

I realized when I heard the sincerity in his voice that the rush of white noise in my ears was gone. I didn't know if it was the fall or if hearing Antonio's voice was God's last gift to me for something I couldn't give words. Not yet. Not until he promised.

"No revenge," I said. "Do not avenge me."

"Theresa—"

"Say it."

"I can't."

"You have to see past all that."

He moved my hair from my face. "I can't see in front of me. You are my life. I have nothing to hope for without you."

"Promise me."

He didn't answer. My lungs weren't holding air, and he was holding himself together with thread. Even in my state, I could see it. I could catch him now. I could get him to promise, then I could remember the thing and I could rest and—

"Promise." I barely breathed it.

He waited forever to answer, as if he couldn't lie to a dead woman so he had to make sure he'd only speak the truth. I kept mouthing the word, waiting for a response, but it got harder with every repetition. Because. The thing.

Promise promise promise

"Yes," he said. "I promise."

"No vengeance?"

"Come vuoi tu."

The thing was the flood of memories of my years on earth. The adult years between the boy and his fingers and the man with the espresso eyes. All those years I was good. All those years I'd chosen happiness. I remembered my sisters and school, and pretty dresses and stupid kindnesses. Katrina. My brother. Rachel. The assistants I'd trained and the good, honest, ethical years of work I gave. None of it made up for what I'd become, but my life hadn't been a waste. Hadn't been a lie.

"Thank you."

I started falling before I even pronounced the first syllable, the gratitude catching my fall into a blackness that grew into the darkness of a truck that smelled like gunpowder and pine, rumbling from Tijuana to Los Angeles. I remembered olive orchards and a life not lived. The wheels under us *hup-shh hup* like a heartbeat. Antonio above me, stroking my eyelids closed and whispering, *This is the day they went to live in the olive orchards. When you close your eyes for the last time, this will be this day you remember as the first day of the long happiness of your life. You will smile your whole journey to heaven.*

Chapter 52

DANIEL

There's an old Italian saying. I can't pronounce it, and I'm probably misquoting it entirely, but it goes, "When the snake is dead, the venom is dead."

I don't think that's true. Not in every case. For me, the venom died when I thought Theresa was dead after the wedding. For Antonio, when he was leaning over Theresa on Donna Maria Carloni's compound, I knew his venom was dead. He was broken. Utterly broken.

It was a fucking mess, the whole thing. I'd rushed to the compound as soon as I realized the sheriff's office wasn't going to call the feds and no one gave a shit because the snake had paid all of them to leave her alone on her land.

I knew that because I'd gotten my share.

I'd seen Valentina chewing her nails on the side of the road. She stood near a silver Mercedes that had been having a make-out session with a chain-link fence and barbed wire. She couldn't explain a word in English, so I put her in the car and took her into the compound, following the divots she'd made with the gate.

I took her hand. I hadn't touched her before, but I had a feeling her husband was dead. She broke down crying. I didn't love her then, but I thought I could, maybe. If I got out of that compound in one piece. They'd already trussed me up and hung me from the ceiling. These families weren't known for lowering the stakes from encounter to encounter. I was unarmed, unskilled, and I'd be unaccounted for for a long time if they decided to bury me here.

In retrospect, I was either really brave or really stupid. At the time, I'd felt as though I didn't have any choice but to, at the very least, witness what was happening. Jesus, what a way to get myself killed.

But I kept going. I told Valentina to stay in the car, and she drew the tops of her fingers under her chin and flung them at me. I think she was telling me to go fuck myself. Must have been, because she got out with me.

I'd never seen the actual compound. It was more modest than I thought it would be, and it was a wreck. In the front yard, two women and four children, from twelve to a few months, huddled in the morning light.

"Are you all right?" I asked one of the women. I recognized her as Irene Carloni.

They didn't answer.

"*Stai bene?*" Valentina asked.

Irene, who I knew spoke English, made the same motion Valentina had, a drawing of the fingers under the chin.

"*Omertà,*" Valentina said as I headed into the house. "They will never say."

I smelled gunpowder, heard the batshit squeal of small animals, and ran out to the back. I saw a man's body, his face in the mud. Simone Fiore and Lorenzo Desano stooped together. Hutches of animals. A bloody grate. My eyes fell on Antonio Spinelli, on his knees next to Theresa.

Blood, everywhere. I mean…everywhere and—

Valentina fell apart, but I couldn't—

So I went to them. Antonio looked up and said—

I didn't know what Lorenzo and Simone were up to. Enzo Priole appeared. There was some conflict. Some questions that hadn't been answered.

Jesus Christ, she'd been gutted. I just—

"Can you kill me?" Antonio's question was absolutely sincere.

He was losing his mind, and I couldn't blame him. I couldn't even process a story around what I was seeing. He had blood pouring from his head, and his bruised and welted torso was bare to the winter air.

"I'm not killing you."

I knelt by her. I thought I looked calm. I pushed back the creeping emotions, but I'd feel them later. I knew that. I was a heartless asshole, except when I wasn't.

"How did this happen?" I asked. Even in death, she was beautiful. I touched her face. I didn't care if I got blood on my hands.

Antonio just shook his head. He was in shock.

"Spin." Lorenzo stood over us.

"Get the fuck away from me," Antonio shouted. "You're so fucking lucky you're not dead."

"The Sicilians. Their boss is dead. She—"

Antonio sprang up, took Lorenzo by the collar, and slammed him against a wall. "This is on you, Zo. On you. You got ambition and no brains."

"If you're gonna kill me, just do it!"

"I can't!" Antonio let him go, and Lorenzo dropped.

"Her people are coming. Donna's dead." Lorenzo pointed at Theresa. "She did it, and she's dead. What the—"

"Fuck you!" Antonio was beyond reason.

Lorenzo had a point. If Theresa had killed Donna, a crazy thought I had to just accept at face value, and Donna killed Theresa, the Carloni family had no leader.

"There's a power vacuum," I mumbled, leaning close to Theresa's face.

"Say you done her," Lorenzo said. "Say it, or they'll crush us. Take charge."

"No! No more. I'm done!"

Their fight fell into the background as I bent over Theresa. I'd seen so many dead people, and the one thing I could say about them was that they looked like statues of themselves. Glass blue eyes and hard lips. I put my thumbs on Theresa's eyelids and closed them, and I felt something I shouldn't have.

Warmth.

"You stupid motherfucker," I said, standing. "There is no power vacuum." I had only a second to see Antonio's red eyes on me before I stared at my phone, trying to figure out who to call.

"What?" Antonio said.

"She's alive."

Chapter 53

ANTONIO

I didn't realize how crazy I was until I came out of it. It was like being on a descending airplane with compressed ears that whooshed until I yawned or swallowed. Then everything cleared up. I didn't even think I was foggy and deaf until the pressure equalized.

Daniel saying she was alive was that pop. I didn't know what I'd been feeling or doing. I only knew what I couldn't do, which was kill Lorenzo. I'd promised her I wouldn't. Not being able to take him out meant I didn't have a distraction. A little shiny violent thing to experience or a problem to solve. I had to lose her and feel it without diversion. I didn't think I could live through actually feeling that level of pain.

I was a child. I'd been naïve and inexperienced. I thought I'd grieved before, but no—I hadn't allowed it. In the seven or so minutes that I lost Theresa, all I saw was a long descent into oblivion. I despaired for myself as much as I did for her. I couldn't handle it. I didn't have the tools to comprehend a part of myself getting ripped away. I couldn't even finish a sentence in my head. I was half a man. Half a human. Immobilized by a promise and sucked dry by the only death that mattered.

That all came to me after the pop.

She was alive and broken. She could still die, but what I'd been missing in those minutes filled me. Hope. It was the nature of clarity. It set off everything against it. In that tension between what

I hoped for and everything else, the world was in focus. I came to myself. I had something to *do*.

I put my hand over Daniel's phone.

"Who are you calling?" I asked.

"Nine one one. We can't move her."

"Trust me."

I made the call crouched over her, noticing the signs of life I'd missed in my despair. The team from Marymount who had taken shrapnel out of Bruno's hand were coming. They were discreet and expensive. I prayed while I told them where we were. I prayed they'd be quick, that I hadn't delayed too long.

Enzo came to me when I got off the phone. "Zo wants—"

"Keep him out of my sight."

"Are you taking charge? Is it you?"

I pulled Enzo away from Daniel. "Did I kill Donna Maria?"

"How should I answer that?" he asked.

"The truth. Who killed her?"

He pointed at Theresa timidly, as if afraid to say.

"There's your capo. Now back up. I said I wouldn't kill anyone. I made no promises about shooting your legs out from under you."

***

In the minutes before the ambulance arrived, Zo, Simone, and Enzo whispered. Two of Donna Maria's men showed up. I heard a car in the driveway, and my three crew, the three betrayers who now officially worked for Theresa, subdued Donna Maria's men. Daniel fidgeted. We were both holding back a panic that Theresa's life was pouring out of her and we couldn't do anything.

"You should go," I said, bending over her, afraid to touch her for fear of something broken inside her.

"Fuck you."

"No, fuck you. Get Valentina out of here."

He nodded. "This won't stay under the radar. Too big. It's too big."

The sound of the siren reached us.

"Go," I said.

He took one last glance at Theresa then jogged into the house, passing a cluster of mob soldiers as if we were all commuters on the same train.

Chapter 54

THERESA

Pain. I remember pain. My insides. My bones. The place where the needles were. And the itching. The itching was so intense, I thought I'd go mad. But I couldn't move, or talk, or even control my own breathing. I was half conscious, immobilized, in a fog as thick as peanut butter.

I knew I was moved. I knew I was cut open and sewn up. I smelled alcohol and latex, so I knew I was in some kind of hospital. But none of that was important. My body became the responsibility of other people, and my job was to stay still and endure it.

I knew I wasn't alone. That was what was important. That kept me from a confined madness. Margie was there. And my mother. Deirdre. Even Daniel.

But Antonio wasn't. I loved my family. I wanted them, craved them. But I had a creeping concern in my half consciousness that my demand that he not take vengeance wasn't the end of the story of that day.

I prayed for him a lot. Every day that passed with the light coming in, diffused by my eyelids and warming my face, my worry grew. He wouldn't just leave me. Something had to have happened. Something terrible.

"Sit." Margie's voice came through. I didn't think she was talking to me.

"I'm on my ass all day." Jonathan. This was his second visit.

"You had a heart transplant three weeks ago. Your ass isn't half finished."

A chair scraped. "I hate this."

"I'll be an old woman one day, and you can make me sit down when I need to."

I listened for a third person, but no one came. Not one of the hundred doctors. Not a nurse. Not Antonio.

Where's Antonio? I tried to say it and failed.

"You're never getting old, Margaret. Not if you can fix it."

"There are some things a fixer can't even fix."

Every time they came and went, I forgot then remembered. They bickered and joked. They did it out of rote. All of them except Deirdre, who'd prayed out her sense of humor. Even Mom could cut deep with a single word, and just that day, I couldn't bear it.

Antonio.

"You need to put that as an exclusion in the contract," Jonathan quipped.

"Once I can get some blood out of you to sign it in."

Antonio. Please.

"Did she just say something?" Margie asked.

A chair creaked.

"Sit down," Margie snapped.

I opened my eyes. The light felt like knives in my head and my tear ducts went into production mode, fogging everything. I blinked. I felt the drops rush down the side of my head. When I opened my eyes again, Margie's face blocked the light.

"Well, hello."

Antonio.

"Eyes open," she said to Jonathan then looked back at me. "How are you?"

"Antonio." I couldn't believe I got the word out. Every syllable was exhausting.

"He's fine."

"Swear?"

She held up her hand. "Pledge open." She pulled two of my fingers off the sheets.

"Open," I whispered.

"Antonio is alive and healthy. He walks, he talks, he is very, very worried about you. I'll tell him you asked about him. He's going to shit a brick with joy, but he can't visit. Don't be mad at him."

"I'm not."

"All right. I'm going to call a doctor to look at you."

"Tell him…" I swallowed. I didn't know what to say. Everything. "Tell him he's my capo."

"Funny you should say that. He says the same about you. Pledge closed."

I had more to say. More questions. More statements. More more more.

But I didn't even have the energy to close the pledge. Consciousness left and was replaced by a worry-free sleep.

Chapter 55

THERESA

would only ever ask Margie about Antonio, and she constantly reassured me that he was fine. She promised she'd tell me everything. She changed the subject. She told me not to say more because I couldn't see who was in the room.

"Talk to me, or I'll scream." I couldn't have screamed if I wanted to, but the threat was enough to get her to lean over and look at my face.

"Oh, someone's feeling better," Margie said.

"I can feel my body."

"You're so lucky you're not paralyzed. Have I mentioned that?" She pulled her chair close.

"Can you tell me where he is? Did he go home? To Italy?" I swallowed. I couldn't do much more than swallow and blink.

"No. He's in California. And by California, I mean...the state of."

California. Huge state. In the geography of love, it was a nanostate. In the geography of need—it was massive.

"Just tell me."

"It can wait," she said.

"Tell me. Please."

She leaned over me, deep in thought, then sat down. I had a view of the grey ceiling again.

"I want you to remember, as I tell you this, that he's fine."

My chest constricted. Had he run off with Valentina? A machine beeped somewhere.

"Easy, kid. If you make the doctors come in, this conversation ends."

I breathed. I felt the ends and edges of my body, calming them. I'd done that when reporters asked me about my cheating fiancé. I'd done it when talking to Donna Maria for the first time. I'd done it my whole life, and I did it on that bed.

"Okay," I said when I was ready.

"Okay."

"Go, Margie. You're stalling."

She sighed then continued. "There wasn't a mob doctor in California who could help you. He made a choice. He turned himself in. He and Daniel hammered out his story. He said he stabbed you in a lover's quarrel and you fell off the veranda. Everyone in the house corroborated. Valentina said she ran the fence in a jealous rage. No grand jury. No indictment. No nothing."

"Wait...I...there were—"

Bodies.

Blood.

Bullets.

"A wall of silence," Margie said. "Donna Maria Carloni and Domenico Uvoli disappeared. Poof. No one's seen them."

There were holes, but I couldn't get my head around them while one question remained. "He turned himself in? What does that mean?"

"We made the indictment over Paulie go away. There was enough evidence to claim self defense for that, but for what happened to you...look...he skipped everything and copped a plea. I shouldn't tell you since I'm not even supposed to know the details, but I arranged his lawyer, and I'm yours, so there's that."

"Where is he?" I couldn't bear saying it, because the answer—

"He's in prison, Theresa." Her hand was on mine. She squeezed it.

"But—"

"Listen to me. You fought over Valentina. He stabbed you. He threw you off a second-story veranda. That's the end of it. If anyone asks you anything, you say you don't remember. Your memory is fucked beyond repair."

"How long, Margie?"

"If you decide to go honest, a lot of people you love are going away for a long time."

"How long is he in? Tell me!"

She breathed hard then spit it out. "Ten."

"Ten years?" I squeaked my last breath, because my god, my god, a decade?

"Listen…"

I was crying before she finished the word. I heard something about parole. I heard something about good behavior and not making it worse. But I was wrecked.

I had to know if I was allowed to forgive the fake stabbing. I had to know who knew what because I'd been holding on to this string of hope and it was about to break. But I couldn't, because I was crying so hard I couldn't speak. Then the doctors came, and I pretended to know nothing about anything.

Chapter 56

THERESA

found it easier to just not talk. When the cops came, I claimed to remember nothing of the incident. So sorry. Shrug. Daniel didn't let the interviewer press too long.

"Dan," I asked when it was over, "the election? It's March, almost."

He smiled at me. "I got out in time. And you're my last case I'm overseeing as DA."

He wasn't actually the prosecutor. He couldn't be. But he seemed to be around all the time.

"Then what?"

"I can do commercial litigation, I think? Private sector stuff. I'm still a good lawyer."

"No public advocacy?" I asked.

"My public life is over. Too many proverbial skeletons in the proverbial closet."

"I'm sorry, Dan. It was all my fault."

"No. It was my fault, and it's better this way." He held up his hands. The nails were unbitten. "Less stress. I swear, I get up in the morning feeling...what's the opposite of overwhelmed?"

"Underwhelmed?"

"Not that."

"I know what you mean."

"It'll all be all right. I promise." He squeezed my hand.

But I wanted to die. I missed Antonio every minute of every day. I wanted his company so much I couldn't go to physical therapy some days, and when they took the nylon cast off with a loud *kkkkt* of Velcro, I wanted his touch on my body so badly, I wished they'd put the damned thing back on me.

"Where do you want to go?" Margie asked on my last day at Sequoia.

"Do I still have my loft?" I sat on the edge of the bed, considering the fact that I'd never see those walls again, and I had to face a world without Antonio.

"Yeah. I had it cleaned."

"Okay." I got on my shoes. I could walk, if slowly.

"There are some guys who want to talk to you before you go."

"I don't remember anything."

"Other guys. Names ending in vowels."

I just looked at her. I knew who she meant, more or less. I had no idea why they'd want anything to do with me though.

"You're safe. I have my guy on them. Sit in the chair, would you?"

I turned slowly and sat. I was in a wide skirt because it was easy to get on and a blouse that hid the hunch in my left shoulder. It would take years to fix me completely, and even then, I'd be at ninety percent.

Ninety percent was a miracle. I had to remember that.

Antonio was alive. That was a miracle as well.

And when Lorenzo, Enzo, and Simone shuffled in with Otto trailing behind them, I discovered another miracle.

"Boss," Lorenzo said handing me a fat manila envelope, "I want to offer you an apology and a tribute. I was trying to help us in the organization, and I done wrong. I can't ever make it up to you, but you have my service if you want it."

The envelope flopped back and forth where he held it.

"I'm not Italian," I said, snapping it from him.

"Yeah. It's gonna be a problem."

He obviously didn't even want to talk to me. Otto dropped his envelope on top.

"This is my month, Otto said. "Been great, gotta say, with the Sicilians off our backs."

I peeked into the envelopes. They were stuffed with twenties and hundreds. I thought I should just step down, but there was a reason that was impossible. Killing a boss didn't come without consequences.

"As far as I'm concerned, Antonio runs this operation," I said. "If you have a question or you need something, you go to him and you ask him. This is done, right? When the boss is put away? You visit?"

"Yes," Lorenzo said.

"You bring me the tributes. I'll take care of it. The rest goes through him. I need you guys to keep the peace. I know you want that." I looked at them each individually, stopping at Zo. "You tried to kill Antonio, and you turned everyone against him. It was for peace. I understand that, so there won't be retribution, but we can never trust you again."

He nodded like a shamefaced dog. I didn't feel sorry for him or envy him.

"Go. Visit Antonio."

They scuttled out. Only Otto made eye contact, and I winked at him.

I had this. Eventually, after enough torment, we'd give it all back to them. Even Lorenzo. He'd been loyal to his men and worked for peace instead of war. He'd do fine.

But first, I would rule.

EIGHTEEN MONTHS LATER

Chapter 57

THERESA

hadn't visited. He didn't want me to. He didn't want the parole board to think he would get out and stab me again. That was what he said, but I thought he just didn't want me to see him behind bulletproof glass. I wrote him letters four times a week, keeping it all above board with newsy news and short declarations of love, and he wrote back with little in the way of prison happenings. It was obvious he didn't want me to know.

The only thing I insisted on telling him over the phone was the only thing that might keep him from returning to me.

"What is it?" he'd said. "It's nothing. I know already. It won't keep me from you."

I'd started crying almost immediately. I missed his voice. I craved his hands. I wasted thirty seconds of a two-minute phone call trying to put myself back into a staid little box.

"Don't tell me," he said. "Whatever it is—"

"I can't..." My breath hitched. Got it together. "Because of the injuries. I can't have children."

"Contessa—"

"I understand if that's a deal-breaker for you."

"I saw what happened, my love. This isn't a surprise."

It was exactly that response that soothed me. If he hadn't already known, I might have thought he was just gathering strength to leave me, or that he hadn't digested what it meant. But he wasn't caught off guard. He'd already dealt with it, and he still wanted me. For months, I didn't know what that meant. Us wanting each other. Us "being with" each other. One year of separation or ten. Anything in between.

Over the course of his time in prison, I continued to insist I didn't remember anything from that night, and Margie pushed for parole from behind the person who actually claimed to be his lawyer.

"For you," she'd insisted. "I'm doing it for you. But if he hurts you, I'm coming down like a hammer."

I'd agree to anything. To get him out, I forked over everything the guys sent in tribute. Cash. Untraceable and convenient as hell for doing stuff like greasing wheels and buying an olive orchard in Temecula. I got a place with multiple buildings for my family and promised the children pony rides.

I thought of him every day. I slept on one side of the bed. I left his dresser drawers empty. I set him up with a desk and a space in the office before I even knew what it meant to run an orchard.

"You have pains," Valentina said as she wiped down a big ceramic bowl in my new kitchen. When she visited the orchard, she acted as if she owned the joint. "You should lie down."

"I'm fine."

She'd arrived that morning and taken on the chores as if she enjoyed them. She'd served Antonio with divorce papers soon after he was sentenced, and there hadn't been much fuss. He was a felon. The Church didn't like it, but the Church didn't have to. She handed him to me on a platter and announced that she didn't expect me to get in the way of her and Daniel.

I wouldn't, but I explained what my ex-fiancé had done and what she could expect from him. Apparently, she expected exactly what he had to give. That day, Daniel had illustrated exactly that by plopping himself on the couch when they arrived and watching a game with the men. He was still an irritating douchebag, but what could I do? He was family now.

"You look a little bent," Sheila said.

"I'm fine. Don't make me say it again."

"Yes, boss," Sheila and Valentina said in unison.

I snapped the dishtowel at both of them.

Zia nudged me to the side. "You're in the way."

"Sorry."

"You want to stand in front of the stove? You can cook." She took the lid off something brown and stewey and stirred it with a wooden spoon.

"No, no, I'm good! You cook."

She held up the sauce-smeared spoon. "Taste."

I blew on it and put my lips to the wood. "Oh my god, what is it?"

She flapped her hand at me. She was always impatient with what I didn't know.

"He's late," Jonathan said, strolling into the kitchen. "Maybe they decided to keep him." He plucked two glasses from the cabinet and filled them with water.

"That's not even funny."

"I'm not laughing," he said.

The children were though. And shouting. They tracked mud all over the kitchen. Bonnie opened the fridge and nearly dropped a gallon of milk.

"You left your wife on the patio to come in here and give me a heart attack?" I said to Jonathan.

He kissed my cheek. "She loves it here. We're buying the place next door."

I couldn't tell if he was serious or not, but I played the odds. "Knock before you visit."

He leaned on the counter. The kids had run back out, and I heard Sheila yelling at them from half a house away. Valentina and Zia had gone to prepare the buffet. Jonathan and I were alone.

He put up his right hand. "Open pledge."

I held up my hand. "Open."

"Swear he didn't stab you and throw you off a balcony."

"It was more of a second-story veranda."

"You're making me nervous."

I held my hand up as if taking the oath of office. "I swear, in pledge, that he didn't stab me and throw me off anything in the architectural lexicon. He has never laid a finger on me in anger or jealousy, and if he did, I'd kill him. Outside pledge, I'm sticking to my story."

I'd made the same pledge to just about every other sibling, in addition to swearing to my mother that it wasn't what it looked like. I tried not to speak to Dad alone, because I didn't have enough forgiveness in my heart for him.

I heard the crunch of dirt and rock and peered out the kitchen window. A black car came through the gate. I put my hand on my chest.

Jonathan flicked my ear. "Close pledge, sister."

"Closed."

I was ready. More than ready. I slapped my towel down and ran to the front door, whipping it open and nearly tripping over Antonin, who stood at the edge of the porch. I took a moment to look at him. He was a serious boy generally, but his sullen face was more thoughtful today than usual.

I stopped and leaned in to him. He was almost my height already.

"It's okay. He won't bite you. We talked about this. He's just a man," I said.

He nodded. I hugged him. He was a good kid, whip smart and acing every single class at Harvard-Westlake. He was a genius under pressure. Valentina said he was more like his father than her, but his sense of humor belonged to his mother. At least he didn't need half a glass of wine to bring it out.

Behind me, a car door slammed. And another as he was let out of the back of the limo.

I didn't think I could turn around, because once I did, the waiting was officially over. My life would begin and preparation would become action. I stood with our families on the porch, waiting.

"Capo," he said.

His voice. Music. An opera in two syllables.

I turned and nearly died, my gasp was so strong.

He was...Antonio.

Everything I remembered and imagined, but in three dimensions. In a white shirt and grey jacket, his thumb hooked on the shoulder strap of his bag, his face shaven, his brown hair falling into a parenthesis on his forehead. When he smiled, the sky opened and God himself showed his favor.

"You lost weight." My bottom lip trembled so hard I could barely get the last word out.

"The second worst part was the food."

I didn't say anything. I was too overwhelmed. I took in every detail. His ebony lashes. His lips, drawn across his face in a grin. I was supposed to ask him the worst part, but the breeze shifted and I was swept away in the scent of campfires and quiet pine forests.

"I missed you," I said. God, would I ever again get a word out without crying? I didn't know how to catalog the relief, the joy, and the feeling of utter liberation, because I'd been in prison with him.

He dropped his bag and engulfed me in his arms.

"I missed you I missed you..." I kept repeating, because I hadn't uttered it in a year and a half and it needed saying.

I felt a hand on my shoulder, and a pair of arms around my legs. I felt the breath and tears of our families as they gathered around us, shielding us with their bodies. I rested my cheek on his shoulder. This was my heaven, with him.

He rocked back and forth, holding me as if I were the last woman in the world. I hadn't been held like that since before the fall. I'd been broken in so many places, I was afraid to embrace anyone, but with Antonio, I wasn't scared to be held. I'd forgotten how safe he made me feel, how loved, how trusted. He could hold me and nothing inside me would break. I was fine.

Better than fine. I was whole.

Epilogue

THERESA

The food was gone. The dishes were put away. The children were bathed and kissed. A few stragglers stayed up for late night TV. All was dark.

Except the bathroom. It was white, and the light was on. I'd loved its brightness. I'd designed it so I could see everything, but now I wanted the light dimmed. Or off. Or warmer. I leaned into the mirror. I'd just gotten out of the shower. Hair stuck to my forehead, and droplets hung under my eyes. I hadn't given myself a good look-see in a long time, and tonight, the first night of Antonio's return, was probably way too late.

I was nervous.

The side of the bed I kept for him was about to be filled, but so much had changed in the meantime, I didn't know if it made sense anymore. I didn't know what he'd been through, done, experienced while he was away. He hadn't spoken about it during dinner or the card game after. He seemed reserved. Standoffish, even. I knew he loved me. I knew from the way he put his hand over mine at dinner and the way he looked at me.

"Hello," he said, leaning against the doorframe.

I jumped. "You scared me."

He crossed his arms, and the way he looked at me made me close the neck of my robe tight. "I'm sorry."

"It's all right."

I tried to get past him, but he didn't budge. His cheeks were darkened with late-day growth, and his eyelids drooped a little with exhaustion. He was still the most beautiful man I'd ever seen.

"Do you like our room?" I asked.

"I like the room."

"You can pick a different one, but this one had the nicest patio onto the orchard."

"Theresa. I—"

"I'm sorry, it's just…" I had constructed a hundred ways to talk to him when he hadn't been in front of me. He pressed his hand to my cheek, and without thinking or intending it, I leaned into him, letting his palm cup me.

"Do you want to wait?" he asked. "I won't force you."

"No, I…this…what happened? I'm not the same. I'm ninety percent. Ninety five, actually but not the same."

I'd forgotten how powerful he was in a room. How the energy surrounding him seemed to squeeze out everything else.

"You aren't the same. I could have told you that."

"I just—" I stopped myself. This was stupid. "Oh, fuck it." I stepped into the bedroom and faced him.

"I want to kiss you," he said. "I haven't thought about anything but kissing you for a year and a half. If you don't want to do anything else until you get used to me again, I accept that. But I'm kissing you before I go to sleep."

"I want you to kiss me. You have no idea how badly I want that kiss, but first I have to show you." I opened the robe. It was the hardest thing I'd ever did, not because I thought there was something wrong with me, but because I didn't know how he'd react.

The scar drew his eyes first, but then they drifted all over me, the way they had that first day, and the second, and the time I swore I felt him touching me.

"I see," he said, touching the scar on my abdomen. "Does it hurt?"

"Itches sometimes. But also, my left shoulder. I told you in the letters, but see, I can't really do this anymore." I shifted my shoulder back as far as it would go. Not very far. It had taken the brunt of the fall.

"You need me to be gentle," he said.

My anxiety fell away and was replaced by irrational joy. He knew it was just as simple as that. I only needed him to know that I felt fragile, even if I wasn't.

"I do."

He pushed the robe off my shoulders. It fell at my feet like a snowdrift. I was naked, and he was there. Right there. My body was on fire for him.

"I want my kiss," he breathed into my cheek, his lips grazing me.

"Come and get it." I barely made a sound saying it, then I thought he hadn't heard me, because he didn't do it.

"Do you know why I haven't kissed you all day?" he asked.

"No."

"If I kissed you, I was going to take you. And I didn't want a rush job in a closet."

"If you can take me like this, you can take me."

His lips were so soft on mine, his mouth so supple, his tongue gentle and sweet. He was slow, savoring every turn and twist of our mouths together. His hands landed on my cheeks and traveled down my neck, over my breasts. I groaned as a shudder went through me.

"I want you like this." He leaned forward, guiding me onto the bed until I was on my back and he was on all fours over me. "And like this." He kissed my chin and moved down to my breasts. "And this." He put his lips on my scar. "Just like this." He kissed my navel and below it. "God, I missed you."

He parted my legs so tenderly yet so firmly that I knew he was still in charge, even if he wasn't rough or demanding. He kissed between my legs, flicking his tongue over me. I hadn't been touched in so long that my back arched, and I knew if he flicked it again—

"Stop," I gasped. "Wait."

He looked up from below, his hand on my knee. "Why?"

"I want to see you. I thought about your first night home all the time. And I always imagined looking at you."

He pecked the inside of my thigh and stood at the foot of the bed. His eyes grazed over me. I thought I'd feel more self-conscious about my scar and my little crookedness. I thought I'd have to apologize for being imperfect and overcome my physical inadequacy in his sight. But I didn't feel the need for that at all. I felt warm and loved, whole and perfect before him.

He unbuttoned his shirt.

"Was it terrible in prison?" I asked.

"It wasn't too bad. Boring mostly. And lonely." He undid the cuffs, shrugged the shirt off, and tossed it over a chair.

"Is it true about the showers?"

He laughed.

"I'm serious!"

"You want to know if I took a bitch in the showers?"

Then I laughed. Of course he'd never imagined anyone would top him. Santa Claus would land on the roof first.

He got out of his pants and crawled over me. His erection pressed on my thigh, and I felt two completely separate longings. One for a deep, slow connection, and the other to be torn apart until I couldn't speak.

"Well?" I said, running my hand over his chest. "I'd forgive you as long as he was ugly."

"They're all ugly. It's in the food or something."

"Except you."

"I wasn't really there. I was always here with you." He ran his lips over mine. It wasn't a kiss but a wakening of skin.

"Capo," I said.

"Yes, Capo?" He kissed my cheek softly.

How did I go so long without feeling his breath in my ear? It was the most exciting and distracting thing ever.

I put my hands on his jaw and pushed his face to the front of mine so we were nose to nose. "I'm sorry."

"For what?"

"That you went to prison for me. I wouldn't have let you, but you did. And I'm grateful to you and mad at myself at the same time."

"I would do it again."

"I hope you don't have to. I want to give the whole thing away. I've set it up so it runs itself. Just let it go. I think I can divide it up nicely," I said.

"*Come vuoi tu.*"

"We can talk about it."

"No talking. Just do it."

I hitched myself and wrapped my legs around him. *"Come vuoi tu."*

He laughed softly. "Your accent, my God."

"No more talking." I rotated my hips, getting myself against his length.

He shifted, getting the head of his dick against me. He pushed forward, and I pushed against him. I'd forgotten about his size, and I laughed.

"What?" he asked.

"I love you. Now, fuck me already."

He smiled, pulled my legs apart, and got on his knees. He entered me in three short bursts, each one making me gasp with pain then pleasure. Then pleasure again. And well, it was all good after that.

That night he came home, he bent over me, pressing our bodies together. I looked in his face while we made love so slowly, it was almost torture. I memorized the lines and curves of him all over again. I touched his cheeks and ran my fingers through his hair. And even when I closed my eyes because I couldn't take the rising tide of my orgasm anymore, I kept his face in my hands and let the scent of burned pine and sweet olive blossoms meld and linger until they became a unique harmony of their own, never to be separated again.

***

I put my head on his chest and listened to him breathe.

"It's a good room," he said.

"It's ours. Just ours. Let me show you the best part."

I rolled away and opened the French doors onto the orchard. The breeze caressed his hair, flicking the ends. I sat on his side of the bed, stroking his forehead. A scar so straight it looked as if it had been drawn with a ruler shot across his temple and past his hairline. I drew my finger along it. No hair grew along its length, even past his ear, where it tapered and disappeared.

"Thank you for waiting for me," he said.

"Tomorrow, I'll show you your orchard. We can walk the rows."

"How's business?"

"Breaking even."

"Good. Very good." He rolled onto his side, draping his arm over my thighs. The moonlight fell on his cheek, and the mating calls of crickets filled the air. "I'm so tired. I didn't realize until now."

"Go to sleep, Antonio. I'm here. You can sleep now."

The last word had barely left my lips before his eyes closed and his breathing turned even and slow. I didn't think I'd ever seen him sleep without a care as to how he woke up. I curled up behind him, putting my lips to the back of his neck, and I thanked God for him, for our life, for the love between us that hadn't died even when we almost did.

I was sure we would pay for our sins in either this life or the next. But maybe there was a little in us that could be saved. In this little room with a half-empty closet and a full bed, maybe salvation would come in the form of love.

Acknowlegements

This is an impossible task.

You can't get everyone who helped make a book happen. That's crazy. But once, there was a blogger who used social media to bemoan not being personally acknowledged at the end of a book because she did a giveaway. Readers piled on, asking for the author's name so they could shun her. And I thought, "Oh my god, I can't possibly mention every wonderful blogger who has done a giveaway for me." This had kind of a paralyzing effect on me. I almost stopped doing blogger giveaways altogether. I'm so terrified, I don't write acknowledgements until the very end of a series, almost guaranteeing I'll forget someone. That's irony for you.

So I'm doing a list. Here it is. I'm not saying what anyone did because you all know what you did. You know you were instrumental in making these books happen, and if you don't, YOU WERE. Writing is a solitary endeavor in bursts, but overall, from betas to editors to cheerleaders, writers need people. And publishing is even more of a team sport. Anyone who says this is a solitary endeavor has never actually published anything. I'm sorry. No one does this alone.

Gabri Canova, Erik Gevers, Tony and Diane, Kaylee, Jean esq, Nina, Roxy, Bella, Irene O, Michelle, Stephanie, Becs, the entire team at iBooks, Maura, Mary, Lisa, Lael, Lynn, Cassie, Goddess of the emotional realm—Angela Smith, Kristy/Lauren/Laurelin, the EC, FYW, BGP, every fan who kept me going when I wanted to announce I wasn't writing this book because it was too damned hard.

Made in the USA
Lexington, KY
24 October 2016